The Lillie Pad
A Southern Tale

Laurie Pfister Taylor

AmEricaHouse
Baltimore

First printing

ISBN: 1-58851-858-2
PUBLISHED BY AMERICA HOUSE BOOK
PUBLISHERS
www.publishamerica.com
Baltimore

Printed in the United States of America

Dedication

For my most wonderful and amazing 2 year old: Molly Mattison Taylor. Without her this novel would have never been possible, all the long hours and patience. We have accomplished this publication together.

For my supportive family and friends.

And in great appreciation, to the town and many friends of Savannah, Georgia, from which much of the description and inspiration came. Savannah is my place of solitude, my escape from the daily hustle and bustle and, ultimately, my destination.

Introduction

The river flows as if it is showing us that life moves on. Life continues to flow faithfully. The currents seem to gather together, travel on and then slowly drift apart onto separate paths. The water carries debris of all sorts. A broken branch proceeds through the roughage as if it knows its destiny. Faded and torn leaves stay afloat with grace. The warmth from the brazen sun beats down, while the breeze sails by with a refreshing breath for all to enjoy. Another tree limb passes through the river with daring speed, ripples in the water blurr and then fade.

Beautiful is not the appropriate word to describe this place. Breathtaking and exhilarating appear to fit. There must be a God to create a scene such as this. The air so refreshing leads callers to believe they are somehow renewing their troubled souls. It is an escape, for however long they choose, from the disturbed disorder in their lives. Just a moment to let everything go, to let it all hang out... so to speak.

The whispers of the river give much needed relaxation to all who come to visit at no cost. All it takes is a gaze out into the distance, a deep breath, and you can feel the calm.

Chapter One

Batson Cannon was in a world all his own as he unwound after a troublesome day at the realty office, where he worked there in town. There had been a handful of calls in the last hour before leaving. With the interest rates so low this year, buyers were rampant in this area. People from all over the place were suddenly looking to settle down in the south. Of course, how could he blame them? Camilla was his home, born and raised there.

Many of Camilla's old homes were extensively restored and new replicas were built to accent the architecture of it all. The once rundown Main Street was now refurbished with new awnings on the aged retail stores. Even the old furniture shop, Turner's, had pitched into the reconstruction and landscaped their designated side of the street. The renewed pride of the town was created from its residents. Anyone visiting could see the town locals were surely pleased that their little town by the river was in bloom. The yards overflowed with enormous magnolia trees that had grown there for years. The Spanish moss continued to hover over the parks and sidewalks of the worn streets. Property values had skyrocketed and that made everyone happy, especially Batson.

This was routine for him to visit the river after a hard day. To sit and slowly watch the sunset was like a muscle relaxer, a stress reliever. A few moments reassured him that the day was almost over and tomorrow would soon come. Every once in a while after work, Batson would take a short drive out to the island, about ten minutes. The island was a heavenly getaway when you were in the mood to be near the ocean. Downtown Camilla ran parallel with the river, it was easier just to walk down here. Two blocks south to be exact. The walk was a familiar one to Batson and quite pleasant with waves and friendly hellos from casual acquaintances, some he had known ever since he was a boy.

Cannon Realty was not new to Camilla. The business had risen and fallen with the best of them. The old three-story office building was situated on the corner of Whitsett and McMillian. It had been passed onto Batson when he turned eighteen. Cannon Realty was rightfully his now. Before it had been operated by both Batson's father and grandfather.

Batson's parents died when he was nine years old, leaving he and his younger sister, Gracie, alone. The only living relative was their dad's mother, Grandma Anna Cannon. Batson and Gracie, who was only five at the time, were sent to live with Anna out on the island.

Grandma Anna had a forever giving heart and did what she could to raise the two children. Batson was understandably angry over the death of his parents; so angry he was consistently in counseling until the age of fifteen. Gracie had been so young; she grew up never really remembering her parents. Anna put her in counseling for a short time, but she would not understand her loss until she was older. The whole incident was tragic and to have left two young children behind was disastrous. The community of Camilla grieved along with the Cannon family.

Anna struggled to get the kids back to a somewhat normal life, while at the same time, devastated by the loss of her own son and daughter-in-law. Life certainly went on though and by the time the kids were adults, dear Anna was completely satisfied that she had done her job well.

Batson was succeeding in the family business and ambitious Gracie had recently moved to Chicago to thrive in her journalism career. Both children had grown to become adults and were living their lives to the fullest. Or so she hoped.

Grandma Anna was tremendously proud of her two gems

and they in return, cherished her and kept in close touch. As Anna got older, both Batson and Gracie faced the fact that the time would soon come when they would take care of her, as she had them. A touchy subject, but one that would soon have to be dealt with.

For now, Grandma Anna was content and still on her toes. She lived in the same house, standing tall on the island edge. The house was built with a beautiful screened back porch; Anna called it her 'haven'. The backyard traveled back about twenty or thirty yards into the marsh and then further out was the sea. Batson and Gracie now understood the love Grandma Anna had for the sea. Growing up there, it had been easy to take advantage of its presence. Now that both were gone from the island house, it sure was easy to miss it.

Anna continued to get around well and accomplished many necessary tasks for herself. Bessie, the housekeeper, came everyday to help out with the cleaning and most all of the cooking. Anna and Bessie had become close after Batson's grandfather, Joseph Cannon, had passed. He died only a few years after Gracie had been born.

Ms. Bessie Mae Callahan was her full name. Bessie was a bit younger than Misses Anna, as she called her. The two were on the same level, enjoying similar hobbies and chatting with one another about pretty much nothing. They would sit quietly at the breakfast table babbling over their coffee and cream. In the early morning or early evening both took a seat in the crooked rockers on the porch out back. Afternoons were just 'too damn hot', as Grandma Anna would put it. She never went out there in the middle of the day; it had always been the mornings and evenings since Joseph had left her.

When Joseph was alive, Anna would sit out on that porch for hours waiting for his fishing boat to pull in. Being the leading man at Cannon realty, Papa Cannon took it upon himself to use as many personal days as possible. He was an

9

outdoorsy type, never cared to sit at a desk all day. For Anna to sit out there in the afternoon now would be like waiting again, but for someone that would never return. It brought back too many heartfelt memories for Anna. Batson and Gracie never knew that story, one of Anna's secrets. Only Bessie knew the reasoning behind it. Whether the two would admit it or not, they had a friendship that many people don't believe even exists.

Not thinking about his troubled past, Batson harped on the workload ahead. Cannon realty employed over twenty agents with dozens of listings all over Camilla and days at the office were understandably stressful. Batson ached through his neck and broad shoulders. His legs were sprawled out in front of him. Batson had always been tall and lanky, tall enough to play good basketball. But he never played much basketball, as softball was his favorite. Anna would say, 'he runs those bases like a mouse tailed by a cat'.

An elderly colored man sat on the weathered bench beside him, throwing one of several lines out into the water. Batson glanced at the man with a squint in his eyes due to the blinding sun and casually threw him a smile. The fisherman responded by nodding, barely noticeable with his wearied gray cap covering as much of his face as possible. The fisherman went about his business and hummed a tune, in a world all his own. A bite pulled from the water. Almost instantly, the fisherman reeled in one of his first catches of the day, by the looks of the empty bucket placed between his denim pant legs.

Batson imagined the pants had rarely been washed from the looks of them, probably reeked of fish and the stale smell of the river water. Neither man mumbled a word, both kept to themselves. The colored man continued to fish and didn't move an inch when Batson leisurely meandered off, loosening his tie.

This 22nd day of August was muggy and extremely hot. The summer had several weeks left to linger on, no one ever seemed to get used to it. Most everyone talked about or complained about the weather, it made for good conversation. Some days were so hot it was a chore to even breathe. Batson listened to the whines of his employees, 'My God! How hot is supposed to get today?' 'It couldn't possibly get any hotter!' or 'I can't even smoke outside, it's just too hot'.

With a sly smirk he would simply say, "Such is life, isn't it?" and walk off like he could care less. The agents would roll their eyes behind his back or gesture to ignore his comments. Batson found it ridiculous to complain about the hot weather, it wouldn't make it any better and in his eyes, that was life. Besides, he got tired of hearing about it.

Batson dropped by his usual pub on the way back to the car, Mary's Bar and Grill. There was a group of younger folks in the back of the house shooting pool and the dedicated two or three VIP's at the end of the bar, marking their stools. By the looks of them, they had probably been there since noon. The rest of the barstools were vacant and Batson placed his briefcase on one and sat down beside it. The bar was dark, a nice change from the glare of the sun outside.

"What can I get for you, Batson?" Sherry asked. Sherry, the bartender, had gone to high school with Batson and had worked at Mary's ever since they were both legal to drink. She had three or four kids, all still very young and now she was divorced for the second time, if he remembered right. Sherry had a pleasant smile and surprisingly kept a cheerful disposition most of the time. Batson sometimes felt sorry for her, being raised with what some would call a rough life. But hell, who's childhood wasn't rough? Oh well, Sherry seemed satisfied and he didn't know. After all, it was her job to be pleasant, right?

"Draft beer," he said, then changing his mind, "No, wait…

11

make it a bottle. Thanks, Sherry."

Sherry no sooner put the bottle in front of him, when a loud voice yelled out calling his name.

"Hey... Bats!" The voice was hoarse and one Batson knew all too well. Coming from a pool table in the back walked a friend of many years – it was Sammy.

"Hey man. How's it going?" Sammy was a smooth talker and as usual, it was hard to get a word in. "Heard about Gracie landed her that good paying job up there in Yankeeville. Wow, man... that's great, huh? She was always a smart one and not bad looking either!" He nudged Bats and then kept on, "Everything's fine at home. Kids are always keeping us busy with all that after school stuff, but Liz handles most of it. I just work all the damned time in this hot sun." He paused, "Sorry man! All this about me... how about you? Been selling a lot lately?" Ah, finally.

"Yeah... had quite a few closings here lately. Things are going really well. So you're still doing that hard work I see?" Batson nudged him back, just to tease.

"Well, hell yeah. You know how those family business things go... gotta stay with it. I'm over all our crews now. Dad does all the paperwork, office stuff," he replied, taking a slug of beer in between sentences. "You just can't find good workers nowadays. You wouldn't believe some of these characters we get... they show up one day and then never come back! It's absolutely crazy." Sam's face scowled with frustration just thinking about it.

Maybe Batson didn't know too much about the hard labor but he knew about the office load of running a business. That was a job in itself.

"So about Liz, she's doing well?" Batson asked, showing his manners, being polite.

"Oh yeah, doing fine. She's still at home with Billy, our youngest. He's going to be three in November. She's signed him up at a daycare for fall and then she wants to go back to work at Smither's, the bakery on Liberty." He continued, "We will have been together eleven years in January! Can you believe that? Man, time flies."

"I'm happy for the two of you. You have certainly done well for yourselves," Batson smiled.

"When are you gonna ever settle down, Bats? You juggle them around enough." Sam patted Batson on the shoulder, a brotherly gesture. Sam was a lot larger than Batson. A bulky frame with a gut emerging underneath his t-shirt, looked like an old football player. Most people were intimidated by him, but on the inside... he was a good ole' boy, wouldn't hurt anyone.

Sammy's speech went on, "Sorry, don't mean to joke... maybe I'm jealous, who knows? See... I like the family thing. The kids are work sometimes, but man, nothing could ever compare. Come on, let me get you another." Sammy had pride in his eyes, a kind of pride Batson had not yet experienced.

Batson complied and the two sat there at Mary's and had themselves a good time. They gossiped like two old ladies, leaning into each other and carrying on. Every once in a while, Sammy's laughter roared out and Sherry would look over their way. Batson told Sammy stories of some of the oddballs he'd gone out with and Sammy tried giving advice. Then he offered to set Batson up with a friend of Liz's, Batson declined. He wasn't looking for Miss Right yet; he liked to play the single game for now.

Batson entertained several women in Camilla, quite a player he was. Most of them were professionals- intelligent, dressed well, attractive and had class, or so he thought so. He only had a couple serious relationships and Batson had let them go, like sand sifting through his fingers.

Men didn't usually discuss personal issues like Sam and Bats, but they had been together as kids and were almost like brothers. Sam grew up on the island with Batson and Gracie.

13

The boys had done all the normal things that children often do while growing up. They rode bikes, fished off the pier at Hudson Point, built forts to play war and late at night, settle down a bit with an amusing board game or gin rummy with Grandma Anna and Bessie. Gracie normally kept to herself. She stayed in her bedroom with her doll collection, reading a book or writing poems. Gracie stayed close to Anna and Bessie. She liked helping Bessie with the cooking or cards with her Grandma Anna. Gracie yearned for her mother's love, although the memory of her was faded. Sometimes she would go into a daze and imagine her mother right there, being part of her life.

Sam remembered the day when Batson and Gracie's parents died. The memory stuck with him as the years passed. Batson and Sam were only summer pals before the accident when Bats visited the island. Before Mr. and Mrs. Cannon died, the family lived inland on Racine Drive. Sam never actually visited the house where they had lived before, but later on when he was older, drove by out of curiosity.

Batson and Gracie were sent to Grandma Anna immediately after the tragic news. Sam remembered standing at the edge of the gravel road, balancing on his bike and watching Bats and Gracie, hand in hand, walking with Anna and Bessie into the house. They were all dressed in their Sunday clothes, worn to the funeral. Bats and Gracie looked so confused, so lost and he could almost feel their pain. What were they going to do without their mom and dad? He thought about them the remainder of the evening.

The following day, Sam and his mom went in town. With all his allowance money he proudly bought a G.I. Joe for Batson and a yarn doll for Gracie. It was all he could afford and he wanted to do something to make them feel better.

Sam and his mom walked up to the Cannon's front-screened

door. Looking in, both children were sitting side by side on the flowered print sofa. Almost everything in Anna's house was floral. They looked like they were lost in the midst of a wild storm, frightened. Sam handed over their gifts he had picked out.

Sam's mom gave Anna a pan of homemade lasagna; they hugged and exchanged kind words. The three kids on the couch sat innocently, hugged quickly as a thank-you to Sammy. Little Gracie, so young, seemed so uncorrupted in the tragedy of it all. The women watched the children with awe, as tears began to disappear from the wells in their eyes. They knew the true devastation; Batson and Gracie Cannon had lost the most important people in their lives. Their parents would not be there for them when they might need to talk or give them a yes or no, even to make Sunday breakfast or go the park. They were gone for good, leaving only Grandma Anna to care for them. She was the one who would need to be there when they cried out at night, to listen when they had a problem, to tuck them into their beds at night and the one that made sure they felt loved.

The ladies walked slowly into the breakfast room to have some tea. The boys went outside and Gracie went into what would soon be her new bedroom. She began arranging what dolls were already there. She didn't understand what was going on. Grannie had said Mama and Daddy were in God's place, a place called Heaven.

Batson and Sam were surprised to hear the wooden clock striking eight times. Sam jumped off his stool, eager to get home.

"Bats, gotta run. Liz will be all over me if I don't hurry up. The kids had soccer practice and they'll be home in about twenty minutes."

"Then you had better get going, pal. Tell Liz hello for me."

Batson said and they shook hands.

"Sure will do. And as for you, take care... it's been fun." Sam hurried out the front door, home to Liz and the kids.

Batson was glad the two had gotten together. For a while it was like old times.

Sherry interrupted his thought, "Need another?" She had noticed a group of women coming in the door and from experience, knew it would take some time getting their drink order. By the looks of them, they would be ordering the fun drinks: daiquiris, martinis and margaritas. She had better take care of Batson while she had the chance. Giving a yes, Batson vowed this one would be the last and then he would head home.

The last swig came quick. He glanced over to the table full of ladies, noticing a few that caught his eye. Forget it. He was overly tired from conversing with people all day long. Batson needed time alone. Time to organize his thoughts or at least try to.

Batson strolled to his car, parked in front of the office. The air felt thick and sticky, resulting from the heat the day had brought. It did not occur to him, of course.

His mind rolled with thoughts. He needed to go visit Grandma Anna sometime soon. Almost a week had passed since he had gone to see her, when normally he would drop by every other day or so. He decided he would call her first thing in the morning. Maybe she will want to go out to eat, he thought. She did not get out of the house much lately and maybe that would be a treat for her. Bessie could take off early and they could try that new seafood place near Barley's old gas station. No, staying in might be better. She's comfortable there and besides, it's almost too hot for her to be out and about.

Arriving in the driveway, falling directly below the staircase leading to the front door of Batson's townhouse, sat Max in his same spot. Max was the collie dog of the house and almost nine years old now. With the house sitting in city limits, Max would normally have to be on a leash but Batson never went by the rules. Max was a good boy and stayed where he was supposed to.

He greeted Batson with a joyful leap, while Batson talked to him to calm him down, "Down boy! Maxie, how was your day, ole boy?"

Batson walked up the stairway, Max trailing his feet respectably into the foyer and immediately hopped up on the couch panting for attention. Baston stumbled into the kitchen with Max following again. Max gobbled up his dog food before Batson could even finish filling up the bowl.

The two settled down on the floor together in front of the TV and munched on a bag of chips. Batson reached over to check the machine for messages. One from each of the two girls he had taken out a few weeks before and one from Grandma Anna. She called daily to check on him and to 'let him know that she was still there'. It was a reassurance type thing between the two of them. Now that Gracie had moved, Grandma Anna had become quite dependent on her grandson. She needed to hear his voice every so often to 'ease her mind', as she would say. He played the message again to hear her voice...

"Bats, it's Grandma Anna." She could be so proper at times, he knew it was her! "Just making my daily call to you, baby. Hope you had a good day. I miss you and hope you'll come out tomorrow. Gracie phoned this evening and wants to hear from you. I think she needs some of that brotherly support, she's a little homesick, you know. Give her a call when you can. We love you. Good night dear." She had made the call at seven, by now she was in bed. Again he made a mental note to call her in the morning.

Bats stripped down and climbed into bed, alone. Loneliness... this is not what it's supposed to be like. Max

17

kept resettling himself until he finally got situated. Batson decided to say a prayer. He prayed silently, hoping God would hear him.

"God, I know you don't hear from me much. I am struggling tonight though. My life is filled with everything I need. But something is missing. Help me to find that love, the love that won't go away. The love that makes you a better person, the one love that you want to be with for all times.

Tonight, I actually envied Sammy. Maybe I'm coming to a point in my life where I need that significant other. The one and only. Am I?"

Batson asked God to watch over Grandma Anna, Gracie and Bessie. He told God that he knew his mom and dad were with him somehow and to tell them... Batson took a deep breath. He looked up at the ceiling, realizing that he had never prayed to God about his parents. Only as a child and after the incident did he pray about them. He nestled down into the pillow, not able to say a word. God knew how he felt... empty, hollow.

Chapter Two

"Bessie, you got the coffee on?" Anna called out to her help.
"Yes, mam. It's been on fer o'er an hour now," Bessie
hollered back from the laundry room at the backside.
Eight thirty and these two were already screeching like hens.
Bessie was folding a basket overflowing with sheets and linens
as Anna stomped through the kitchen looking for her mug.
Anna drank out of the same coffee mug faithfully every
morning, one of her many routines. The mug was always in the
same space so the search didn't require too much effort. Clean
and ready to go, Anna filled it up.
"It's nice out dis' mornin, Misses, so I went on 'head an
opened up. 'Cept the winder' down da' hall baf' is stuck."
Bessie swigged her coffee, "Maybe Bats can come on out to
fits' it sometime."
"I sure hope he can find time for us out here. That boy
works all the damned time, won't take time off to enjoy his life
a 'tall."
"He will, Misses Anna. He jus' gots to find a reason to."
She finished folding and joined Anna at the table. "Whoa,
Misses! My day is jus' startin' and I'm already pooped.' Anna
rose from her chair, grabbed Bessie's mug and fixed it all up
for her the way she liked it. Anna handed her old friend the
coffee and their eyes met. Usually there was no need for words
between them, their actions spoke stronger than their words.
A breeze gently carried throughout the house. Soon
enough, the afternoon temperatures would rise and Bessie
would then turn on the ceiling fans. Batson had tried endlessly
to convince Anna to install central air, but she refused. God
knows they could afford it, but she insisted the house stay as it
was. She was a real stickler when she chose to be.

Anna picked up her mug and strolled out back to the porch, Bessie followed. They sat in the rockers and stared out at the water, so calm. The pier was badly weathered and Anna made a note to tell Batson about it. It would need to be replaced at some time. If she ever got any great grandchildren, they would need something to fish off of.

The silence was short; they soon fell into a new discussion.

"Have you seen that Mister Habersham's new car?" Anna loved to gossip. "I'll tell you what, I've got plenty more money than he's ever had and you don't see me drivin' somethin' that fancy!"

Bessie laughed at her, "You can't drive anyways, crazy woman. We is too old to git round in a car dat big!" Anna smiled, knowing how damn right she always was.

"Well, it's awful foolish to be out spending money on something so materialistic, if you ask me. I save my pennies for a rainy day and that old Mr. Habersham's gonna run out of his before he knows it." She waited for a minute, "I mean, he can't make that much with that rinky-dink hardware store of his, selling shovels and nails. I don't know, maybe he does."

"Don't know. He mus' be doin' somethin' right to be drivin' a caboose like 'dat one," Bessie cackled. Her teeth shining like stars when she opened her mouth.

They waved to Merv Tempton as he passed on by in his fishing boat. The water in the marsh rippled and the pier rocked slightly. As soon as they relaxed back into their chairs, the phone rang and Bessie went inside to answer it. It was Batson.

Anna followed to get the call, "Hello dear, how's my boy this morning?"

"I'm good. You sound cheerful. Already had your coffee this morning, I assume," he said sarcastically, referring to her overly friendly disposition.

"Yes sir, you know my Bessie. She gets me up so early.

Are you calling from home? I don't hear the bustle of the office in the back?"

"Yep, I'm home. Decided to take the day off today, if you can believe that one." He was finding it hard to believe it himself.

"Well, good Lord! I don't believe it!" She held the phone down on her lap and relayed the news to Bessie. Bessie got a strange look on her face, 'Somethin's up with dat boy,' she thought. "He's coming out this afternoon to fix all our problems." It made Anna feel good to know she was still loved.

Anna got to her grocery list for Bessie. They would need something good to eat for dinner since Bats was coming out. Anna insisted on a pot of country boil with the andoulee sausage, shrimp, corncobs and potatoes.

Bessie agreed, only if the shrimp were fresh at the market. She was a perfectionist when it came to her cooking. Ah, cooking was among the few things that they always agreed on.

Batson lounged around in his loose boxers, savoring every sip of coffee. No need to rush. He couldn't remember the last time he took a day off from work. Today must be well spent. The to-do list for the house could be put off another day. His time alone last night was taking a toll on him; Batson had decided to begin taking advantage of all the little things life had to offer. Turning over a new leaf.

He wanted to stop by the bookstore to check out some of the bestsellers. That was down on Main and Max would certainly appreciate that often promised walk in the park.

This was a treat to sit and actually drink a full cup of coffee. He read the entire newspaper, which normally ended up stacked up in the straw basket beside the door, unread and wasted. He showered, shaved and was dressed in twenty minutes tops.

"Today's gonna be great, Max."

Batson phoned Gracie at her new job in Chicago. Her voice filled with excitement about the articles she had worked so hard on, mentioning only a few friends she had met so far. She sounded lonely; the big city was a major change for her. Batson had faith in her; Gracie had always been a strong girl. Still, he worried. He assured her that soon she would be a huge success.

"You'll be running that paper, girl!" They said a quick goodbye, not wanting to let it linger and Gracie swallowed hard.

"I love you, Grace. Hang in there, okay?" She held in her tears, noticing the dozen other journalists working away.

The bookstore was practically void of customers. Small and privately owned, it prided itself on old-fashioned charm. To the left was a section devoted to newspapers and magazines and instinctively, Batson went down that path first. There it was-the Chicago Tribune, Gracie's Chicago Tribune. He picked up the top copy and the two books that he wanted off the best seller pile and took a seat at a table. The café was a newer addition to the store. The art students at the college had helped design it, matting the tables with artwork of all sorts and some mosaic pieces. To Batson, they were a distraction from what he was reading. He liked to examine each piece carefully, trying to see into the work.

People of all ages wandered in and he found himself watching the door open and close, open and close. He was surprised to see the door open and noticed the legs, then traveling upward to see that it was Liz, Sammy's wife. She had Billy attached to her hand, leading him inside while telling him not to touch anything. Batson waved to her and they began walking towards him.

"Well, hello stranger," Liz spoke first, "How's it going?" Billy pulling her fingers apart, trying to loosen the grip.

"Good, good. Just taking the day off today, needed a break." Liz looked at him with envy; she could use a day off. "You guys want to join me?" Was that a good idea? Batson wasn't sure.

"Sure. I'm meeting a friend here in a minute." She sat down, placing Billy on her knee. "So, Sammy said you guys got to see each other last night, huh?"

"Yeh, had quite a time."

"Well, good. He doesn't get out of the house anymore, you know. I've got him under lock and key. You need to come by sometime." Everything was so normal, so casual, and friendly with her.

"Is that a formal invitation?" Sammy just doesn't know what he's got... her.

"Yeah, whatever... formal. Ha. You know you're welcome anytime. Oh, there she is." Liz acknowledged another woman walking in with her toddler attached to her as well. "Gotta go. See you later?"

"Uh-huh. See you later." And she was gone.

The walk in the park with Max idea was down the tubes. Batson headed out to the island instead. He stopped in at an oyster bar on the beach with a crowd full of drunken fishermen. Some sat in their boats in circles, like their own little cult, making fun of some of the tourists walking by. Soon they would all be back on the water, out and about, never imagining life away from the sea.

Batson sat at a table by the window, ordered a bowl of crab bisque and thought of Gracie. He was so proud of her, doing exactly what she had set out to do. She wanted so badly to get out of Camilla and that's what she did, got out.

He jumped when the waitress returned with his drink.

"Sorry." She realized she had startled him. "Didn't mean to come up on ya like that."

"Oh no, no. You're fine. I'm a little off beat today." He flushed and he watched her walk away. She went to mingle and wait on other customers and Batson eyed her up and down. Something about her, she reminded him of someone he had known years before.

Bats pushed the thought further away, took a drink but still the idea crept upon him. Gradually, the image of Kate got clearer and clearer. She had moved to Camilla her freshman year of high school, the new girl everyone was talking about. Her father had been transferred here through some big corporation and they moved down from Boston or somewhere. She was the most beautiful creature he had ever laid his eyes on.

Kate had history class with Batson and it took all he had to pass that damned class. He would daydream about her during lecture, never enough to get the nerve up to ask her out.

The last year of school, on a Friday, the entire student body was in an uproar for the big game. The pep rally was carrying on inside the gym; Kate chose to go on home. Her dying Volvo wasn't cooperating and Batson was there to step in. He offered her a ride and that day was the beginning of a wonderful memory that would linger on until it finally faded away. God, she was so beautiful.

Chapter Three

Anna rested in her bedroom, while Bessie had taken a trip to the market in town. Anna had a bedroom full of character. Anna believed you could tell a lot about someone by what's inside his or her bedroom. She looked around, admiring the photographs on the wall; it occurred to her how comforting her room was. One window faced the waterfront and the bay window looked out to the right of the lot. Anna's bedroom expressed her own uniqueness with the handmade cedar bench that edged the lowest part of the rear window. She tilted her head, as she looked it over from across the room, remembering the day Papa Joe had finished it. Still newlyweds, kids, she and Joe had gone into town to buy some special fabric to cover it. Anna spent many hours cross-stitching a pattern that read as follows:

"Joe and Anna Cannon, married March 9, 1942. May we Love and Cherish each other for many Years to come, United in our Peaceful Home by the Briny Sea." APC 1943

She embroidered wild flowers all around the edge complimenting the academy blue and Cornish yellow threads. This was a prime example of Anna's renowned creativity and polished style. Joe had built it especially for her after their first year anniversary. They purchased this three-bedroom home, at the time it was brand new, just so Anna could live by the water. The first year had been awkward for Anna; they lived in a cramped studio apartment above the office building, which eventually became Cannon Realty. Before they married, it was Joe's pad. The office below was a bank, belonging to a family friend of Joe's parents. Joe had recently finished school and the young couple's life together was just beginning. Joe inherited money from his grandfather and so they had an instant nest egg. After Joe passed away, the remainder of the inheritance had helped out tremendously when Anna took guardianship over Batson and Gracie.

Anna had been raised beside the ocean and she insisted she could not live in town. She always apologized to Joe for being so choosy, but Joe took it all in stride. That was just the way she was, love was blind. Wasn't it? Every single thing about her made her the woman she was and in Joe's mind, that was what made her so special... those little things. And when they decided to hire some help around the house, Anna got to choose. She chose Bessie.

Anna would have never guessed that Bessie, the little colored girl, would have stayed around forever. But she had. Bessie was a wise woman, set in her ways... a spiritual woman with insights into the trials and tribulations of life. She was the one that was there when Anna delivered her first and only son. Bessie was there when all the people Anna had loved, died. She was Anna's security, offering compassion, guidance and encouragement. All it took was the comfort of knowing that she had Bessie beside her, holding her up when she felt drained and weary. Thinking back, like she often did, Anna could not imagine her life without Bessie. Bessie listened when Anna needed to talk, shut her mouth when she knew better than to say anything, and held Anna's hand when she needed strength and reassurance. Misses Anna was not strong all the time and Bessie was there when her armor came down. The two sort of grew up together and Bessie turned out to be her most trusted confidant and the oldest, dearest friend Misses Anna would ever have.

Anna treasured her inviting seat at the window. It was a habit to crack the window at night before she lay down and listen to the soothing roll of the sea. Her childhood bedroom had faced the sea as well, so it was like second nature to her. Everyone in the south knows if you live on the ocean, the bedroom with windows facing the ocean is the first to get gone.

Her closet was relatively small but managed to occupy clusters of cherished memorabilia. There were various pictures of days past, paperwork on the family business, photo albums, scrapbooks, bits and pieces of events long ago. The whole life of Anna Cannon was in that closet. The stacks had gotten so tall, that many years ago, Anna decided to move her clothes into one of the other bedroom closets. Anything to avoid actually cleaning it out. The closet was overflowing and Bessie offered countless times to go through it all with her, but Anna refused. Anna said that they would save that job for a rainy day, with a bewildered glitter in her eyes. Rainy days came and went, the closet remained untouched. Bessie knew the task of cleaning it out might cause sparks to fly, all that it contained, Anna had packed away deep inside of her.

Anna jumped when she heard the car door shut. Startled, she realized it was coming from the house next door. Who could be over there? That house has been vacant for years. The couple that had lived there had moved away, died or something, Anna never kept close tabs on them. They were always strange anyway, keeping to themselves and hardly ever coming out. Months ago, a moving van came and loaded everything, locked it up and that was that.

Anna sat up and Cecilia, the cat, hopped off the bed, obviously disgruntled that Anna had interrupted her afternoon nap. Anna slowly went to sit up on the side edge of her bed, her petal slippers on the hard wood beneath. She leaned on her arm, trying to push herself up. In a second, Anna's fragile frame crashed hard against the floor. Her head slammed onto the corner of the night stand causing a long gash to her forehead.

"Oh Gooood! Oh, dear God." Anna cried out with frustration, she lay helplessly in a heap, alone. Her whole bottom half burned with pain and the tears rushed out. Cecilia howled out, sensing her friend was in serious trouble. Anna was terrified. The severe pain and shock had numbed her entire body. She cussed herself for falling, "How damned clumsy I am, now look what I've gone and done!" She noticed the blood trailing down her cheek from her forehead, and then it occurred to her… the car door! Someone is out there!

"Help! Somebody please… help me!" her voice faded out, she had no strength. The right side of her head was now smothered with blood from the gash and she managed to grab the blanket that had fallen with her and put pressure to it. She wiped and pressed the best she could, but the pain was almost unbearable.

Thoughts meandered through her mind as she lay still. Anna flashed back to the numerous times that the children had fallen and been hurt. Stitches were routine for Batson and Gracie had broken her arm once, you would have thought the world had ended. She could see Gracie, fear in her eyes, 'It hurts. It hurts, Granny', she would sob. Gracie was her little angel. And Batson, well, Batson was always so brave. He knew when he was going to need a stitch, almost as if it he were proud. Anna closed her eyes and thought of the two at that moment. She struggled to call out again, "Heeelp! Somebodyyy!"

"Hello. Hello, is someone here?" A young voice carried through the screen door. Anna could not move, even her trembling arm ached from trying to put pressure on her head. She didn't care who was at the door; it was someone, someone that could help. Anyone.

Anna's voice sounded horse and scratchy. She pleaded, "Help me, dear. I'm in here!"

The girl rushed in with what appeared to be her daughter, although she sure did not seem old enough to have a child.

28

Anna calmed down a bit and looked the young girl up and down. Do I know this person? The child was straddled on her hip, as if that is what God had made hips for.

"Oh my God! Oh..." The girl took a breath and covered her mouth with her free hand. The sight alarmed her. The little girl dangled her feet, then slid down to stand on her own. "Find a phone, honey. Dial 9-1-1." Anna listened to the girl as she tried to reassure her that everything would be all right, over and over.

"Oh no, now don't do that. It will take them forever to get out here. Call Batson, my grandson, at his house. He'll come n' carry me to the hospital. If you could just grab that towel in the bath, right in there," she pointed. "Wet it and bring it in here for my head."

"No, no mam. I mean, yes. Yes, I'll get you a towel. But let me carry you to the emergency room." She grabbed the towel, "Do you think we can get you to the car?"

The girl's eyes were wide open; she was in shock. She had a tiny build; her hair hung straight several inches below her shoulders, with a small golden barrette to hold the top layers back. Her long hair was lovely, made her look almost angelic.

"No, just..." she paused, resting herself, "just call Batson. The number is right there on that piece of paper."

The girl dialed the number, letting it ring numerous times. No answer.

"No one's there." She began getting impatient. "The machine picked up." She would have to carry her to the car, hoping she wouldn't do anymore damage.

"Dammit now. Where could he be? The one day he takes off and something like this happens. Let me see if I can get off this floor." She glanced over at the child, "I'm sorry, I didn't mean... agh!" She fought to work herself up, Abby gently tugged with her hands underneath for support.

"I'm sorry. Is it hurting?" Anna looked at her like she'd

lost all sense. Is it hurting? Well, hell yes. She was up and standing, but not for long and so the three moved quickly to the car. Abby helped Anna lie down across the back seat, "Careful, careful," Anna whispered.

Abby's daughter, Lillie, hurried into the front seat and popped her seat belt on.

"I'm in my seat, mama. See? Seeee?"

"Yes, baby. I see." She was busy trying to make Anna as comfortable as possible. Abby listened attentively to Anna's detailed directions to the hospital, as she wasn't from Camilla.

Bats left the Oyster Bar at Hudson Point and headed on over to Grandma Anna's. The drive was a short one; her house lay a few streets over from the main road, cut a left down a two-mile winding road and her house sat there at the end. Both Batson and Gracie knew that winding road like the back of their hands. The street had few houses facing it; most were hidden back into the scattered woods of the island.

Batson remembered when they first moved here with Grandma Anna, he had been scared to ride his bike too far out. The kids at school made up these horror stories of the monstrous gators that lived close by. 'They could even eat one of us, the whole body! In one big gulp too, others a limb at a time!' Kids can have such gross, tormented minds. But in all the years that Batson lived here, he had yet to see one. The fear had gone away after a while.

He noticed the heavy door shut and the car gone. That's strange, they must have stepped out for a minute. After all, he told her this morning that he wouldn't be over until this evening, and it was only three o'clock or so.

He checked the door. Yep, it was unlocked, but that was the usual. He hollered out several times, neither answered, so he made himself at home. He dozed off and woke to the sound of the car pulling in the drive.

Bessie came through the door with a bag in each arm.

"Well... long time, no see." Bessie smiled from ear to ear, those teeth just a shining. Batson and Gracie were like her children too; she loved them both as much as Misses Anna.

"Hey, hey, hey. Where've y'all been?" He grabbed the two bags from her arms and motioned for her to go on in the kitchen, he would get the rest.

"Y'all? What you mean y'all?"

"You and Grandma."

"I been to dah market. Misses ain't wif' me."

"She's not here. I thought she was with you. Where is she?" Bessie rushed to the back door, knowing good and well that Misses Anna wouldn't be on that back porch. Batson and Bessie walked together into Anna's bedroom and gasped when they saw blood drops on the floor. The phone broke the silence.

"Cannons."

"Is this Batson?"

"Yes, uh-huh."

"This is Abby Logan. Listen, before you start freaking out, your grandmother is with me and doing fine. She slipped off her bed earlier and I brought her here, to the emergency room."

"You did what? She's okay though? Who are you again? Wait... never mind. We'll be right there." Batson dropped the phone on the hook.

Bessie held an open hand over her heart, while Batson explained. The groceries were left on the counter; Bats grabbed the keys and headed quickly to the hospital.

The emergency room was nearly empty. There was one middle-aged gentleman to the right sitting quietly, as if he were just waiting for someone. A mother was trying to occupy her busy toddler with a toy truck, who looked over at Batson as he

31

walked in with Bessie hooked on his arm, then the boy continued, "Vroom. Vroom."

"Calm down now. Misses Anna needs you son."

"Can I help you, sir?" The receptionist asked, after swinging open the glass pane that separated them.

"We need to see Anna Cannon, my grandmother... she's here."

"Come on back." She pointed to the doors, the monitor on the wall beeped and the doors opened automatically.

The emergency room was small but noticeably well kept. The lady at the front desk asked one of the nurses to take them back. The mint green curtain was pulled open and there she was, like a prize on 'Let's Make a Deal' or something, 'Behind curtain number 3...'

Anna looked drained but relaxed. Beside her in the chair sat Abby, she stood up immediately. With Lillie snuggled against her leg, she offered her hand to Batson, then Bessie. After quick introductions, Batson felt his heartbeat slow down a little, no more panic.

The same nurse that had led them inside returned and gave a detailed explanation of Anna's injuries. Anna had bruised both of her hips; she must have fallen directly on her front. The gash on the head was not serious, just a couple of stitches.

Anna smiled, while the nurse continued. They had given her some magic pills to ease the pain and suffering, the nurse handed the prescription slips to Batson and said she was ready to go home.

"Now?" Batson interjected.

"Just keep a close eye on her. She needs to stay in bed, off her feet, for at least a couple of weeks. Let those bones rest," she pointed to her own hips while speaking.

Batson was at a loss of words as he looked at this Abby Logan. Thank goodness she had been there. "But what had she been doing there?" Oops, he let that one out in the open. "I

32

mean, what were you doing there? Around the house?"

"I know it's kind of coincidental, but Lillie... she's my daughter here... well, we were out for a drive and happened to take a wrong turn. I noticed that abandoned house next door to hers, went to take a look in the windows and heard her holler out for help. See, we're sort of looking for a place." She paused, realizing how unimportant that really was, "Anyway, that's how it all happened. We then managed to get her into my car and made it here." Bessie glanced over at the girl and nodded as though she were satisfied with the story.

"I am just so grateful that you happened to be there. I can't thank you enough." Batson shook her hand, then smiled at her sincerely. "Grandma, I'm sorry I wasn't there."

"Well, it's alright now. Over and done with... kaput! But little Abby here, she was there. Now, we must have you two girls out for dinner or something special. Batson? Batson! Write her number down for me, please dear."

Bats pulled his wallet out of his back pocket and was ready to jot it down on one of the several scraps of paper inside. He listened to Abby Logan as she recited their hotel number. He noticed her eyes as she spoke, so deep and having their own story to tell. Abby told all three to call anytime if Anna needed anything. She hugged Anna.

"I'm glad I was there to help. I promise we'll come visit." They had to get going, it was almost suppertime already.

Bats and Bessie settled Misses Anna comfortably in her ruffled bed, turned on her new TV, the one Gracie had bought her for Christmas last year, and dimmed the lights. The sheets were washed yesterday and so they still had that fresh, crisp smell. Bessie still hung sheets, afghans and comforters out on the line that ran alongside the house. 'Gives em' a kiss of sunshine'. It sure did.

There was nothing quite like climbing in your own bed,

leaving that crack in the window and falling asleep to the stillness of night. Life was so peaceful there by the water. Anna had determined that this was where God had meant for her to be. This cottage was hers and she was not leaving it until her time to go. She and Bessie managed just fine around here. As long as they had each other, everything that needed to be accomplished got accomplished. It felt so good to be home.

Bessie made her way into the kitchen and had decided to go on and cook the country boil. Batson especially liked it and Bessie knew he would presumably be staying there for the night.

"Bessie? I'm going into town right fast and feed Max. Listen out for her while I'm gone."

"Take yo'r time. It'll be a while 'for dinner is ready."

Batson went on his way. He was awful curious about this Abby Logan. She seemed to be a likable girl, not his type, but nice. She looked almost like a lost child. He felt for sure she was unattached and with Lillie too. Seemed scary to him... being in a different town, not knowing anyone. That in itself showed strength, major independence, independence from whom though? Why was he worried with this and making all these assumptions?

He liked the way she looked up at him and he at her. She had on jeans, a shapely t-shirt that he couldn't help but notice, and sandals. Plain.

Her daughter, Lillie, was a darling child. Big brown eyes like her mom's, but bashful, clinging to her mama for sure. She was probably four, maybe five.

Abby had a natural look about her, the image stuck in his head. Her brown eyes, her long hair, a no-make-up kind of girl. Probably was a tomboy when she was younger, he thought. Where did she say she was from? Did she even say? And where was her husband? It just seemed so bizarre for a girl her age to just appear out of nowhere... and in Camilla, why?

What did she do for a living? She was looking for a place. Something about the house next door? Batson couldn't remember. Pulling in his driveway, he realized that he had thought about her the whole way home.

"Bessie?" Anna hollered from her room.
"Yes-um?"
"Could you bring me another one of those Tylenol? I think it's time for another."
"Yes-um."
"What you watchin'?"
"It's Jeopardy. Sit down, watch it with me." Anna pointed to the rocking chair beside the bed. The two tried to answer question after question, quite a competition. During commercials, Bessie checked on dinner.
"Batson should be back any minute now, guess we better make up his old bed." She paused. "Well, you know… in case he decides to sleep o'er." Anna knew her grandson was not about to leave her side. He would do anything he could to make her feel better and Bessie as well. "I'll probably go to sleep early tonight. Before dinner, more than likely. Maybe the two of y'all can play rummy without me."
"Yes-um. I is stayin' too, ya know. I'll take Gracie's bed, if dat's awlright?"
"Yes. Yes, of course." She liked it when Bessie stayed over; they would often stay up late and sit on the back porch. Anna always made hot tea for them both to sip on. Before Joe died, Bessie would stay over only on occasion. Joe would always go on to bed early, so they had their private time sitting out back. He never cared what the two talked about anyways. It was tradition now, to sit on that porch, chat about how the years had passed quickly enough, reminisce and tease about the old hairstyles, ridiculous clothes, or what Joe Blow and Sally Sue were doing down the road. Stories of times past, funny and

golden, silly and precious, they would come out over and over. Bessie and Anna were the closest of friends.

Bessie lived on the other side of the island. There were lined, rundown houses on what was dubbed Orr Street. Bessie had lived there all her life. Once a peaceful neighborhood, now days it filled with violence, graffiti and a bad name. Only the coloreds lived there. Anna forbade Bessie to walk home past dark. If she was able at the time, she continuously drove Bessie home.

Bessie had never married. Anna and Joe had been all she had, except as a child. Anna asked her about marriage once before, Bessie just said she'd never had the desire. Her ma and pop passed away years ago, leaving Bessie living alone in that house- she liked it. She kept her house up well, same house she'd been born and raised in. All her sisters and brothers lived in town now, they didn't want anything to do with that ole' place. Bessie took pride in that house though, it being the only thing to call her own.

She never purchased a car either, 'my legs do jus' fine'. Every single day, Bessie would walk to and from Misses Anna's house and only used the Cannon's car to run errands.

Bessie ladled out the country boil, all which would fit in the generous serving bowls. Batson bolted in the front door, hung up his work clothes for the next day and grabbed his bowl. The day had been a long one for all of them.

Anna read in her bed with her glasses tucked neatly on the tip of her nose. Batson waved hello and went back into the kitchen to eat dinner. She seemed to be doing well, but that fall had to have been painful and exhausting. She took it all in stride but it made Batson very aware that she was becoming less independent. Maybe it was time to make some changes around here.

Changes would be difficult, Anna being so bull-headed

sometimes. The ideal would be for her to move in town with him, but he knew that was out of the question. Anna would refuse before he would be able to get out the first few words. Wonder if Bessie would move in? They would have each other to depend on, perfect idea! Bessie might not be willing to leave her house though, but Batson felt sure she would do it for Anna. Right now was too soon to decide the matter, he would have to talk to Gracie and get her input.

Bessie walked in.

"This is great, Bess. I was starved. I grabbed a bowl of bisque earlier today but that didn't fill me up."

Bessie fixed up a bowl for Anna and placed it on a tray. She added a glass of lemonade, a soup spoon and an abundance of napkins to the side; this dish was a messy one.

Anna was still reading when Bessie went in to bring her dinner. Anna looked up at her friend, placed the book down and took off her glasses. Bessie went back in the kitchen to get her bowl and then joined Anna in her room.

Batson sat comfortably at the table, dazed and tired from the whole episode. The country boil hit the spot and was exactly what he needed, a home cooked meal. It helped him to relax and put things into perspective while his mind shuffled through the many hassles of work. He had a banquet to organize for Christmas, a luncheon with the human resource director of the Depot Mart account and the monthly staff meeting coming up on the first of September. The banquet was always important to him. He made the effort every year to conjure up an enjoyable and unforgettable evening for his employees. After all, they were what made Cannon Realty the success that it was.

Cannon Realty was not only the oldest realty company in Camilla, it was one of the largest and unmistakably the most reputable and prestigious to work with. Most of the realtors took pride in their accrued experience and admired Batson for following in his family footsteps.

Batson stepped into Anna's room and found Bessie sitting in the rocker. Anna had fallen fast asleep and Bessie had already set their empty bowls aside. She watched as Anna lay resting with the lights, still dim and the window remaining cracked open. They collected the dishes, Bessie turned off the light completely, and closed the door.

"She is worn slap out."

"It's been a hard day for her," Bats continued, "She's getting on up there and I'm worried about her staying out here all alone. I think it's time to make some decisions about her living arrangements."

"Oh, no. Batson, Misses Anna would has a fit if she hear you sayin' dat."

"Bessie, I know how close the two of you are. It's almost been as though you were sisters. I can't remember a day growing up when you weren't here. I have something to say, well something to ask you about... don't answer me now, okay? Just think about it."

Bessie knew where this was going.

"I think Grandma needs to have someone here with her around the clock. Now, I don't want to hire a nurse, or aide or whatever you call em'. What I would really like is for you to move in here, move in with her." Bessie's eyes wandered around the room, looking everywhere but at Batson. "It doesn't need to happen immediately, just sometime soon. We'll have to be very casual about this around her, you know... I don't want her to think we're pushing this on her."

"Uh-huh. I understand." A deep breathe, "I is gettin' old too, you know. I'll think 'bout it din' an not says a word, I promise you."

Bessie's heart ached with the reality of his proposition. Misses Anna was so healthy, only she was thinner than she used to be and obviously, a lot more fragile as well. God's telling us that our lives on earth might fin' come to an end, movin' on to a life wif' him.

Bessie's faith was one of her best traits. She had such courage through all that life had dealt her. When Misses Anna grieved, she grieved. They had seen loved ones pass on, all just part of God's big plan. Bessie believed that everything that happened was for a reason. The people we meet along the way, well, we are supposed to meet. The joys and celebrations that we share, are all part of the plan. Each and every person carries their own spiritual energy, this determines who we bring into our lives. Everything in its place. Bessie's view on life astounded Batson, always had. In her own way, she had instilled her beliefs in both Batson and Gracie. She was passing along a little bit of herself, as if they were her children as well. Batson and Gracie were the children that she had never had.

Chapter Four

Abby and Lillie settled into the double bed at the Super 8 out on Highway 90. Lillie had had her bath and was beginning to nod off. Lillie snuggled up against her Mama and held her stuffed bunny tightly in her arms. Abby held her daughter close, running her fingers through Lillie's curls. She must have gotten them from her father's side. Abby cringed at the thought of him, but it still hurt. Tears filled up her hazy, swollen eyes. Her emotions began to overwhelm her. Is this a mistake? Maybe I'm not strong enough to do this on my own. Chills spread over her body and she felt suffocated. She slowly lifted Lillie's arm off of her and stepped over to the table near the window. The drapes covered the large panes of glass completely. She plugged in her typewriter to the outlet directly below the window, reached into the faded leather briefcase. Her father had given it to her years ago when she had been interested in journalism. Abby typed, corrected and typed; over and over she worked up a half-dozen resumes. Looking through the classifieds as she went along, it seemed that there were plenty of opportunities in this town. She didn't have much professional working experience, she could type fast and knew quite a bit about computers. Surely there would be something out there for her. High hopes led her to believe she could find something! She and Lillie had enough money to get them settled in. The car had been paid off for over a year now, which helped out tremendously. All they had brought along were the necessities, enough to start over. Abby would need to get furniture and hoped she could find some relatively inexpensive pieces.

Lillie slept soundly, moving from time to time, obviously dreaming. Abby looked over at her child. She took an unintentional break in her work and thought to herself. That child was all she had. Abby had done the best she could, having to raise her alone and realizing that she wasn't even half way there. Lillie was so precious to her, words could not begin to describe the love between a mother and her child. She had been so good throughout it all. Abby began to cry, tears of joy and some out of desperation. She was determined to make a life for Lillie, the best any child could ever ask for. Her tiny face had the same profile that Abby's had had as a child. Lillie had ravishing blonde curls atop her head; Abby imagined the sun of Camilla would only accentuate the brightness of her tresses. One would think she would have sky blue eyes to match, but she didn't. Her eyes were a nut brown color, similar to her mama's but not as dark. Abby wondered what went through Lillie's head, what she thought about all this moving around business.

She continued to type after her short delay. Soon after, her hands started to ache and she decided it was time to turn in. She finished the page she had been adamantly working on and put everything into its place before climbing into bed. If she left it out, the little hands of Lillie would soon find it come morning and have her way with it.

Abby flipped on the reading light above the headboard and pulled out her journal; a pencil marked the last spot.

August 23rd

How long have I waited for this moment? I am still daydreaming aren't I? The day that I would finally move on with my life and make it my own. Lillie sleeps peacefully beside me. I met some wonderful people today, the Cannons... Ms. Anna Cannon, she lives out on the island with a lady named Bessie, I suppose she's a maid of some sort. Quite interesting how we met but it's too long of a story to tell right now. They said they would be in touch.

For now I believe we will continue to stay here at this hotel until I am able to find a home for us. I saw an adorable one beside Ms. Cannon's house. I think it will need a lot of work but I will see what I can find out about it. Not sure what her grandson, Batson, does for a living.

He was very kindhearted and thanked me for all I had done. My mind is weary and writing is difficult tonight.

I am trying not to think about mom and dad. I'll have to call tomorrow, they worry so much about us. Lillie misses them desperately and so do I. Let God watch over us and tomorrow will bring good news I hope. Good night.

Rain poured all through the night in Camilla. The hot air made for ferocious thunderstorms down along the coast. It was always to be expected for thunder to roll at any given moment during the late summer months. Batson had always been captivated by the power of nature. The threat of hurricanes was also a scare for the residents of Camilla, but it had been nearly forty years since one had even come close. They would usually roll on up the coast north of Camilla. Camilla sat in somewhat of a nook, the town was usually spared any horrific destruction. But not far north, the coastal cities that did get hit by storms would certainly need assistance. When Batson and Gracie were younger, Anna would take them up the way and all three would aid anyone that needed it. Anna felt it was important to let the kids see what sort of damage a storm could do and more so, how to handle the results. The Red Cross was the rescue squad they worked with and Batson remembered seeing demolished, irreparable homes and both adults and children crying out for food and water. Batson and Gracie would graciously pass out bottled water, help make sandwiches and try to keep the younger ones entertained. Living by the sea could sure have its drawbacks and this was one of them.

The storm hitting Camilla tonight was common. The winds blew strong, sweeping sand and debris all over the island. Thunder boomed and lightning flashed. The cat snuggled close to Anna, who slept quite soundly in her bed. With her window still cracked, the marvelous breeze would keep her asleep. Bessie, on the other hand, lay with her eyes slightly open. She enjoyed storms but was hesitant on a good nights sleep.

Batson was wide-awake in his old room. He got up and raised the window a couple of inches, then gradually fell back into deep dreams.

Abby held on tightly to Lillie while the winds blew even harder outside. The panes of the window sounded as if they could shatter at any given moment. She hoped the noise of the storm would not unsettle Lillie; it would most definitely frighten her. She was sure the storm would soon be over and before she knew it the sunrays would streak through with an early hello.

Nearly two weeks had gone by and Anna had not called Abby. The morning was extraordinarily cool and everyone was busy with their normal routines. Batson would be at the office and Bessie had been continuously staying at Anna's. Batson and Bessie had made an agreement for the time being; Bessie just wouldn't leave Anna home alone. Batson would go to the market if need be and run errands as necessary. Bessie and Anna could go together if he could not be reached, but for now Anna was with someone at all times. Bessie was staying over at night until she made the definite decision to move in permanently, sort of a trial run. Anna did not even notice the arrangement between the two; life seemed ordinary and normal to her. She just assumed Batson and Bessie were being overprotective of her, trying to accommodate her since the fall.

Abby was still looking for work in the meantime. She found a Montessori school in downtown Camilla that seemed to work out great for Lillie. She was in K-4 now. It was a private school, which meant more individualized care, smaller classrooms and many qualified caretakers. Abby trusted that her daughter was in the best care. She was lucky to have taken the last spot available. Most of the enrollment was done in August, but the school had one child drop out at the last minute. Lillie filled the spot the first week of September. This gave Abby the opportunity to make her job-hunting full time.

Abby had two interviews today, one at an optometrist office near the mall looking for a receptionist, the other at a law firm downtown on Whitsett. Wolfe and Richmond was the name of the firm and little did Abby know that right beside it, on the corner sat Cannon Realty.

Batson Cannon situated at his desk, hovering over his ancient, out-of-date typewriter. Batson refused to bow down to the computer technology that was invading human intelligence. He was old-fashioned and tried holding on to a world that had died long ago, a working environment that existed before computers came along.

Abby's high hopes seemed to darken as she left the optometrist office. It was only a receptionist position. They were only willing to pay a minimum salary and it was not enough. Once again, she had found a dead end. She took a deep breath as she started her car and headed on to her second and final interview of the day. She just could not accept that position... she was worth more than that.

The law firm of Wolfe and Richmond had advertised for a legal secretary, willing to train if needed. Abby had sent her resume in, doubtful that they would call, but they did. Two years before she had taken some paralegal courses at the tech school near home, she had noted that on her resume. Maybe this one will be better. She was confident it would pay better.

She found a parking spot directly on Whitsett and saw the sign, Wolfe and Richmond in brass letters on the door. Abby noticed the line of magnolia trees across the street. Whitsett was a charming street with awnings on most of the small business stores along it.

Abby greeted the receptionist, took a seat and five minutes later a young gentleman came to meet her. He appeared to be about her age but his manner was like an old man, very professional too. He introduced himself as Thomas Richmond, understandably one of the partners in the firm. They exchanged a handshake and he led her down the hall to his office. She marveled at the view outside his window. Down below were the same magnolias that she had admired when walking in and there appeared to be a small park beyond them.

Abby found Mr. Richmond quite intriguing, as he explained in detail what the job responsibilities would entail. He had a prominent southern accent but spoke with firmness and stressed the confidentiality of the job position. Someone so wise and unquestionably sophisticated would normally have easily intimidated Abby, but instead she found herself very comfortable with him. She smiled, even blushed a couple of times out of nervousness as the interview continued. Abby needed to show him that she would be the perfect candidate for the job. She nodded in agreement and was attentive to every word that flew out of his mouth.

"Now that we have gotten it all over with, I need to tell you that I have a couple more interviews today," he paused. "But I am very pleased with our interview. I should contact you sometime tomorrow and let you know what I've decided." The decision would ultimately be left up to him; he was the one that needed the help.

"Yes. Yes, of course. Mr. Richmond, it's been a pleasure."

"Yes, it has."

"Thank you so much for your time." Abby shook his hand

once again with a firm grip and she showed herself out. The interview could not have gone any smoother and the two seemed to have enough chemistry to incorporate a stable working relationship. Abby Logan contained herself from jumping with excitement as left the building.

Batson Cannon noticed Abby from his window as she got into her car and sped off. He remembered her small frame and long, straight hair. That was her, Abby Logan. Wasn't it? What had she been doing down here?

Batson left his typewriter on and walked over to talk with Thom. He went on back, waving to Patricia at the front desk. Thom had been an old friend of his and he knew if Abby had been in there, Thom would let him know all about it.

"Hey there, Bats. What brings you over?"

"Just wanted to see if that was Abby Logan in here?"

"She just left. She was interviewing to be my assistant… why? Do you know her?"

"Well, no, not really. She helped my grandmother a couple of weeks ago when she fell and I was just curious." He sounded unconcerned, an effort.

"She seems like she'd be a great addition for us here. Young, outgoing and a lot of potential." Thom complimented her, if only she knew.

"Yeah. I really need to call her sometime or Grandma does. Hey, could you do me a favor and give me her number?"

"Bats… you know I'm not really supposed to do that."

Batson interrupted, "Yeah, that's alright. Don't want to make waves… I'll just pick it up from Grandma. We need to have her out to the island, a thank-you kind of thing."

"Well, sure." Thom looked over at Abby's resume and wrote down the number. It was the direct number to her hotel room, but Batson was sure Thom didn't know the girl was staying in a hotel. He remembered the first couple of digits from the first and only time she had given it to him. "Here you go… just don't mention my name."

Batson promised and went back to his office. He sat the number beside the typewriter and thought about it. He really did not understand his sudden urge to get her number. What made him so damn curious about her? Was it her innocent look? Maybe he just felt sorry for her. Why do that though?

She looked a lot different when he saw her from the window. Her dress fell to her ankles and her hair was neatly brushed, pulled back into a braid. Abby looked so young, but Batson saw something in her that he hadn't seen too often. This was a woman with an enormous amount of potential, guts. She was trying to make her way in this town. He admired her, that's what it was. She was an original and like he had decided before, nothing like the women he was used to dating and being in the company of.

If there was one characteristic to describe Batson Cannon, it would be his persistence. He was determined to call Abby. How would he go about it though? She seemed so secluded, almost as if she didn't want anyone around. Batson did not want to frighten her off. Then there was Lillie, her little girl. Wow. How would he fit into the picture there? Maybe he should not even start up anything? A woman with a child was a totally different ball field and one he had never played in.

The afternoon hours crawled by, minute on minute. Batson's hesitation had frustrated him. He decided that he wanted to call her, but oddly enough, he didn't know what to say. It was getting close to closing time and he finally picked up the phone, only he didn't dial Abby's number, he called someone else.

She answered.

"It's me. Can I see you?"

"I'll be at your place at six."

Chapter Five

The temperature was rising even more and the humidity was close to boiling. Abby was pouring with sweat as she and Lillie waited in the drive-thru line at McDonald's. The air conditioner never worked in this car. Abby swore to buy a new one, which was on her list of goals.

Ice cream cones were always a treat after school. Lillie would continually make a mess with it, so as usual they pulled to a side street to enjoy. Lillie talked the entire time in between licks off her cone. She really enjoyed school and being around the other children. It was at this age that they truly did enjoy school; it was the later years that kids normally faked sick or tried to get their temperature to rise. Abby could remember.

Abby had gotten to stay at home with Lillie for a while after she was born. She was two when she started at the church daycare. The change was an adjustment for both of them. Abby would cry just as much, if not more than Lillie did on most mornings when she had to leave her. This time had not been nearly as difficult. Abby still had an empty feeling down deep about it though, hollowness. Her sadness was now because of the reality of Lillie growing up. To be a mother is so hard, to sit and watch your child grow and change. Yet, at the same time, it brings intense joy to see how they learn, memorizing the many milestones that they accomplish each and every day. Daydreaming, Abby tried to divert her attention back to Lillie, who was excitedly telling stories about her day.

Lillie grabbed a napkin and wiped off to the best of her ability. Abby's attention caught a figure out to the side. She squinted her eyes, as if it helped her focus any better. It was Batson Cannon, Anna's grandson. He was parking his car into a spot below an amazing flight of stairs, leading to a quite luxurious townhouse. She watched him loosen his tie and rush inside. He must live there.

"Wow, that's quite a place."

"What Mama?" Bless her heart, so inquisitive.

"Nothing. Let's go back to the room." So they did and that was that.

The red light on the phone was blinking. Someone had tried to call. She dialed the front desk and was told that Anna Cannon had called and left her number for Abby to return the call. Great! Abby couldn't believe today was turning out so well. First, the interview with the law firm and now, her only friend in Camilla had phoned.

Bessie answered, followed by a holler, "Misses Anna... Phone's for you."

"Yes. Hello, this is Anna."

"Hello, Ms. Cannon?"

"Um-hum."

"It's Abby... Abby Logan. Did you try to reach me earlier?" Abby tried to slow her voice down a bit, she felt like a racehorse, one that was still running even after the finish line.

"Yes, dear. I sure did. How are you?"

"Good, very good."

"Well, see... I wanted to see if you and your daughter... will you please forgive me, I cannot recall her name."

"Oh, of course. Her name is Lillie."

"Lillie, yes... that's it. I wanted to see if you and Lillie would like to join us for dinner." She was so polite, so soft mannered.

"Yes, mam. That would be so nice. Thank you so much for asking. What time would you like us to come?"

"Whenever you guys get rested a bit, just head on o'er. Bessie's got salmon stew on, you know, nothing fancy. Oh, and probably some grilled cheese for the baby... she'll like that, of course."

Without hesitation, Abby got off the phone and began to get ready. Lillie changed into some fresh clothes and Abby dressed casually in a pair of denim shorts, a nice blouse and sandals. They made a quick stop at the grocery store, where Abby picked up a small bottle of white wine and a big 7up for Lil'. She wasn't sure if Anna or Bessie drank or not, but the idea of it with salmon stew made her even hungrier. She hoped they wouldn't mind.

Batson showered and grabbed a beer from the fridge. She would be there any minute now. It was wrong to see each other like this and both of them knew it. Their relationship had gone way back several years, even before she had married Sammy. He needed to see her. She was like that old, comfortable pair of jeans, that notebook cover that you doodled on, the one he just couldn't get rid of.

Batson heard her footsteps climbing the back stairs. Liz always parked her car down at her best friend's house and then walked through the alley to his house. That was the routine.

She only had to knock twice and Batson threw the door open, embraced her and led her in. The time they had together was limited and they wasted none of it. In only minutes, the two of them joined together in Batson's bed. The release of stored energy and baffled emotions filled the entire room. Liz loved her husband, but he was never around for she and the kids. She spent her days alone. Being with Batson was her escape; he filled her fantasies and made her soar to a different place. She knew that what she was doing was wrong; it was something people would look down upon. Like an addiction, she needed Batson as bad as he needed her.

His body wanted hers so desperately, every time. She was desirable. Did he love her? No, it wasn't love, far from it. The two of them together was a habit, a bad one. It was so awful to

51

do something that could be so beautiful and use it in such a cheap way. Never were the words of love or tenderness exchanged. It was a sexual relationship, so private and so fast lived every time.

Sam would never forgive him for this or forgive Liz either, for that matter. Batson found her so hard to resist. She was the ideal woman to him. Liz was beautiful. Batson felt the only reason he was persistent on spending this intimate time with her was because of the absence of someone of his own, someone he could trust to share himself with.

Liz was in it for different reasons, or so he thought. She had no feelings for Batson, which hurt. Batson was an object to her when she visited, something to play with. Batson found himself wishing that while taking such a risk to be with each other, it could at least mean something to her, but it didn't. Batson had accepted it though. She had Sam, whether she wanted him or not.

Liz sat up on the edge of the bed and ran her fingers through her hair. "I don't know if I can do this anymore, Batson. It's eating me up inside."

Batson's fingers felt the small of her back and he agreed. Feelings of regret and guilt shadowed over her, a cloud of evil and deceit.

"It's been going on too long, Liz. I'm sorry... I shouldn't have called." He whispered the words into her ear.

"No, we are both to blame. We did good there for a while, but we just can't continue like this." She paused. "I mean, I can't. You know how much I love Sam and the kids... Oh God. I've got to go." She turned around, "Don't call anymore, Batson. I can't do this."

Batson watched as she dressed without saying a word and walked out the back door, not looking back. Batson got up to get another beer and mellowed in his bed for the remainder of the night. He thought about Liz. She was hurting from all of this. What they had done was something they could never take back. It would remain forever in their pasts. How could he have ever done such a thing? Well, this was definitely the end of it. He could not look at her as he did before.

All three of them had been such good friends long ago, inseparable. He remembered Sam picking him up, Liz in the front seat and going out with all the guys. Liz always came along when they went camping or out to a party. She fit in perfectly; she belonged to Sam. He had been the only real boyfriend she had ever had, or so everyone thought. Batson and Liz had started way back then, having this intense attraction between them.

They were never able to see each other intimately until years later. Liz was planning her wedding. She and Batson met up downtown, then went out to the island together. It was casual at first. Sam had gone on a fishing trip with his dad for the weekend. And there, in a secluded area on the beach, near Hudson, they made love for the first time. The two went on with their separate lives from then on and only on occasion repeated that moment they had shared. Now, it was all coming to an end, over for good.

The stew had turned out perfectly and though Lillie did not care for it, she filled up on a grilled cheese and chips. Bessie showed her to Gracie's room, where she found a collection of dolls to play with. Abby and Anna sat outside on the back porch, while Bessie straightened the kitchen up.

The water was still and the air was pleasant. Abby complimented several times on Bessie's cooking, Anna's interior decorating and the beauty of the island. There was peacefulness about it, like something out of a movie or a dream. The landscape was so undisturbed, so natural. Abby had been born and raised in the south, but had never lived on the water. She remembered visiting the beaches when she was a young girl. That was a long time ago. Breathing in the fresh air, she took in as much of it as she could. The whole evening had gone so well. Abby needed to know that she had someone here for her, she felt right at home.

"Did you find out anything about the house next door?" Anna was sipping her wine, though Bessie would have no part in it.

"No, I haven't. I didn't know exactly where to look to find out the information on it… I've been job-hunting, you know."

"Well, I'll have to ask Batson about it. I thought I told you, he runs our family realty company downtown… he's a great person to work with."

"That'd be great! I really am interested in it… just not so sure we can afford it. It's on Whitsett Street, right? The realty company that is."

"Sure is. Have you seen it?" Abby nodded, telling her about her interview.

"Yes, yes. Batson went to school with one of those boys, can't remember which one though. Maybe he can put in a good word for you. I'll ask him about it when he comes out."

"Did you know the people that lived in the house last?"

Abby seemed disinterested in talking about Batson, she kept on track with discussion about the house.

"No, not really. We didn't see much of them, did we Bessie?"

"No, mam."

"They came and went most of the time without paying much attention to us over here."

"Well, that's not very nice. I guess it was their loss, huh?" They carried on and on for a little while longer before Lillie came running out. She found a favorite out of the doll collection. Anna said she could keep it for a while and when Gracie came home, she might let her keep it for good. Gracie had collected those dolls for years, but missing one wouldn't

54

hurt.

Bessie strolled out from the kitchen, tired of hollering outside. The day had worn her, you could see it in her eyes.

"I gots some coffee on in here, if any y'all wants some."

Everyone joined at the kitchen table for a quick cup before Abby and Lillie left. Abby noticed the trophies gathering dust on a bookshelf in the hall.

"Who do these belong to, Anna?"

"Oh, those things are Batson's. All his years of playing ball and now, here they sit, at my house instead of his. He was an all-star player, that's for sure. I can brag, you know, he is my grandson." Abby smiled at her. "Now, Gracie is so very different from Bats. I can't wait for you two to meet. She's in Chicago and writes for the paper up there. We are all so proud of our Gracie, aren't we, Bessie?" Bessie agreed with her.

Abby admired Anna for all that she was, not knowing the terrible circumstances that brought she and her grandchildren to live together. A parent's death was surely the reason, unless they had moved away or something. Maybe one day she would find out, or not, it didn't matter right now. She just knew that Anna and Bessie would at least be there for she and Lillie... that was important to her.

"Well, we'd better get going. It's late and I know you two are tired. Bessie, would you like a ride home or will you stay here?" Abby offered, not knowing the situation.

"I stay here, Misses Abby." She patted Abby on the shoulder, thanking her for her thoughtfulness.

Abby thanked them both once again and she and Lillie went back to the dreaded hotel room. It was not fun now, but Abby promised Lillie that soon they would have a house to call their own.

"I know, Mama. It's okay." But Abby meant it, they had already stayed way too long in the hotel, it was time to get a move on. She hoped that either Anna or her grandson would call tomorrow with some information on that house out there. It needed plenty of work and if she did get to rent it or even buy it, it would take some time just cleaning it up.

Liz lay in the bed beside Sammy, closing her eyes as if she were sleeping. She was overwhelmed with guilt. Sammy sat watching the news, as her mind repeated what had happened only hours earlier. She thought about all of it and knew in her heart that Sam could never know the truth. It would wreck the lives of too many innocent people. Besides, it was never going to happen again and all of it lay in the past. What would be the justification of telling him now? She nuzzled herself up to Sammy and he gently placed his arm around her. He loved her so much and the two had made a good life for themselves. Together they brought three beautiful children into the world and lived in an immaculate home. How could she ever destroy this? Liz took all the memories of she and Batson, placed them way down deep inside her, and vowed never to let them float to the top.

Chapter Six

"Lillie! Are you not ready yet?" Abby hollered to her from the bathroom, just stepping out of her morning shower. "We've got to get going or you'll be late for school... let's get a move on."

"Yes, Mama," Lillie ran to the bathroom door, "This is for you." She handed over a picture out of her coloring book, a picture of Big Bird and Oscar scribbled in with a rainbow of colors.

"How pretty, honey." Abby complimented her. "Will you put it on the table over there for me so I can keep it in my briefcase. That way I can see it all day long." Lillie did as she was asked, a well-mannered child with her curls going everywhere this morning. Lillie had taken her bath the night before and so her hair was wrecked from going to bed with it wet. Abby tried to tame it, but it was no use. The curls were impossible to comb, it only made them frizz. Abby love her curls and usually decided to let them go where they wished. Abby called her a 'blonde Raggedy', insinuating a Raggedy Ann with blond curls instead of red. Lillie always grinned when she called her that, it made her feel special.

About fifteen minutes later, Abby was dropping Lillie off at school. She walked her inside as always and Lillie was quick to run and meet with her classmates. Miss Brenda was the teacher and Abby admired her tremendously. She was gregarious and clever, always full of new and creative ideas for the children. Lillie especially liked Story Time with Miss Brenda and the other teachers. They would join together and recite plays, sometimes even with costumes on. The children got so excited when Story Time came around. With the absence of her father, Abby wanted Lillie to thrive just as much as the others. It had not been a big adjustment for Lillie because she had been so young and he was never around anyway. She only hoped Lillie wouldn't remember the especially hard times she had had with her father. The agreement they had made was that Lillie stay with her mother, he was overly pleased with that. He never cared, one way or the other. Abby burned with fury when she thought about it.

Abby dropped by and filled her thermos with coffee at the Quickmart. She needed to make a couple phone calls and could now relax a little, but hoped to hear from the law firm downtown. Her first priority was to call back home to talk to her mom and dad.

It rang twice before she picked up. Her mom was elated to hear from her, finally. Abby told her that she was looking for a job and about the nursery school she had found for Lillie. Her voice was filled with excitement as she talked about Anna and Bessie. Her mom was relieved to hear the self-assurance in her daughter's voice. A long time had passed since Abby sounded like the 'old Abby' she used to know. Abby had gotten so depressed while she was at home every day with Lillie and after the hectic separation with Will.

One day she reached and found her true spirit, it had been there all along. Abby's mom knew she had a light inside of her; it had only flickered out during that one stormy phase of her life. Now, it was shining again. She understood Abby's desire to move further from home, on her own… they believed in her and later helped out with the moving expenses. Abby was an only child, so of course, they gave her everything she needed. They wanted to see Abby and Lillie find all the good that life had to offer. By the sound in Abby's voice, they would. Things just took time.

Abby cried, suddenly yearning for her mom to squeeze her between her arms, some reassurance that everything was going to be all right. Abby missed her parents desperately, but promised as soon as they got settled, they would be invited to come and stay. She would call again later to talk with her dad, Lillie would definitely want to talk to her Papa. Tears ran down all four cheeks, as they said their goodbyes.

Wiping her face off with the edge of her top, she tucked her knees up into her chest, bowed her head between them and cried some more, like a child. It was so hard for her to find strength. Feeling isolated, Abby lingered on her bed in that same position, long enough to renew herself. There was not a single feeling in the world, like the one you feel when you get homesick. Your stomach feels all empty and nauseated, like worms crawling inside there. Ooh. What a thought. And when you hear your mom or dad's voice it really doesn't calm you, if anything, it makes you wish for them and weep even more.

She lifted her head and wiped the remaining tears in the corners of her eyes. All right, that's enough! She had to finish up her calls. First, a cup of hot coffee was what she needed. Abby poured a generous capful in the mug from the thermos and took a seat at the table. Her typewriter sat motionless on top of the table, her briefcase lying open on the floor with Lillie's picture dangling out and those damned tacky drapes still closed. Abby opened them up; let the warm sun replenish the darkened room. The difference the sun made to their small room was like an astronomical makeover. She felt refreshed and nuzzled in the sunken leather chair and sipped her hot java. Outside sat their car that had brought them to Camilla. The empty luggage sat next to the front door. The thought reminded Abby of one of the calls she needed to make. She needed to call Anna to see if she found out any news about the house out on the island. She felt a twinge as she reached out to make the call, chills went up her arms. Her eyes left the phone and drifted over to the window to see a shadow standing outside her door. The hazy silhouette startled her and she jumped up to hide behind the door.

Batson Cannon got up the nerve and finally extended his hand to knock. Abby hesitated to answer and without a peephole, she would have to look out the window. Who could this be? She glanced around the curtain piece to see the admirable face of Batson Cannon. Her eyes widened and she paused once more before opening the door to welcome him in. She felt her face flush with embarrassment, trying to imagine what she looked like at the moment. Company was the last thing she had expected! Why hadn't he called first? God! Oh, he looks so handsome too. What am I thinking? Okay.

Surprisingly, Batson was dressed in jeans, a collared shirt and tennis shoes. Abby tried to calm herself down. Only minutes ago, she had been wailing on the phone, feeling so alone and now, here she was with this charming, attractive man lurking at the door. It had not even occurred to her at the hospital, but after seeing him climb the stairs at his house and now, he was certainly a sight to see. He apologized immediately for stopping by unannounced.

"Oh, that's alright. Come on in. I must look like a mess. I just took Lillie, my daughter, to school and um, I am just beginning to start my day. You surprised me. How... how did you find out where I was staying?" The thought was just now coming to her as well, how did he find me?

"Grandma told me. I apologize again for bothering you, but I found out some good news and thought I'd tell you in person. It will make you happy, I'm sure." He was smooth and so polite. "Can I tell you about it over some breakfast and um... more coffee?" He must have noticed her gigantic thermos standing straight on the nightstand.

Who could resist breakfast with this guy?

"Sure. That'd be great. Could you give me just a minute?" she asked, obviously wanting some privacy. What was this good news about?

Batson suddenly felt his face redden; he had invaded her space.

"I'll just step down here in the office and get a cup of coffee myself. Take your time and dress comfortably." As the words came out of his mouth, he noticed a feeling of nervousness come over him. What was wrong with him? He couldn't be nervous; he was just taking her out for a drive. Actually, it was an exciting drive, one that would hopefully lead her to what would be her new home. He walked out the door and closed it behind him.

Abby was all smiles. She wondered what the news was about. Was it her house? Her possible job? Abby trembled as she scurried around the room looking for something halfway decent to wear. When she looked in the mirror, she saw a different person than she had seen only months ago. She took a brush to her long hair and quickly found a barrette to pull back just the few strands that hung in her face. Thank goodness she had already showered this morning. She found a pair of khakis that were hanging on the rod near the sink and a simple, pink knit shirt to go with them. When Batson came back to the room, she was putting her shoes and socks on.

"Ready to go?"

"Yep, just let me get my purse." She did and Batson led her to the car, opening the door for her. Batson watched her as they drove. He noticed the way the sun danced on her strands of long hair. Abby turned her face away, sat quietly, not quite sure what to say. She hope the law firm would call, but now since she had left, found herself worrying that they might not leave a message.

Batson recommended a pancake house down near the Bershire Shopping Center and five minutes later they arrived.

"Mind if we sit in smoking?" Abby didn't mind at all. She used to be a smoker before Lillie came along. The hostess showed them to a booth near the front window.

A waitress, probably in her fifties, greeted them with a pot of coffee and Batson asked her to give them a few minutes. Batson and Abby sat looking directly at one another. He was unable to quit noticing her beauty; her skin was so natural, so real. Abby was so captivating to him. He wondered what her story was but decided there would hopefully be time for that later. She had a mystery about her, like a past that she wouldn't want to reveal. What am I thinking? Order something!

Abby spoke up first. She talked about Lillie and her new school. She was a proud mother. Batson liked to listen to her as she told about a picture Lillie had brought home the day before and about what actually came out of her mouth the day before that. It was so easy to make conversation about Lillie, who was the most precious thing to her, all which mattered. Her eyes lit up naturally when Lillie's name came out of her mouth. From what Batson gathered, that little girl was all Abby had. He admired the small dimples that were noticeable at the sides of her mouth when she smiled.

"So I guess I'll stop rambling now. Tell me, where are we going and what's this good news all about? I can't wait too much longer."

"Well, I wanted to just take you there. But... I suppose I can go ahead and tell you," he smiled, anxious to tell her, "The house that you liked so much beside my Grandma's... well, it's marked down in price tremendously. Apparently, the owners left the place in a disaster and it needs quite a bit of work, mostly on the inside. It's been marked down to fifty-seven." Abby's eyes began to awaken as the words spewed out of his mouth.

"Ahh. Uh-huh."

"Now, the possession belongs to a Mr. Harold Edwin who lives up in Raven County. I got in touch with him and he was very surprised to find someone with interest in it. He is willing to do a lease-purchase option or whatever it is you can do money-wise for now. You will, however, be responsible for all repairs and cleaning since the price has been cut so much. Is this in your price range or what do you think?"

"Yes, of course! I mean, I think that's in my price range… what do you think? Ohh, I'm so excited. Can we go see it?"

"That's what I picked you up for. I have an extra key, got it this morning. We can go and have a look." From what Grandma Anna had said, Abby adored this house and would be willing to do pretty much anything to get in it. She was so eager to find a home for she and Lillie and Batson was elated to be the one to help her. "Now, I don't know what kind of condition it's in or what we might find, so be prepared. It's been vacant for quite a while. We will have to get an inspection done and check for termites… the whole nine yards, okay?"

"I know, I know." Abby could barely contain herself. The waitress came back and they each ordered a stack of pancakes and sides of bacon. Abby was thrilled with the news; she could hardly swallow anything. She was ready to go. Batson was so happy for her, but hoped she would understand that it would certainly need a lot of work. He could help her find a carpenter, a painter and people to help. And if she needed financial support, he could give her a small loan. Batson found himself willing to help Abby out in any way he could. He wanted her to succeed and more so, for some reason, he wanted to make sure she was happy.

Chapter Seven

The old house beside Anna's stood tall, dark, reflecting its much weathered siding and bent, rusted gutters. Leaves were still green and rustled on the trees alongside the house and driveway. Camilla's island was filled with serenity and brought ease to the toils of everyday life. Abby gasped as they pulled directly in front. Her dark eyes scanned her new surroundings. She felt like she was finally home. The door was locked as Batson had said it would be and with the key to it all, he opened the jarred door for his new- found friend.

The smell was like a stench from long ago, which was to be expected from a house that had no life dwelling in it for so many years. The air was lonely and cool through the front hallway, cobwebs reached from the corners and dragged along the tops of the sticky walls. To the right was a living room with leftover odds and ends that Abby instantly took priority to, examining each piece with curious eyes. Every house had a story buried inside it and these were simply clues left to tell a bit of that story.

The floor plan was similar to Anna's, except for an added loft area above, which Abby favored quite a bit. The kitchen's linoleum floor was rotted and sunken in several spots. It would definitely have to be replaced. The smell seemed to worsen as they kept walking through and finally Batson opened a window on the backside of the kitchen. Most of the other windows were painted shut and too hard to pry open without a tool of some kind. The brisk sensation of the island air blew through the house like it was giving it a first breath of life. Abby felt it brush against her arms and uncrossed them slowly, smiling with satisfaction.

"I want this house, Batson." He was not surprised in the

least.

She could move in immediately, once she met the owner and they decided on a payment arrangement, signed a few papers and so forth. First there would be cleaning to do and painting that was by far, way over due. Abby didn't mind doing the hard work at all, this would be their new home after all and it would be perfect.

They walked over to visit with Anna and Bessie, and Batson decided to go ahead and call Mr. Edwin, the owner of the home next door. Abby was on cloud nine and her tiny face glowed as she relayed the news to Bessie and Anna, her arms flying with excitement.

"We are going to be neighbors! Can you believe that?" She was ecstatic. "It needs quite a bit of work, so I'll be over here next week and probably the next getting it ready. Ohh- I'm so thrilled. This is such a blessing for me."

"Well, I'm volunteering."

"Volunteering for what, Batson?" she asked.

"To help. I can take a couple days off work and we can go pick out paint and paper and... it will be fun, a new project."

"Well, alright, but you really don't have to."

"I insist."

Anna's eyes watched as the two rattled off ideas and a future 'to-do' list. She caught the look in her grandson's eyes and began to imagine something even greater about to happen. It was something beyond anyone's control, but not wanting to ruin it, she kept quiet and to herself. Bessie kept icing her rolls, thinking that she had better finish them up so the kids could enjoy one before they hit the road.

Anna remembered when she and her Joe had first moved into this, then new, house. So long ago and yet the memories were so vivid and strong, like it was only yesterday. Anna and Joe had walked hand in hand to the front door. Anna trying to contain herself from exploding with excitement, it was quite overwhelming to finally own something of your own. This was Anna's ideal house; right on the water and Joe had known she would fall in love with it as soon as he saw it. He knew this would make her happy, and he was right, it had. Joe remembered the small talk from conversations between them, what she dreamed her house would be like, the colors, the furniture, and her porch. Joe remembered it all; he was always so good about that. For instance, Joe could remember what shirt she wore on a certain night or what they had ordered at dinner- like he memorized every moment they shared. That was one of the characteristics that drew Anna to him. He was such a unique and special person. When she would ask him about it, he would simply say, 'I just have to remember all of you; it's captured inside so I'll have it if you aren't around'. The thought of him brought Anna to a place in time when things had been so different.

Without realizing it, Anna had been the center of his soul since the day they had met. Because of her, he had grown to make a success out of his life. The times before Anna were confusing and lonely for Joe. She straightened him out, so to speak. They were soul mates, meant only for each other. Anna forced herself back into the conversation in the kitchen. She felt her heart squeeze tightly, like Joe's spirit tugging at it. "Oh," she sighed deeply, how she missed that man of hers.

The conversation with Mr. Edwin was brief, but everything seemed to have been agreed on and then they were headed to Bat's office. Abby found herself curious about Batson, just as he had been about her earlier. He was easy going and strangely enough, eager to go out of his way for her. Abby found herself already fond of him. He appeared to be a very kind and compassionate person. But why was he so willing to help her out? She had never in her life liked the so-called 'good guys', which is how she would describe Batson. Nope. Abby always managed to scoop out the ones at the bottom of the barrel. Her mom would say, 'You sure can pick em', Abby' and it would drive her up the wall.

She tossed those thoughts to the side and went back to thinking about the arrangements that she would have to make about the house. Batson mentioned several different options on how to go about purchasing it. This was scary, a big step. Batson assured her that he would explain everything in laymen terms and that she would understand completely. Finding a job would be the first priority. Mr. Edwin knew about her situation and was generously willing to cooperate with her since the house had sat vacant for such a long time, but she needed a job and quickly.

Anna told Batson about the law office interview the day before and he listened as if he never knew anything about it. Both found themselves very comfortable with the other, like they had known each other for years- it happened that way sometimes. She could remember being in high school and even in the last couple of years dating some new guy and having that old shoe feeling with them. It's as if at first they are meant to be, then the dirt settles and you're left with a pile of mud. Abby promised herself not to get sucked into this one. Batson Cannon was going to be a good friend and that was it. She did not move down here to Camilla to begin some new estranged love affair, she moved to begin a new life for she and Lillie. For once in her life, she was not going to screw it up. She had too much to contend with for now. Abby came back to earth and shook her head to forget the thoughts that had been roaming there.

The realty company was right beside the law firm and Abby pointed to the firm where she had had her interview. A quick idea of checking in crossed her mind and before she could say anything, Batson read her thoughts.

"Go on, stop by. Can't hurt anything, can it?"

"I look a mess though. If they see me like this, there is no way they'll hire me." She adjusted the mirror and used her fingers to brush through the tangled hair.

"Don't be silly, you look fine. He's an old friend of mine, so just explain that we've been out and about... he will understand, I promise." He caught himself touching her hand as he spoke to her, and then slowly pulled away.

Abby flushed and told herself it was only a friendly gesture; he was going for the reassurance bit. So in she went and Batson went next door.

The law firm appeared exactly the same as it had the day before. The lady at the desk showed Abby on back to Thom's office and there he sat, perched behind the oversized oak desk. He seemed surprised to see her once again and she explained her day trip in town with Batson.

"Yes, Batson and I go back a long way," he answered her and then sat quietly, waiting for her to explain further.

"Basically, I just thought I'd drop by and see if you had any good news for me. I am really interested in this position and I hope you don't think I'm nuts for coming by." She stopped and began doubting her initial decision to come.

"No, no. Actually, I'm glad you did. I tried to phone you this morning. I was impressed with our interview yesterday and I'd like you to come work with us... I mean, as my assistant." Abby smiled uncontrollably. "You will have to meet my partner whenever you're available and the pay will need to be discussed, since you don't have any prior experience with a law firm. But please, don't let that discourage you... once I get you trained, you'll be comfortable here and in what you'll be making."

She was flabbergasted. This couldn't possibly be happening, could it? It was.

"I can meet with him anytime. I am obviously available now... well, not right now." She motioned down at her clothes, insinuating her dress code for the day.

"Sure, well, you could come by tomorrow morning. Say… around nine?"

"Of course. Thank you so much. I'll be here at nine then." She stood up and shook his hand with her new found confidence. Her life was on a roll now; this was beyond the start she had been looking for. Abby Logan had a job and now she was on her way to acquiring her very own home, one that she and Lillie so desperately needed. Everyone in this town was so inviting… this was where she belonged.

Batson was on the phone and from the window motioned for her to come into his spacious office. His office was a busy place with phones ringing and bookshelves crammed full of files, folders and stationary of all sorts. The floors were hardwood and had been noticeably kept up and polished. The agents looked her up and down as she walked in, not knowing exactly whom she was or why she was there. Mrs. Dalviny showed her upstairs and smiled pleasantly at Abby, making her feel more comfortable and less out of place.

The office had a simple pine table for a desk where Batson's typewriter sat and there were shelves on either side of the room, filled with more books, office supplies and everything imaginable. Abby couldn't help noticing the disorganization, but thought it fit the man talking on the phone. He was a busy man, after all. Then her eyes saw the most breathtaking photograph on the wall. The woman was radiant in the black and white that trickled through with a shine. It had an embossed emblem at the bottom, a professional one.

"That's my mother." Batson pointed to the picture after noticing that Abby had been admiring it. Then he continued with his conversation with the person on the other end of the line. Abby smiled sincerely and then blushed, embarrassed that he might think she was prying.

She looked back at the woman on the wall and saw that her hair was curled tightly around the nape of her neck and darkly colored lipstick that perfected the sensual curves of her lips. A floral scarf was tied neatly in a bow at the top of her blouse and for a moment, her eyes looked like those of a child, so young, so delicate.

"Sorry about that. That was an agent from another firm looking for a new position over here with us. Go ahead, take a seat," pointing to the two leather seats situated on the opposite side of his desk. "Well, everything looks good. As soon as we can confirm employment, we can complete all the paperwork. Mr. Edwin is going to handle the financing for the first year and then after you get more settled, you can look elsewhere for more secure financing. Sound good to you?"

It sounded better than good, it sounded fantastic. How could she get a better deal? She told Batson about the offer from next door and he insisted they celebrate.

She declined.

"It's just... so much has happened here today and I'm exhausted just thinking about it all. I have to pick up Lillie at two anyway." She saw his disappointment.

"Sure. Well, maybe we can get together tomorrow evening after your first day on the job. And no need to worry about a sitter. Believe me, Grandma and Bessie would be flattered if you asked them to keep Lillie for a while. You haven't been in town long and that would give me some time to show you around," would give me some time with you, he thought. He didn't want to sound pushy, but he wanted to see her again soon, very soon, didn't want it to linger off.

Abby agreed to the invitation.

Batson carried Abby back to the hotel and could easily see her exhaustion, the shock and feelings were overwhelming. It was a lot for anyone to digest, let alone a single mom, in a new town, with a new job and now, a new home. He tried to put

71

himself in her shoes for only a moment. Hopefully she would take him up on his offer for tomorrow night, she needed to.

The parking lot in front of their door was nearly empty. Abby hurriedly went in and waved goodbye. The temperature had skyrocketed, so she cut on the air first thing, shut the tacky drapes and crashed on the bed, eyes open and sighed. It was almost 11:30 and Abby felt her stomach grumble. She closed her eyes and tried to let everything sink in. She and Lillie would soon be living in a home of their very own home! How exciting this was!

She phoned home to announce the good news to her mom and dad. They would be so proud. Her mother was ecstatic and relieved that her puzzle of a life was finally fitting together. Abby deserved every bit of it; all of her hard work was paying off. Once again, her father was out, so she asked her mom to relay the news. She had a ton of things to do this afternoon and this evening.

The rumble of hunger roared again and a quiet lunch alone would be the perfect thing. There was a small deli across the street that she and Lillie had already tried out. She looked in the mirror and noticed the glow on her face, almost close to the one she got when she was pregnant. How accomplished she felt, how relieved and how overjoyed she was today. As she walked over, she could feel the skin stretching, her smile beaming from ear to ear.

The deli was packed with people, the line was long but Abby was patient and didn't mind a bit. Finally getting her sandwich and sitting down, she saw how large it actually was. Her favorite tuna salad was piled high, a slice of provolone, two thin pieces of homegrown tomatoes stuffed into the gigantic bun, with chips overflowing the side of the paper plate. Saying a silent grace, she took the first bite. Heavenly. Sometimes it was such a nice feeling to sit and eat alone. Abby savored the time she got to spend with Lillie, but moments alone were savored as well. It was a treat, a small reward to her for the day.

Abby's thoughts took over once again and she found herself in a daydream, the kind where the noise around you disappears and the eyes focus on some random object and then it just gets all gray. She pictured she and Lillie in their new house. She saw the colors of paint that would spread on the walls, a plate rack running along the top of the dining room, rocking chairs from a garage sale sitting on the front patio and finally, she saw herself tucking her sweet Lillie into her very own bed and in her very own room. Then there she would sit relaxing on the sofa, having the time to read that novel, or watch a favorite program, her mind rested and light. The kitchen was neatly complemented with bright, beachy colors, teapots galore and a breakfast table with a history of its own, big enough for she and Lil. She could almost smell the sea and feel the sweet breezes that would flow through her hair as she would walk to the mailbox. Abby folded her two hands together, softly, thankful for all her blessings. She could not wait to begin, again.

Abby picked Lillie up early to share the good news and then planned a few hours of bargain hunting. Lillie loved to shop with her mama, they had just never really had much money to do it before. But today, they would splurge a little, enjoy life and live for this moment. The coming weekend would really be the time for the yard sales, but they could look around for now, maybe grab a few small knick-knacks. Lillie was thrilled about the idea of having her own room. She and Abby had always shared a room up until now.

Batson was out and about himself. He grabbed a quick bite at Mary's for lunch and decided to ride out to Grandma Anna's for a short while to visit. Bessie was sweeping the cracked sidewalk pieces that lead to the front steps. They had always been broken up like that.

"Hello there, girlie," he shouted to her, impossible to see a black woman blush. She placed her hand on her forehead to block the glare, and then kept on with her work.

"Oh hi, Bats." She still swept, "Misses Anna's inside."

Batson walked on up the steps and met Anna at the door. Bessie soon followed, with her broom in hand. She wanted to make sure she didn't miss anything too exciting.

"Well guys... Abby got the house!"

Anna and Bessie were delighted to see their new young friend find her way, especially her moving right next door. They started in with ideas of what to take over, what might need to be done and Batson escaped through the front door.

"I'm gonna run over next door right quick. I told Abby I'd check on some things." They didn't even acknowledge his exit, just kept on rattling.

Bessie got up to get a couple glasses of iced tea and they met up in Anna's bedroom. The window, as always, was cracked open and Bessie took her seat in the rocker, Anna placed herself on the sunken bed. The room was darkened and cool; the sheer shades covered most of the sunlight that would normally shine strongly through the upper parts of the windows.

"Well, this is certainly joyous news." Anna smiled and looked over at Bessie's dark and mysterious eyes. You never could tell what was going through that head of hers. "So, how can we help... I mean, what are we going to do? The kitchen. We can definitely work through that kitchen o'er there- get it all cleaned up for her."

Anna felt she owed Abby quite a bit. After all, it was she who was there for her when no one else was. Anna would soon take Abby under her wing, one of her own, and Bessie read every unspoken word. Bessie knew what was going on in Anna's mind. Bessie noticed an interest in Abby from Batson, but Abby in Batson? Bessie was not quite as sure as Misses

Anna. But Bessie didn't say anything aloud; it was understood. They brainstormed for a few more minutes and then it was soon forgotten.

The day began finishing itself off with a graying darkness and Batson left Anna and Bessie at the crooked kitchen table playing rummy. He drove past the houses on the street, his eyes waving from side to side noticing little changes here and there. The image of Abby floated through his thoughts. All of his heart sinking deeper into his chest, he imagined her, all of her. He was touching her face gently with his tanned fingers to calm her restlessness. She seemed so distant and looked away. All day he had thought about her, Liz was forgotten. Abby's eyes, her hair, her voice. His mouth twitched, his eyes blinked and he threw it in park and sat.

The pier stood strong while calling him to it. The old pier was cracked about a million times throughout, marks from fishing hooks, cigarette burns and butts. It was still warm to the touch from the afternoon rays. Batson walked up it and then back down. He had memorized her reaction when she found out about the house, the light in her skin, the wrinkles that formed from excitement on her forehead. He remembered her mannerisms and the way her hands moved when she spoke, graceful and feminine. She had moved closer to him when they spoke as the day progressed. Her hair dripping over her shoulders and down her back, he pictured her right there, right then.

The waves rolled to and fro' and the musical notes of the ocean soothed his desire for her presence. Would she even be interested in him? He would take things slow and plan it out just right. Batson did not want to play games like with the others, not with Abby. No. This one he wanted to last. The more he drifted into the idea of her, the more he knew his intuitions were right and that she was the one for him. He could feel it inside. Strangely, Batson thought of his mom and a familiar sensation ran through his body. Batson felt her pushing this one on, she would have approved of Abby for sure. He left the pier pleased and with a purpose, to have Abby and Lillie Logan in his life.

Abby lounged in her dim-lit room, her hand busy with a pencil, writing and writing while Lillie lay in bed asleep.

Another magnificent day in Camilla. It looks as though Lillie and I have found somewhere to call home. Oddly enough, it's right on the island beside Anna and Bessie, the ones I mentioned before.

God is being extremely good to me, isn't he? I am so grateful.

Strangely I find myself thinking of Will. Is he thinking about us at all? I wonder if he even misses seeing Lillie?

How can you still think of someone who hurt you so badly? I am annoyed at myself for even writing his name. It is the loneliness. The absence of having someone around is eroding my emotions. I can't help but wonder if one day he'll show up or call, a changed man wanting time with his daughter.

What will I say then? Sorry, you're too late?

Oh well, I have Tommy to dream of. He will forever be embedded in my head, my memories, my fantasies.

Lillie won't even remember her dad and is that bad or good?

It's his loss, but it is hers as well. What child doesn't want a father around? Damn him for being the way he is.

Damn him.

She is so beautiful, an angel. I need strength, I pray for it every day. We can make this work, can't we? I remember how scared I was of raising her alone. I don't

see myself with anyone else. Will is still with me... in my mind, touching my body, part of me... I hate that. I suppose feelings for him will always be there in some way, after all – he gave me one of my greatest accomplishments... my sweet Lillie.
Good night- A.

Chapter Eight

The next day flew by with the tick of the clock. Abby and Lillie were up and running early, Lillie to school and Abby to her first day on the job. Batson had gone over around lunchtime to make an entrance and possibly invite Abby to lunch, but Thom beat him to it. Abby and Thom left about ten minutes before Bats had arrived. He shrugged it off... no big deal, right?

The afternoon was humid and miserable, but Abby sat at her desk unaware of how high the temperature had risen in the past hour or so. Before she knew it, Thom was knocking on her door to let her know it was time to go home. She felt weary, her brain warped with new information, all the new files, the office area- every bit of it. She asked to take a little bit of paperwork with her to become more familiar with it. Thom allowed it, happy to see her interest.

Batson saw the two walking side by side making friendly conversation and she looked so professional. He was happy for her and couldn't wait to see her later that evening. He would call her in an hour or so to make definite plans.

Abby picked up Lillie from school and drove on out to the house with the back seat full of small things to take in. She had found a piece of stained glass to hang in the kitchen window, a framed picture for her bathroom and a couple of folding chairs that would have to do for now. Lillie had a stack of books in her lap and a container of blocks beside her; she smiled the whole way there.

Abby opened the front door and proceeded into the living room.

"Well, this is it, babe! What do you think?"

"Where's my room?" The most important question of all,

Abby showed her to it.

Back in the living room, Abby found a huge cardboard box with a variety of paint cans, brushes and brand new tools. There was a plastic toolbox filled with nails, screws, toggle bolts and a hammer. Abby read the note taped on top:

Dear Abby-
Hope you don't mind my interfering, but here are a few starters. I couldn't help myself. Looking forward to tonight... See you soon- Bats

She sunk down between her bent knees, staring at the box of hardware. Everything felt so right. Seconds later, tears began rolling down her face, the reality of the new home had finally sunken in. She looked around her and knew that all of it belonged to her. It was a moment she would never forget. How thoughtful he was to bring all this over.

She glanced down at the note, rereading it then noticing the 'looking forward to tonight' part. She remembered the conversation from yesterday and realized that she had totally dismissed the invitation. Should she go? Of course... especially after all this, how could she say no? It couldn't hurt anyway and obviously it was just as friends... new friends. Yes, she should go.

Lillie listened carefully to mom's plans and was thrilled at the chance to stay with Anna and Bessie. Abby hoped that Batson had already mentioned it to them, surely. So over they walked, hand in hand and yes, it had been confirmed.

"Of course, dear. Bats called this morning and we were so excited about having her. Bessie went to the store earlier and picked up snacks and stuff for dinner, so don't you worry yourself about it one bit. You two just go out and have a marvelous time."

"Well, alright then... I need to make a quick trip back to the hotel to change and all. Did Batson say he would pick me up here?"

"I don't know... he didn't say. Better give him a call to see." Anna dialed the number for her and handed the phone over.

For some reason she got shaky when he answered the phone. She thanked him for the box he had left and they began making their plans. He would pick her up at Anna's. Abby would need to pick up Lillie's pajamas in case they ran late. Anna hurried her out the door.

An hour later, Abby showed back up wearing a simple sundress with her favorite and only pair of brown sandals. Batson was already there and on the floor goofing off with Lillie. Abby smiled, glad to see them having fun, and thought of Lillie's father for only a moment and then it was gone.

"Ready to go?" he asked, looking her over. He seemed pleased with what he saw. "You look wonderful."

"Thanks." The compliment made her face light up with a boost of confidence. "Now, Lil, you behave for Misses Anna and Miss Bessie, alright?"

"Yes mam."

"Of course she will. Now you two get on out that door before you change your mind." Abby hadn't had many sitters in the past, so it was not easy to leave. But she felt comfortable leaving her there. Lillie was in good hands... almost like leaving her with her own parents back home.

The two found themselves driving down historical streets with Batson commenting on every landmark and telling stories of what used to be. Abby listened closely for a while and after it got boring, she just enjoyed the sound of his voice. With the windows rolled down, the breeze came through as they laughed, welcoming each other's company. It was as if they had been friends for years… they bonded.

Batson had reservations at a five star restaurant down by the river, recognized for its most appealing cuisine. They had a table reserved overlooking the water; the sun was just in the process of retiring. The view was splendid and Abby noticed how the water unruffled time after time. The tablecloth hung motionless over the corner edges of the table, a skinny, moss green candle divided them, and the light reflected on the sides of their wine goblets.

"See anything you might like?" Batson broke the silence.

"Lots! Everything looks so good. Let's see…"

"Pick out whatever you want. This is my treat, your first real night out and I'm delighted to be spending it with you." She blushed.

After ordering, they fell into talking about the new house. Abby had plenty of ideas rolling in her head, but explained that first and foremost she would have to make some most necessary purchases, of which furniture was at the top of the list. Batson offered to take her by Turner's Furniture Store, they had financing and it was a small family business. He liked to support them.

Lillie was a major topic for conversation. She was the mainstream of Abby's life and so it seemed only natural to talk about her. Batson was mesmerized by the excitement and glow she got as she talked about her daughter. Lillie this and Lillie that… that little girl was undeniably the star that had kept her going. Batson sank further and further into her.

"So did you always want to be in real estate or was there something else before that that you wanted to do? I mean, I know it's the family business, but was there ever anything else?"

"Well, after college, I really went straight into the office, so there wasn't much of a chance to do much anything else. When I was younger, I studied a lot of history and had thought about teaching."

"Wow, that's interesting. I could see you doing that. I write quite a bit. Well, not publishable material, but just for me." She felt herself getting too personal and it felt awkward at first, letting it go. "I have always written. It releases so much and when I was younger, I cherished my journals. Gosh, they were so sacred to me." She giggled, feeling like that little girl, the one who wrote of crushes, first kisses and her deepest thoughts.

"That's interesting. I think Gracie used to have a diary. Gracie's my sister."

"Probably so... it's a common thing for girls to do, at least it used to be."

"Yeah... I suppose." He smiled.

It was time to move onto something different. Earlier, it seemed he had a ton of ideas of where to take her, but now... he hadn't a clue. Maybe she would like Mary's... or that lounge on Easterly... nah, too dressy. Maybe a walk on the beach... just ask her for Christ's sake... go ahead.

"It's still early. Where would you like to go?" Then realizing that she probably had no idea of where to go. "Well, what I meant is, what kind of places do you like to go to?"

"You choose, I'm not that hard to please, I promise. Wherever is fine with me." He decided on Mary's. It was a favorite of his and she seemed flexible.

Mary's was only a short walk down the street and Batson led the way. The two were a perfect pair, walking at a leisurely pace and pretending to admire the surroundings. Abby felt a tingle rise up her arm as Batson carefully slipped his hand in hers, letting their fingers twist together until finally getting it right. She noticed the tenderness on the tips of his fingers and gazed ahead of them and then at him with wonder, imagining where the night might take them.

Batson remained collected on the outside but his insides were jittery, he couldn't believe it himself... tense over the simple gesture of holding her hand. It was she, just she. She captivated him as no woman had ever done before. Remembering back to when he first saw her, so ordinary, so plain. Now with his hand clasped into hers, Batson thought she was amazing. Absolutely amazing. Abby was one-of-a-kind and she was his, at least for tonight.

Walking in the door, the lights glared and it was hard to focus. There stood Sherry in her usual spot behind the bar and she greeted them as they came closer. Batson waved and led Abby to a corner table near the well-embellished wall, then turned to get some drinks.

Abby admired a few peculiar photographs on the wall while her eyes tried to refocus from the lights, some were of old newspaper clippings and memorabilia, others were of racing cars, football teams. Mary's had a certain charm though, an abundance of spirit and she felt quite comfortable. She could tell the majority of customers knew one another well, regulars. She thought about Cheers and how she used to love to watch it, liked to watch Woody do his thing behind the bar. She glanced down and swore that the two at the end of Mary's bar could have passed for Norm and Cliff Claven. Even one of the waitresses had a disgruntled look on her face and stomped around like she didn't give a shit whether they tipped her or not. Anyway, she missed that show.

She stood up as Batson returned and said she needed to call to check up on Lillie, he pointed her down the hallway where the payphones were. Batson watched her walk, unwilling to direct his eyes anywhere else.

"Wha's up!" A voice behind him distracted his concentration and he knew in a second who was standing over his head. It was Sam, of course and... oh, my God- Liz! Bats sat erect in his seat before standing up to greet his friends. Trying to act normal as physically possible, he couldn't lose it now... he hugged Liz as if he hadn't seen her in ages. She was as cool as a cucumber throughout the whole ordeal and for some reason, it sort of pissed him off. Although not planning to join them, Sam insisted on sitting down. He pulled over a chair for Liz and Bats grabbed a second.

"Who's that for? You gotta girlie?" Sam asked in his quite normal for him, boisterous voice.

"Actually, yes and you'd better be nice." Bats nonchalantly eyed Liz to see her reaction, just in time to see Abby walking up behind her with a surprised, but pleasant look on her face.

"Hi there. Everything okay?"

"Um-hum."

"Abby, want you to meet some very good friends of mine. This is Sam and his wife, Liz."

"Hi there. Liz Borders. It's so nice to meet you." Liz didn't hesitate to extend her hand and act so... so right.

Abby took a seat close to Batson and he smiled, hiding the dilemma going through his mind. There he was... with Abby, who he dreamed of having more than just a friendship with and then across the table sat his best friend from high school and his wife. Yes, yes, dammit- the one he had slept with only a week before. This is unfreakin' believable. How in the hell did he ever get into this predicament?

Meanwhile, Liz didn't hesitate a bit on the twenty questions for Abby. 'Where do you work? Where are you from? How old is your little girl? How long have you been seeing Batson?'

It went on and on while Batson tried having a conversation with Sam and halfway listening in to the girls' conversation at the same time. Sam seemed to jabber on and after only thirty minutes, Batson decided it was time for he and Abby to move on. Finding it hard to break into the conversation between Abby and Liz, Batson finally gestured that he was ready to leave and Abby nodded.

Finally, the four said their goodbyes. Batson thought he would vomit as they pushed through the crowd. Hold on to

85

it… hold on. How could this happen to him? Now he had Liz to worry about. If she and Abby got too close, there was no telling where he and Liz's past would end up. But it wasn't exactly in the past; it was more recent than years past. Damn. He cussed himself in his head.

Abby nudged, "Something wrong?"

"Oh, no. No, I'm sorry. I just went into a daze for a minute. Crowds can get to me sometimes and plus, the uh, the beer. Are you cold?"

"No, I'm fine."

"Well, there's a cool breeze out tonight." He went ahead and laid his coat over her shoulders. She smiled and he knew she'd liked the gesture.

No need for her to answer, she leaned over into his arm, tired. It wasn't that late, maybe ten o'clock or so, but Batson realized that she had Lillie to go home to. Abby was exhausted. She wouldn't dare say anything, but she wanted to get Lillie and get back to the hotel. It wasn't that she hadn't had a good time, not that at all, just that she was weary and ready to get off her feet.

Lillie lay asleep on Gracie's four-poster bed in her old bedroom. Anna and Bessie sat on the couch with the cards strewn out, covering every inch of the coffee table.

"Did y'all have yourselves a good time?" Anna inquired, optimistic about their first night out.

Abby tilted her head up to see Batson's reaction.

"We had a great time, but I think this one is ready for the sack."

"Slightly." She paused, "How was Lillie tonight? Did she wear you guys out?"

"Hardly. I think it was the other way around." Anna and Bessie clearly agreed. "She knocked out about an hour ago. Oh… we played with all Gracie's dolls after we bathed her and then she played by herself in there. We went to check on her, not even fifteen minutes later and she was curled up in a ball and out like a light."

"Gosh, I hate to get her up." She yawned.

"Well, don't then, honey." Anna suggested and quickly offered her a nightshirt and the other side of Gracie's bed. "You two just stay over here for tonight. There's no sense in dragging her up and out. We'll wake you up bright and early and you'll have plenty of time." What a nice idea and Abby couldn't turn this one down. The hotel sure didn't sound too inviting and besides, they should have plenty of time. Batson looked pleased that she'd chosen to stay. He took her hand and led her out on the front porch.

Outside the wind still blew cool and their first date was now officially over. Abby removed Batson's jacket from her shoulders and he looked into her eyes for the last time of the evening. The night had turned out relatively well, even with the run-in between he and Liz. He was not thinking of Liz though. No, not at this moment. Only Abby.

Batson ran his hand through the back of her long hair and pulled her close. Abby succumbed into his arms as they wrapped around her. She let her head nestle into his chest and they stood frozen, embracing one another. Slowly she lifted her chin and permitted his lips to open onto hers. Abby felt the softness of his soul and couldn't bring herself to let go. She found her body longing for him, and then they broke apart. He walked away. Her body crawled with the memory of his touch for the remainder of the night, and later it was that memory that rocked her into a deep sleep.

Chapter Nine

The sky is painted with white sashes of cotton and the radiant streaks of sun weave in and out. There are Abby and Batson, was that Batson? Maybe it was Will. Abby's eyes fluttered as her dreams drifted on. The roaming sea, thrashing onto the shore with a relaxing rumble, and the two of them beaming with exhilaration and delight. Strong winds braid Abby's long hair with beads of salty sand. She dances in circles, the dark strands tack onto her damp, sweating skin. The man stands to the side, watching her, admiring her impulsiveness and amusement to be in a world all her own. Her problems vanishing before them. She grants the sea spirits to embrace her spirit, her soul. She searches the waves for her spot and flees to the water, letting it cover her entirely. The man takes a seat and Abby can sense his eyes upon her. She is a goddess of the sea in this dream. The man sees that this is where she belongs, where she has always belonged. He rises to his feet and walks off slowly, leaving her there, not looking back.

Abby's eyes exposed themselves to the morning light coming through the thin drape over the bedroom window. She sits up quietly, so not to wake Lillie and tiptoes over to the cracked window. Looking out the clouded pane, she can see a glimpse of the water to the right. Her dream still fresh in her mind, she repeated the parts she liked best.

What did it mean? Was that Batson in the dream or was it Will? Oh hell, it was just a dream. It was silly anyway. She left Lillie lying fast asleep and snuck into the kitchen to find Anna and Bessie still in their nightgowns, having coffee.

"Did you sleep well, dear?" Anna asked, looking awful groggy.

"Like a log. But this morning I had this really strange

dream."

"Well, com'on girl. Tell us 'bout it." Bessie said.

"Oh, well... it was just about me on the beach, running, happy and free. Sounds silly I know, but it was that simple. I was like a goddess of the sea or something. Isn't that crazy?" Now she was embarrassed for even telling them about it.

Bessie looked her over, "Goddess of da' sea, you say?"

"Yep." Abby answered back, peeping over at the coffee pot to see if it had quite a bit left or not. She went over to get a cup and Bessie motioned for her to sit down.

"Abby, I thinks you done stumbled on an ole' folks tale, girl. You is gonna thinks I is crazy when I tells you all this, but..." Anna peered over and watched her go to work. "Well, 'dey say 'dat girls who dreams about sea fairies, goddesses, have special powers, if you believe in em'. Powers like da' witches do, like wif' spirits an stuffs. The spiritful peoples 'round here in da' south ain't really knowed as witches but as doctors, voodoo doctors that is. You might have some inside stuff needs to be dealt wif'."

Abby interrupted before she could continue any further, "That's crazy, Bessie. Interesting stuff, but just not up my alley- I'm a mom for Christ's sake, a mom that needs to get a move on or I'll be late for work." She stopped and saw Bessie's eyes swerved the other way. "Sorry, Bess. Maybe we can talk about it all later. I can be a grump before I finish my first cup of joe." She smiled and knew everything would be fine.

Lillie put on her school clothes, Abby showered and yet, another day in Camilla had begun. Abby arrived at work on time thankfully, greeted with a stack of paperwork on her desk. She found herself overjoyed to come to work, to have the chance to study something she enjoyed. Thom waved as he passed her door and she started sorting through the files. She put the dream and Bessie's evaluation on the back burner and dug into her workload.

Lunchtime arrived quickly and she skipped the invitation from Thom and instead walked next door to go eat with Batson. Unfortunately, Bats had gone to a business meeting with a group of his associates, so Abby went alone. She chose a small Chinese restaurant that advertised daily specials on their board, situated in the sidewalk cracks outside. Her food was placed in front of her in no time at all and she gobbled it up, thinking about the dream without meaning to. Looking at her watch, it was time to head back to the office.

A note lay on her desk when she got back.

"Hey. How's it going?" Thom peeped in.

"Fine. Just fine."

"Are you enjoying it here so far?"

"Of course, I find everything very interesting."

"Yes, good. Well, this afternoon I would like you to go on, take off early." Abby looked puzzled and questioned his gracious offer. He insisted she would need some extra time to herself, to get the house together and all. "Once you get settled at home, I think you'll excel here at the office. So go on, try to get some things done and I'll see you in the morning, bright and early." Abby was thrilled at the opportunity.

Without much hesitation, but a teaspoon of guilt, Abby drove right past Lillie's school. She could get so much more accomplished without her little helper. The house seemed so peaceful; she unlocked the door and pried it open, then carried load after load from the car. Abby had snatched the small radio and plugged it up immediately. Music would raise her spirits and within minutes she was setting up her workstation to paint the living room. Batson had left a two-step ladder to reach the hard spots and when she first noticed its presence, she thought about him.

Abby cleared cobwebs, windexed the front panes, and scrubbed the kitchen sink, bathroom tub and tile floors. The afternoon was a productive one for one person. Singing out loud, the eighties blaring out the radio speakers. She heard a faint knock at the door. There stood Batson, dressed in baggy khaki shorts and a t-shirt, obviously used before to work in. The two didn't exchange too many words and instead went straight back to work. Batson took up the job of painting Lillie's room, they had chosen a teal green and Abby was slaving away at the paint job in her own room.

After a couple of hours, it was time for a breather. Abby grabbed two Cokes and they took their seats in the two folding lawn chairs that were placed in the middle of the otherwise empty, living room. There they sat, breathlessly admiring what they had accomplished so far and laughed aloud at what a sight they must be.

Batson bent over the first chance he got and kissed her, then saw the surprise in her eyes at his gesture. "I had a great time last night. Did you?" So perfect he was, so unbelievable.

"Yes, it was nice. To be out and, and the food was incredible." She then broke into a snicker and pointed to a rounded blot of paint on the tip of his nose. "I need to go get Lillie. She will be thrilled to see all we've done, especially her room."

"I think she'll just like the idea that I did it." She nodded. "Alright. Well, why don't I grab us a bit to eat and bring it back, then I'll meet the two of you back here."

Abby looked relieved. How lucky she was to have Batson here to help, to contribute and be strong. She knew he could never understand how much all this meant to her. He led her to the car and stole one more quick kiss before heading off.

Liz was at home doing her daily duties, cleaning the kitchen, washing gobs of laundry and keeping the kids occupied. Sam would be home from work soon and she had cooked a ham for dinner, with veggies, ones the kids would actually eat. The phone rang as she was setting the table, a friend of hers to chat for a few free minutes, also a stay-at-home mom. Liz seemed to spend half of her days talking on the phone with the other moms in the neighborhood. It was always something, organizing for this fundraiser, a class picnic, planning ideas for someone's party... always. Sometimes they would swap recipes or gossip in the morning hours with their first pots of coffee. This was the lifestyle she had chosen. Sam agreed that she should stay at home; it was best for the children. Some days could be dreadfully boring and dry, others flew by and she would actually feel privileged to get to be at home. Billy, the youngest one, was the only one left at home, the other two were students at Lakewood Elementary. So with just she and Billy, they liked to get out quite a bit, do the fun stuff, giving Liz the chance to enjoy the baby, her youngest.

The kids were in the playroom; she could hear the video game echoing down the stairway. Liz sat down in the woven kitchen chair; the table was set orderly with plates, napkins, glasses and silverware marked for a nightly feast. She envisioned the night before, the feelings that boiled up in her body after seeing Batson with another woman. She had never felt so threatened, but last night had been odd. There was a mystery about this one and she couldn't figure it out. Even if it were envy that she felt, what right did she possibly have to feel it? This Abby was so different compared to the women Batson had dated before.

Liz concluded that the reason she and Abby had gotten along so well was because they were so much alike, somehow connected. What would happen if they got to be good friends? How would Batson react to that? She wanted to see Abby again, study up on her. She decided to call her, maybe this weekend even. Maybe she should talk to Batson about it first, like out of courtesy. After all, only a week had gone by since they had been together and decided their relationship with each other would be over.

Sam traipsed in the back door, sweaty, exhausted and without fail, starving. He kissed his wife gently and went to shower right quick before dinner. The kids darted down the hall and then sat in their seats at the table, trying not to finger the food that sat in front of them.

"We always have to wait on Dad."

"Of course you do. Sit down in your seat, Billy, and you two, keep your hands to yourselves." It was the normal winding down of an ordinary day at the Borders house.

Batson dropped by and picked up a basket of fried chicken, mashed potatoes and a few ears of buttered corn for dinner. He had also stopped in the grocery to pick up a few things for the kitchen, drinks, ice, and snacks. Anna and Bessie were outside the front door when he returned. They followed him inside and toured the house, making compliments on the colors Abby had chosen and how splendid it was looking.

"Abby needs to hear the compliments, Grandma, not me. They should be here soon." He meandered on into the kitchen and began putting things away.

"She doesn't even have a table to eat on?" Anna noticed.

"No, not yet. She said she needed to shop for furniture, a bit of an understatement."

"Well, that's just pathetic now." Bessie shook her head to agree. "Do me a favor please, go on over to the house, outside in the shed is that old farm table. It will be perfect in here. There should be four chairs to go along with it, maybe even five of em'. God knows I don't have room for it."

"That's a great idea! Oh, she'll love it too. She loves antiques." Before he stepped out, "Look under the sink and see if there's any polish. We can clean it up before she makes it home."

Anna began thinking about what all else was in the shed. There might be a couple other pieces Abby could use. Papa Cannon had accumulated so much junk in that shed and Anna hated the idea of looking through all of it. He was a packrat, a garage sale regular and auctions were something they both used to enjoy going to. When they bought anything, they always had a plan for it but then, it all just added to the pile and was soon forgotten, some never even looked at a second time. What a bad habit that was, she thought, but grinned at what fun it used to be. Papa had come home one night with an old pair of ice skates, insisting that they were antiques. He wanted to hang them on the wall for decoration, 'character', he had said, but Anna wouldn't hear of it. To the shed he carried them and there they hung on the pegboard. No matter how many times she complained, his bad buying habits never ceased.

Batson struggled getting the table in through the doorway and then returned to get the chairs. It took several trips. Bessie found the polish and got to work. The table was in remarkable condition and would serve its purpose for now. Anna hoped Abby wouldn't mind their small contribution.

The two old ladies heard her car pull up just as Bats was bringing in the last of the chairs. There had been five. They hurriedly dusted them off and fixed the table in the center below the light fixture dangling from above.

"She's taking awhile, Batson. Why don't you go see if she needs some help?" Anna ordered.

"Um-hum. She's probably got stuff to bring in, honey. Go'n out 'dere and see if you can help." Bessie added.

As Batson reached for the doorknob, in she swung.

"I was coming to help." He looked down at the plastic bags hanging from her wrists and began slipping them off one by one. "Here, let me get those. Where's Lillie?"

"Here I am," the young voice cried out from behind her

95

mom's figure, part of her small face peeking around Abby's left leg.

"Hey sweet. G'on inside with Grandma Anna and Bessie. Let your mom and I get the rest, okay?" Lillie relented into the kitchen and then remembering what her mom had said about her room, dashed down the other way to see it.

Batson put the next load of bags on Abby's new kitchen table and she noticed it immediately.

"Where'd that come from?"

Anna was quick to offer an answer, "We had it stashed in the shed next door and I thought it might be just the thing for you and Lillie to use."

"It's beautiful. I love pine." She ran her fingers along the grain of the wood and looked up adoringly, "Ohhh, thank you so much y'all. It's perfect." She reached out to hug each of them, so thankful to have friends. That would save some money and she liked this one much better than the newer ones she'd looked at in the stores. "Y'all are so good to us. How would I have done all this without you?"

Batson burst through their group with the last load, Lillie pounced in and out, full of energy, and Bessie and Anna began dishing out their dinner so they could eat.

It was a wonderful beginning and Abby fought to keep her tears. What a relief to get so much done in one afternoon and she reminded herself of what Thom had said and how right he was. Once she and Lillie got settled in, she would be more productive, not only at work but in her life as a whole. They could forget about the cramped nights in the hotel and fast food was now a last resort, at least for a long while. She admired the plate shelf that wrapped around the entire kitchen wall, anxious to fit her collection of teapots there. The house was rich with charm and character, typical of older homes. Abby had ideas churning of what curtains would drape over the slender windows, the bright colors she'd like to see in the breakfast hours, prints of art to accompany her new table and most of all, the idea of seeing that wonderful man at her table for coffee every morning. She smiled secretly to herself and a few hours later, watched them all walk out the door, leaving she and Lillie content in their new home.

Chapter Ten

The night brought cooler skies and an abundance of ocean breezes through Camilla. Fall had arrived as October approached quickly. It would soon be time for fall festivals, Halloween ghouls and goblins, costumes and candy. Leaves would breeze by on the rundown streets and the winds would pick up with a brisk breath. The sand on the shores lay damp and unable to move. The waves brushed into the land with grace, while palms swished with ease.

It was still dark outside when Batson found himself stumped for sleep. The young man decided to get up, no need to lie around if he couldn't get any shuteye. Max watched him with weary eyes as he walked past him into the kitchen. Max looked as if he'd made up his mind to stay at the foot of the bed. Batson glanced at the clock, unsurprised when he noticed the hands pointing towards the five o'clock marker. He put coffee on to brew and moved on to the shower.

Max opened his eyes once again, curious as to why his friend was up at this hour. The shower was a fast one and Bats slipped on a pair of jeans. Max watched as he cracked a couple blinds on the window open, "No paper yet," he murmured. The man that delivered the paper in his neighborhood had been doing the same route for years. He had full-time work during the day but delivering papers brought in extra income. Batson was friendly with the paper man and they chatted on occasion, but that was the extent of it.

He bounced onto the couch to catch the morning news. His eyes flickered at the brightness of the television and he listened attentively to what was going on in the town of Camilla. "… cooler temperatures and a possible low of 52, possibility of rain showers…" the man's voice was annoying, he switched

99

stations. Max dragged in a few minutes later and they lay back listening to the music videos from the favorite VH-1.

Abby entered his thoughts once again- so beautiful she was. Maybe they would get to spend some quality time together this weekend. He wanted to know everything about her. What about Liz though? The reality of what the two of them had done began to sink in deeper, more so since he'd met Abby. Why was that? Was it because he was actually falling in love with someone? His anger and frustration was directed at no one but himself. He would take full responsibility of his affair with Liz if it ever came out. What had he been looking for in Liz? She was already married to Sam, had children and was supposedly in love with her husband. Looking back now, it was so easy to see another side to it all. What he and Liz had done was so unthinkable, so disgusting and so very unfair. If that ever did surface, there were more people that could be hurt by it... his concern was Abby. Maybe he should let her know about the affair. It would show his truthfulness, but then also his dishonesty, his repulsive behavior. No, that was way too much for any person to take. She could turn on him in a heartbeat, appalled at what kind of person he was. He could only hope that nothing would ever be said.

He mulled over all they could accomplish at Abby's house, though it was hard to think of work without dreaming about her. He fantasized touching her, holding her, merely being close to her. The thoughts became too much and he dove into some paperwork from the office.

The alarm rang through Abby's ears, the phone placed especially close to her head. It was 6:30, time to get up, start another new day. Today was Friday and she was already looking forward to getting it over with, anxious to get some furniture moved into their new house and finally get out of this hotel room.

Lillie lay quietly, still sleeping soundly and Abby hopped up to shower before she woke. She was overly ready to get a move on things this morning.

Abby washed and scrubbed, dried off and then dressed in twenty minutes. She nuzzled at Lillie softly, her foot dangling out the side of the covers and over the side of the bed.

"Get up baby. Gotta get ready for school now."

Lillie wiped the blonde curls tucked into her eyes and moved slowly to cut the television on for cartoons. Her swollen eyes dazed at the screen while Abby picked out her clothes, jeans and a top she had bought for her last year with flowers crawling on the bottom half and "Flower Girl" as the logo. Lillie wore jeans often. Abby insisted she could remember how chilly it would get in school with the air condition running full blast.

"Good morning dear," Patty greeted her as soon as she rushed through the front door. Ms. Patricia Drake was her name. She was an older woman that ran the front desk and everything else in the office as far as Abby could tell. The partners had extended her office just months before Abby had started there. She had already told Abby all about it, beaming and gloating about how much she appreciated it. As Abby understood it, Patty handled all the accounting, payroll, answering phones, filing; basically all the office legwork that kept the firm up and running. Abby was impressed by what this lady was capable of handling, especially her ability to keep her cool under pressure.

"Good morning to you. Ready for the weekend?" Abby answered her.

"I'm always ready for a weekend. You know how they run me ragged around here!" She always bragged about her load as well.

"Of course."

"I believe we are the only two here this morning. Theresa has the day off today. She and her husband were going away for the weekend and both Thom and Bill are luckily out on the golf course." She knew everyone's whereabouts and was obviously pleased to have the office to herself.

"So it will be a quiet day here today, huh?"

"We can only hope, dear… we can only hope." The croak in her voice trailed off as Abby escaped back to her office space. She looked around the desk and on top; it didn't appear that there was much work for her to do either. There sat two files that Thom had asked her to look over, which would only take about an hour or so. Without a load of work to do, there was no doubt the time would pass slowly.

She placed her purse in the bottom drawer and grabbed a cup of coffee before sorting through the files. She looked out her window and saw the sky starting to darken slightly. Without much hesitating, she dug into her work. She read through and through, taking notes and organizing them afterwards. She took this job very seriously, learning everything possible. She was a career woman now, a professional. Not only was she a professional, she was a single mom and she and Lillie's lives depended on her success.

An hour or so later, Patty buzzed. There was a phone call for her, it was Batson.

"Hi'ya. Only calling to check in," he sounded like he was in a good mood. "Friday Fever," her mom used to say.

"Hi. Doing great, just awful quiet over here. Everyone's gone."

"Do you want me to pick up some lunch for you?"

"Uh," she paused, "well, I wanted to swing by that furniture shop at lunch. I thought I'd just grab a quick bite and head on over there, but you can join me."

"Sounds good, just call me when you're ready."

Abby helped herself to a second cup of coffee and sat down. Her files had been thoroughly arranged and gone over, now she was bored. She held up her picture of Lillie in the prize frame she remembered buying long ago when she didn't have much to spend. Lillie had just been born and she had strolled her down to the shopping strip down from their house. It had costs nearly five dollars for that frame and she debated forever on whether she should get it or not.

Lillie looked perfect in that shot, when did she not? Abby's mom had paid for the photo shoot at a professional studio and it thrilled them both. Will was still part of her life back then, she shuttered at the thought.

Looking over at Lillie again she saw how shiny her eyes were and how simply innocent her smile was. To Abby, she was everything good in the world. Without realizing it, she had begun humming a lullaby she used to sing when Lillie was cradled in her arms. Patty happened to peek in the door, but continued on her way, smiling to herself to have witnessed such a moment. Abby caught a glimpse of her passing. Terribly embarrassed, she began to explain but Patty interrupted, "Listen, I have four of my own, Abby. They are all grown now and left me behind long ago. Would you believe that not a one of them live here any more?"

"Really?"

"Oh yes, dear. I remember singing to mine, oh, about thirty years ago. They grow up so fast. Before you know it, you'll be battling the teen years, then college and suddenly, they walk out the door for a final time, or until they find the urge to come home, usually for a home-cooked meal."

"Yes, I know. You see, my baby is all I have here in this town. It seems like only yesterday I had her dressed in her baby gown, holding onto her so tight and warm… don't you miss that?"

"Well, of course. How long ago was this taken?" She picked up the photo.

"This was taken when she was not quite two yet. She has

changed a lot since this picture. Lillie will be four in January, blows my mind."

"You will have to bring her in sometime so we can all see her. She is a real doll. Well, enough of my chitchat. I just came up to let you know that I'm about to go on to lunch and thought you'd like to go ahead as well. This way I can lock up since we're the only two here."

"Sure. Let me make one call and I'll be right down."

Abby phoned Batson and five minutes later she was outside waving bye to Patty. She and Batson decided on sandwiches from Cosmo's and walked towards Turner's. He suggested they take a seat on the bench outside and finish up. Abby laughed at him. Of course, they would finish before going into the store. Geez.

Turner's had the most extraordinary pieces and Abby marveled over nearly everything. She traveled on to the back of the store for mattresses on sale and miscellaneous bedroom pieces. She saw many appealing price tags, but nothing that she'd like to take home. She wanted to get excited about buying her furniture, to find the perfect, meant-to-be parts and pieces to make up her new house.

There was a white wicker little girl's set that wasn't on sale, but that she had to get for Lillie. Now she began to get excited. She also decided on a Shaker style pine bed for her room that had a nightstand to match- it was on sale. Dressers might be found at Goodwill or even a garage sale; they were outrageous in here. And she couldn't afford anything else really. The couches were way over her budget too. She shrugged and they talked to Mr. Turner and arranged a payment plan for Abby. It would be delivered as soon as this afternoon! Abby was ecstatic and Batson offered to be there when they delivered it, in case she wasn't home yet. Lillie would be thrilled.

And so, it was all going according to plan. Batson met up with the deliver guys around four o'clock, even helping with the smaller pieces. He arranged them all carefully, hoping it would suit. Batson wanted Lillie to walk into her splendid new room with a sparkle in her eyes at the sight of it. He found himself catering to the little girl. She deserved it, no father around and all.

Bats rearranged the furniture over and over until he was finally pleased. Lillie's new bed, canopy and all faced her window that looked onto the yard and a side view of the marsh. He had set Abby's the same way, towards the most scenic window. Grandma Anna's ways weaved into everything he did. Both of the girls would be able to hear the roll of the sea at the crack of a window.

The living room was a scattered mess, with garage sale finds and boxes, Batson did the best he could with it. He managed to arrange the two of the antique lamps on the nightstands in the bedrooms and then attempted to make it look more, well, cleaned up. He hoped he wasn't overstepping his bounds and felt Abby would truly appreciate even the smallest contribution.

There he stood in the middle of the hallway, glancing into one room and then the other. The house that once stood vacant and unappreciated was now beginning to look like a home. He walked outside to wait on the porch for the proud new owners.

Anna and Bessie sat inside with the fans cranked on high, watching another game show. Bessie cross-stitching a new pattern she had picked up the day before, this one with seashells. She thought Abby might like it for the bathroom or somewhere. Anna would mat and frame it for her, a little house warming gift from the two of them.

"What is that man thinking? I could've answered that one." Anna hollered at the television.

"Misses Anna, do you think Abby is gonna git it all in der'

dis' weekend? I'm is so excited 'bout her being next to you." Bessie continued. Anna thought she must have just had a burst of talkative energy after humming for over an hour.

"For goodness sakes, I hope to God so. Batson is over there now and I saw some moving guys earlier. I know she's good and ready to get out of that hotel room, you know?" Anna still glued to the screen. "What do you think will ever come of she and Bats?" She looked over at her friend, begging for something positive. Anna wanted so badly for Bats to find someone... this Misses Right might turn out to be Abby.

"Misses Anna! Now you knows I don't wanna git in all dat'. Batson will fend for hisself. Abby is a sweet baby girl, we knows dat', but Batson gonna hafta find love for him. You know what I thinks... well, Abby is out on her own and she needs some time to find her own self. Das' what I think. Just let it lie Misses and times will surely tell." Bessie sounded confident, but never looked up to see Anna's reaction. Anna sat staring at the show, but no longer paying attention to the contestants or the questions asked. She motioned that she was going to lie down and Bessie nodded as she walked out the doorway, no words necessary.

The horn from Abby's car wailed as she and Lillie pulled in the drive. Lillie jumped out of her seat with excitement to see Batson and ready to see her new room. Abby couldn't keep the news a secret and let it out on the way home.

"Wait up now, Lillie. We have to wait on your mama. She will want to go in with you, don't you know?" Batson held his hand out to hers and she looked up at Abby, her heart pounding.

"It's here! It's here!" she squealed.

"Come in and see," Batson opened the front door.

"Come on, Mama. Faster. Faster." Lillie was hardly able to control herself.

Abby rushed towards the two of them, a bag on each arm and they stepped through the door. Abby's eyes scanned over the room and Lillie was quickly out of sight. They followed.

"Mama! Mama! Look at my room! And look at my bed!" She pounced up and down on the mattress, and then proceeded to look through all her new dresser drawers.

"There's not anything in there yet, Lil. We have to put all your things in there." She did not seem to care too much about the drawers after seeing they were empty. "Let's go see Mama's room now, okay?" Abby's skin was crawling, like the skin of a child.

Looking into the room you could see the bottom half of the bed from the doorway. All three walked in a line and only seconds later, Lillie was trying out her mom's bed as well. Everything was placed wonderfully and so welcoming. Abby saw the lamp on the bed stand and looked into the mirror at her own reflection, wiping the tears before they fell. She closed her lids, took the deepest breath and all she could imagine at that moment was the thought of clean sheets on those new beds. Always a mom.

"Don't cry, Mama." Lillie tagged onto her legs.

"I don't mean to. I'm just so happy right now, do you understand that? People sometimes cry when they are happy and other times when they are sad, but Mama is happy right now." Abby stroked at her eyes once again and Batson put his arm around her shoulders. This must mean a lot more to her than he could ever imagine. Abby turned towards him and watched his eyes flutter, then hugged him with all her strength.

"What you have done is amazing, all your help, your support... how could I have done this without you?" She couldn't quit hugging him. If only she knew how much it meant to him to share a moment like this with her. "How will I ever make this up to you? Ever?"

"Abby, this has meant so much to me, but I think we can

think of some things." He smirked and she knew he was
playing with her. All she would have to do was simply be a
part of his life, he thought. That wouldn't be so hard, would it?
He sat on the bed and watched the two girls cackle back and
forth over where to put what. Seeing the two of them so filled
with joy gave him tremendous satisfaction. He knew he would
leave with the knowledge that he had, in a small way,
contributed to one small miracle.

Lillie was running through the house like a wild chicken,
Abby and Bats got stuck carrying the rest of the bags up from
the car. Abby had stopped by the grocery and picked up a stock
of food, hotdogs, lunchmeat, potato chips, pimento cheese,
fruit, more Cokes and a huge bottle of Cabernet for a small
celebration later on. She would soon have the pantry packed
with goodies. Before checking out, she picked up a couple
packs of cigarettes for Batson, thinking of sneaking one in for
herself later with her glass of wine. They were officially home.

Batson made the kind offer of stopping by the hotel to make
sure they had gotten everything, but Abby insisted she go.
Lillie wanted to stay with Batson, so that was settled. But first,
they finished the groceries and Lillie set out her belongings on
the floor in her room. Batson brought in a small box full of
board games, a pack of cards and some home decorating
magazines he'd picked out for Abby. She thanked him as he
handed them over and he knew she was impressed. Never in
her existing life had she known anyone like Batson Cannon.
She was beginning to realize how lucky she was to have him
around.

"Alright guys... Lillie?" Abby stated aloud. "I'm going
back into town to gather whatever is leftover at the hotel.
You're sure you want to stay here, Lil?" She nodded. "Alright,
well, you have to behave yourself, okay?" Abby kissed her on
both cheeks and left right away.

"Hey, Abby. Wait. What do you want to do for dinner? I mean, do you want me and Lillie to go get something, or cook here?" After the words left his mouth, he hoped once again that he wasn't pushing too hard.

"Um, let's see. I bought all kinds of stuff. There are hotdogs or I bought some hamburger meat. Do you cook too?" She knew better than that.

"Why, of course, my dear."

"When did I get so lucky?" She laughed and he chased her to the couch and pecked her on the mouth. Lillie giggled. "Quit now, I've got to get going." Ah, he was absolutely amazing. It was like they had known each other for years and his company felt so natural. He hugged her once again and she smiled, trying to walk to the car without stumbling. She knew he was watching every step, his eyes tracing her figure. They waved and Batson went back inside. They began to work on the organization of Lillie's clothes in the dresser, shorts in middle, shirts on the bottom and panties and socks on top. He knew he wasn't just falling in love with Abby, he was falling head over heels for her little Lillie.

Abby drove along the crooked road until she reached the highway. The whole idea of them together blew her mind. Her life could not possibly be going this good, could it? She thought of Will. What was he into now? She wondered if he was still in their old place. Why should she even care? He abandoned her, he abandoned Lillie, and without a second thought. Lazy and selfish he was, in a world all his own. They had been nothing but a burden to his lifestyle. Who cared now, he was gone for good.

Then she thought of Tommy, the first real boyfriend in high school. Tommy Blackwell was his name. They had kept in close touch for many years, but lately it had slowed. She had many memories of him, clear and vivid. That first love was always the one that stuck in your mind, the one thing you could go back to and think of, just for a smile. He was that one she could always rely on; he would be there for her through day or night. Only thing was, in recent years, she only called when things were bad and he had gotten tired of the routine. When they were together they would goof off, spending quite a bit of time alone. They were the big-ticket item back then, but looking back, she assumed it was never meant to be. His memories were alive and with her all the time though. She wondered what he would say if he saw her now, a mother, a proud new homeowner and finally, away from Will for good.

"What am I thinking?" she said, talking to no one but herself. "Why am I even thinking of Tommy? Of Will? He's probably married now with four kids or something. I really am losing my mind. Besides, look what I have waiting for me at home." A look of grace danced upon her face, she knew her life was going somewhere, somewhere in the right direction. Letting old emotions wander from their hiding places did not serve any kind of purpose. Batson was the most incredible guy and she should savor their time together, make new memories. She shrugged her shoulders up and down, at first in reaction to her thoughts and then just because it felt good. She pulled into the parking lot, walked in with a job to do and later turned that key in for good.

Chapter Eleven

Gracie sat on the lined couch at home, ready to go out with friends when the phone rang. It was Grandma Anna.

"Hello there, dear. I'm calling to touch base with you, see how things are going." Anna's cheerful Southern Belle voice rang through the line loud and clear.

"Grannie! Oh, your voice sounds so good. I miss you so much, but I can only talk for a sec. I'm meeting friends in a minute."

"Oh, well good. Meet some new people?" she asked.

"No, not really. These are just some I work with. We have reservations at Harvey's, a restaurant up here, really classy place too. Then we'll probably head out to some dance clubs or something, but... how are things down there?"

"Very good, very good. Bessie and I are sitting here enjoying this fall weather that is about to breeze through. It's been so cool at night, well, you know how it is." Anna missed her sweet girl, hearing her voice never failed to bring tears to her eyes. All she could do was worry about Gracie in that big city life, all alone. But tonight, Gracie sounded a little more upbeat and that came as a relief to Anna.

"How's Bats?" It's been forever since I've talked to his crazy..." she stopped, almost forgot who she was talking to.

"Oh, he's doing great, honey. You won't believe this when I tell you, but your brother is taking a turn for the better and I mean, much better."

"What's that mean? He's always been a good one."

"Well, lately he just seems to have loosened up quite a bit, taking days off from work and seems to be a lot more relaxed than I ever remember him being."

"Really?" Gracie nearly in shock at the idea of Batson being carefree.

"Oh, yes. He has taken onto our new friend and now, new neighbor, Abby Logan."

"Who?" Gracie didn't recognize the name at first, then, "Oh yeah. That's the girl that helped you when you fell, right?"

"If you prefer to bring that up, yes, that's her. She is such a cute girl, Gracie. You are going to simply adore her and I think that's exactly how Bats feels."

"Wow. You are serious."

"Very." Grandma Anna continued telling her about all the recent Camilla news. Gracie loved to be filled in on all the latest.

Gracie looked over at the clock beside the closet door, "Well, I've got to go, Grannie. Oh, almost forgot, I might get to come home for Thanksgiving!"

"Oh Gracie, that's wonderful news! Please do. We all miss you so very much." Anna knew she would cry now.

"Well, we'll see but I think they can manage without me for a couple of days at the office and I already talked it over with my boss lady. Now I am just waiting for the definite okay, so keep your fingers crossed!"

"We will, sweetheart. I love you and be careful tonight, alright?" Anna held onto the phone tight, her aging fingers cramped together. Gracie said her goodbyes back and that was that.

Bessie was in the kitchen making hot tea, but caught in on most of the conversation, "Got good news, Misses Anna?"

"Gracie's coming home for Thanksgiving!" They hugged and jumped in circles, then she ran next door to tell Batson.

Abby was pulling up, startled when she saw Anna hurrying on the tips of her toes across the lawn.

"What is it, Anna?" What's wrong?" praying that nothing had happened to Lillie.

"Nothing's wrong, honey. Don't panic. Things are great. I just got off the phone with Gracie and she's coming for Thanksgiving! I was only coming over to tell Batson; he will be thrilled."

"Oh, oh. Thank God. I saw you taking off in the yard and just knew she had fallen or cracked a tooth. You never know, you know."

Anna noticed how tense Abby was, more so in the past week with the house and all. It concerned her, Bessie insisted it was stress. She ordered her to lie down and relax.

"What's wrong with her?" Batson asked. Abby's face was flushed in red and white, her leg muscles felt like they never intended to move again.

"I just scared her, that's all. I was coming over to tell you Gracie is going to be home for Thanksgiving! Isn't that great?"

"She is?"

"Well, we think so. But Abby saw me running over here and had thought that something might have happened to Lillie."

Bats walked over and sat down on the edge of the bed. Anna handed over a damp washcloth to put on her forehead and he patted it gently to her face. Abby was embarrassed for overreacting, but when she moved, the room began to blur and then chills covered her skin.

"Are you alright?"

"Sure. I'm gonna be fine, just overly tired and with so much going on, I guess I'm a little on edge. I just panicked. It's a mom thing."

Anna winked, she understood. "Well, here she is now." Lillie strolled on the hardwoods in her sock feet and gown, climbed up in the bed and lay in Abby's arms.

"What's wrong, Mama?"

"Nothing, baby. The sun got to me is all." The words seemed to make her feel less frightened at seeing Abby laid up and sick looking. Her eyes were heavy and Abby traced her eyebrows with her fingers.

"Mama will feel a lot better in the morning, I promise. Let's go in the kitchen and find you something small to drink before dinner."

"No tea." Mama knew best and Anna took the child's hand in hers.

Batson didn't leave her side. She let in and closed her eyes, soft and sunken they were. Batson covered her legs with the afghan that had been folded neatly at the foot of the bed. She was so bushed, it was hard to get into those clean sheets that she knew would feel so wonderful.

He closed her bedroom door and joined Lillie and Grandma Anna in the kitchen.

"Maybe one of us should stay the night, do you think?"

She offered, but in a calm and soft whisper so Lillie couldn't hear.

"She's just worn out. All this moving and the new job, everything has finally taken the toll on her. She's asleep now; I'll stay and watch over Lillie. We'll see if she wants one of us to stay later on."

"I want my Mama." Worried and unsure, Lillie leaned into Batson, then tugged at his hand. "I want Mama."

"She's resting, Lillie. You and I get to play for a while. How about that?"

She stood still, but looked up when Anna mentioned dinner. "I bet Bessie has got something cooked up next door. Do you want to come with me and see?" She agreed. "How about you, Bats?"

"No, you two go along, I'll eat later."

Bessie was in the kitchen working a casserole together, another favorite of the household. Shepherd's Pie was the special on for tonight. She filled it with sweet corn kernels, tomatoes, potatoes, beef and cheese- great for the skinny-minnie that

Lillie was. Of course, the two women agreed she needed something wholesome in her tummy, lots of veggies.

Anna told Bessie what had happened and Bessie then made an obvious effort to keep the little one busy.

Batson did what he could to the house, cleaned out the windowsills and washed off the front and back patios. Abby slept nearly two hours. When she woke it took her a minute to figure out where she was and then remembering, the sweetest of thoughts went through her mind. Sitting up, she was still a bit uneasy. The floorboards creaked as she walked one foot in front of the other; they were especially cool on her bare feet. Where was Lillie? For once she wasn't worried, she knew for certain she was taken care of with Bats, Anna or Bessie. She looked up and met face to face with Batson.

"Hello, sleepyhead." He saw how creased her eyes were from her nap, then how beautiful she was when she woke up. Her lids blinked several times to focus, it was pitch black out now and the light above the kitchen table was unbelievably bright.

"Where's Lil'?"

"She's over there. They ate dinner and all, but they just called and she's still awake. Waiting on you, I suppose," he answered.

"Geez," she yawned. "What time is it anyway?"

"Around eight. You just knocked out when we gave you the chance." He grinned at her, "We were worried about you. Maybe you've got too much going right now."

"What's that supposed to mean?"

"Nothin. I just thought if… well, if I get in the way at all, you just let me know. Okay?" He had a good manner about him and she could see that he was only being sincere.

"No, no. I already said how much I needed you throughout all of this. Bats…"

115

"Okay, okay."

"Wow, I feel like I've been asleep for days, maybe months even. It's been so overwhelming for me."

"Sit down, I'll get you something to drink. Tea? Coke?"

"Actually, I'm going to check on Lillie. Go ahead and open up that bottle of wine, I think I deserve it. She's probably just as exhausted as I was, but at least we'll get to sleep in tomorrow morning." She had the sweetest smile, and then he noticed the creases in her eyes had faded and her face was beginning to shine again.

"I'll go with you."

Without knocking, they pushed open the front screen door. There was a marvelous breeze rolling through and the fresh air was stimulating. Inside sat all three girls on the sofa, cuddled like sardines. Soda cans sat on the floor and what was left of a bowl of popcorn had been pushed to one corner of the coffee table.

Lillie's eyes flew open and she rushed for Abby's legs, squeezing as tight as she could, "Mama!"

"Hey there, sweet girl. I had the most wonderful nap. Are you ready to go to sleep in your brand new bed, in your brand new bedroom?" She stretched it out, adding the extra exciting faces to go with it. "It's all waiting for you next door! Oh, boy!"

Lillie tilted her head up and down, more down than up. She looked pitiful, bless her heart. Abby hoped she would sleep soundly in the new place and not get frightened in the night. Maybe she should put her in her bed, might be a good idea.

"Thanks so much y'all, for keeping her and everything. I didn't mean to doze off like that, I don't know what got into me."

"Wif' good reasons, child. You is a worn out shoe wif' all 'dis excitement, tuggin this way and 'datta way.

116

Lord be wif you. I knows if I was doin haf' as much, I'd beez crashin' out too, uh-huh."

"I think you're right, Bessie. But soon enough, we'll be all settled in and things will be running smoothly, all will be done."

"I know you can't wait for that day to come." Batson added.

Anna sat unusually quiet, obviously keeping Lillie for a few hours had worn them out. She mumbled goodnight softly to the kids and walked on into her bedroom.

"Night, y'all." Bessie locked the door behind them.

The sound of crickets flurried around them as they walked through the grass. The roll of ocean waves thundered in the distance and the marsh grass whistled. Abby knew how gratifying their lives would be here. She saw this as her choice, the choice to live where they could be refreshed every day by the salt scents of the sea.

Lillie held onto her mama's hand as they walked up the stairs and into the house. She looked around and then stood still, waiting for Abby to help her to bed.

"So, princess, what do you think? Nice, right?" She found a nightgown and popped it over the blonde curls.

"Yes, mam. It's gonna be dark in here. Can't you stay with me?"

"Sure, honey. Here, look at this... I got it for you today." Abby handed over the nightlight. Lillie smiled and gave it back, pointing to different outlets until Abby had found the right one. "I have more in the kitchen. One for the hall, the living room, my bath and the kitchen. See, so if you get scared, you'll be able to find your way to me, in my room." She pointed in that direction.

Lillie was still a little apprehensive about this sleeping arrangement. Abby tucked her in tightly, blankets curled below her chin, pulled a favorite book from a box on the floor and began to read. When she went to reach for a second book, her blonde Raggedy was fast in slumber.

Looking down at her, Abby said a silent prayer, thanking God for all her many blessings, this one especially. Lillie was such a dear child, but growing up way too fast. Abby fingered her ringlets behind her ears and then traced her soft, porcelain face. How lucky she was to have such a healthy child, one so beautiful and strong. Bats peeked in and her private moment disappeared.

"She's asleep already?" Poor Batson, he didn't know too much about kids.

"Oh, definitely. She's full of energy all day, but when it comes time to go to bed, she's never had any trouble." Abby watched his face study Lillie, then ran her fingers through Lillie's curls once again. They circled around her bed, Abby thinking up some new ideas.

"Looks great in here. I think I'm going to do stenciling or some kind of border up there. Don't you think?" She spoke in a whisper.

"Now, that question is directed at the wrong person. I have no decorating talent, what looks bad, what looks good. Nothing. I just know where furniture pieces generally fit the best, that's all." He laughed and she followed his lead. Lillie stirred slightly and Abby warned him by raising her finger to her mouth, "Shhh."

She kissed Lillie on the forehead, turned off the light beside her bed and cracked the door. Batson was already at the table with the bottle of wine.

"Well, here we are. Do you want some chips or something?" This was her house, she could play hostess now.

"Nah. Here's your glass of wine." He handed over the glass and their eyes met for what seemed to be the first time this evening. The night was still early and Abby was wide-awake after her nap. She took a seat beside him.

"It feels so good to be here, you just don't know. So nice to unwind and relax."

"Oh, I think I can relate."

"So we never got the chance to talk a lot the other night. Let's do that, alright?" She wanted to know about Batson, his life.

"Okay, what do you want to know about?"

"Well, I'll tell you a little more about me and then you take it from there. Ask me something."

"I don't want to be out of line or anything, but my curiosity is killing me- where is Lillie's dad? Are y'all married still or were you married?" He couldn't help himself, she started it.

"You aren't out of line. It doesn't bother me at all to talk about him. Let's see... Lillie's dad is a one-of-a-kind, William Concord Logan. I've always called him Will. He's still living back home I suppose." Abby began the saga, "We were married briefly, about two years I think it was. When I became pregnant, we began having serious problems. I wanted to change for the better, he didn't." He listened carefully.

"Will never had that many responsibilities. When you first fall in love, well, I'm sure you know, a lot of that stuff didn't seem to matter, or at least it didn't to me. We were both young at the time and liked to go out quite a bit, you know, the normal stuff. He always had a drinking problem but I never acknowledged it until later, when I was pregnant with Lillie. That's when I decided to make a change for the better, for Lillie and me. I tried to put my foot down, some limits, but it just wasn't a good situation."

"So he was an alcoholic?"

"Yes. It was, I think, the most difficult thing I've ever had to deal with. There were many nights when I wouldn't know where he was, if he was coming home or if he was even alive. It was that kind of thing all the time." She talked freely about the subject, but Batson knew it had to hurt inside. She amazed him. Many people wouldn't have the guts to leave. Little did

119

he know, this was only the beginning of it.

"I don't know you and Lillie that well yet, but I cannot imagine anyone treating you like that."

"Well, it was an experience, that's for sure. One night he fell asleep with a cigarette in his hand and thankfully, I went upstairs to check on him. The comforter already had a huge hole burning in it. That's when I knew, something had to be done." Abby remembered more; "I just thought how easy it would have been for that to catch fire and Lillie right down the hall in her crib. That thought terrified me. I didn't want to live my life like that."

"You shouldn't have to. No one should."

"Well, after that, I couldn't sleep soundly at night until I was sure he was out. It became a routine to check after him, make sure the doors were locked, the oven was off, the cigarettes were out and all the beer cans were in the trash before morning."

Batson sat in his chair staring out into the space in front of him, imagining Abby in that situation. She got up and brought the bottle of wine to the table, easily accessible. He looked at her, wanting her to continue.

"It was like having another child to tend to, literally. Guys would call the house, asking me to relay messages that they needed their money. For what, I didn't even want to know. I'm not sure if he was gambling, doing drugs or what. It took all I had to leave though, because I thought he was all I had and with Lillie only months old, I thought I needed his support. Then I realized, hey, there is no support. It took all the courage deep inside myself, the support of my parents and few friends that I had to pull me out of it. After all that, I vowed never to marry again." She sat still for several minutes and sipped her wine fast, over and over. What could he say?

Abby had more, "See, his mother had sheltered him and waited on him hand and foot all of his life. His father left and was never heard from again when he was just a baby, a sad situation. Now look, that's what he's done to Lillie. He just abandoned her. It was a crazy situation. It's so easy to look back and see all the signs and clues in hindsight. Somewhere along the way, you lose all sight of yourself, your true self. Then you think, how did I get to this point? Growing up I was a normal kid, did all the right things. I mean, granted, I made my mistakes too, but what in the hell did I do to deserve this? Life can take us in so many different directions and only if you're strong you know when to switch avenues and when not to. For Lillie and me, it was time to switch."

Batson reached across the table, took her hand in his, "I don't know what to say, Abby. I had no idea you went through all this, you're too good of a person."

"Well, we're okay now. Look at us." She spread her arms out, so proud that they finally had somewhere to live. "It's all over with now and I thank God every day. It was something that I obviously had to go through and I've learned a lot from that. I am too strong a person to fall back into a situation like that." Batson could see she was over it, ready to move on with her life. Maybe she truly wouldn't get married again, only time would tell. He decided right then and there that he wasn't going to push her into anything that might make her uncomfortable. She had been through enough.

"Let's move onto something else," she said.

"Yes, let's do."

"I wish I had a sofa in there. Maybe I'll find time to get out this weekend and look at some."

"You'll find one. This wine is great. I think I needed this too. I've got to go smoke. You want to step out back with me?" He pointed to the back door.

"Sure. Let me run and check on Lillie right quick." She walked down the hallway and peeked in the bedroom door. Her eyes were closed and her bunny tucked up under her arm.

She checked the lock on the front door and then proceeded out the back.

The moon was shining and you could see far out onto the water. The view was incredible and Abby took a seat on the back steps beside him. The sounds were exactly the same as they were earlier and the world seemed at peace.

"I can't wait until morning, so I can come out here with my coffee and enjoy this view at daybreak. It must be amazing." She pictured herself sitting in the morning sun, barefoot and cupping her coffee.

"Oh, you are going to love it out here. I can remember when I was little and the summers we spent getting up early to fish on the dock. My grandfather was an unprecedented fisherman. After he passed away, I always came out to fish with Sam. You remember, my friend."

"Yes, I remember. And his wife... gosh," she stumped, "What was her name again? I'm horrible with names."

"Liz," he replied, thinking how ironic it was that Abby couldn't even remember her name. Yes, she was gone for good.

"Yes, Liz. She seemed really sweet. They are good people, huh?"

"Yeah, old friends. Like I said, Sam and I have been fishing together since we were probably old enough to toddle around." He smiled, the memories easy to picture in his head.

"That's neat."

Batson smoked about a third of his cigarette when Abby asked for one.

"I thought you quit?" he asked her.

"I did. But when I have a drink or want to relax, I like to have one or two. Lillie has never seen me smoke though."

"The closet smoker," he said sarcastically and she laughed, but only to make him feel good. The wine was doing its duty and was unintentionally bringing them closer as they chatted, telling stories of their pasts.

Looking up at the bright stars hanging freely in the night sky, both Batson and Abby became fascinated with each other. They held hands and flirted with the idea of taking it further, but instead immersed themselves in the charming adventure of new romance. Batson held the sides of Abby's face and pressed it closely to his. Their lips rubbing together, sensing the desires of one another. The light of the moon lurked over the two of them. There couldn't have been a more romantic moment, Abby thought to herself.

After several hours passed, Abby whispered that he had better go on home. It was a quarter after midnight and she needed her rest for the next day. Batson relented, not wanting to leave, but knowing she was right. She walked him to the door and they kissed several times to end the night.

"I'll call you tomorrow when we get up, alright?" Abby told him as he began to pull away.

"You had better. You've got me in a corner now, you know that, don't you?" His eyes shined from the glow of light beaming from the bulb dangling above them. She smiled and giggled, the wine.

Batson kissed her one last time and walked to his car to head home for the night. Abby locked the door and went into her room. The night had been perfect. She glanced again into Lillie's room and opened the door so she could listen out for her. Without hesitation, she climbed into bed, her window cracked a notch, and fell fast to sleep.

Chapter Twelve

The sea swayed in and out with its tide and the wind picked up speed as the night went through its cycle. The moon still shined brightly and stood guard, watching over Camilla and its diminutive islands. Out near the pier at Hudson, you could hear squawks of pelicans and other birds of the coast. They would ramble on constantly, never sleeping. Sand dust was blowing across the streets of the island and then gathered in small piles randomly along the pavement. There weren't too many trees out here this close to the water. The skinny ones that did make their way were tossed side to side because of the strong winds that often traveled through. Sometimes it looked like they would have been pulled out of the earth, roots and all, and then carried to the sea for digestion.

The moon gradually descended to the edge of the earth as the sun emerged from the horizon. The view was unlike any other. Of all the places in the world, this is the one where Abby Logan had chosen to be. Leaving her home place with family and friends to take a chance and live where she had always wanted.

Abby would sometimes wonder if it sounded strange to other people when she told them why she was moving. Older people, not wanting to ever change their lifestyle just couldn't understand. Even Abby's parents would ask how she could just pack it all up and leave.

Not only was it significant to her, she would tell them, it was important for her to raise Lillie near the water. Her explanation was that ever since she was a little girl, the family vacations to the beach would always calm the rough edges of their lives. Just to sit on the sand, close your eyes and listen. The essence of taking it all in brought peace of mind, it cleansed your soul.

It was one of the most magnificent works of God. The sea would soon attract the growing Abby like a fly, visiting with whoever would ride, several times a year.

There were even times that she had traveled by herself, without her mom and dad knowing of course. Even for the day, she would race her car down old highways and back roads to have time to herself. She would pass fruit and vegetable stands, antique shops, rotted slave quarters and fields of tobacco, corn and God knows what else. This was her time alone. Abby's backpack traveled with her on these solitary excursions, filled with the necessities. She would always have her camera, extra packs of film, journal, a small book or two, pencils and her wallet. Without a single familiar face around, she still felt safe.

Walking one foot in front of the other, she carried herself around downtown areas, admiring all sorts of buildings and people. The people were her favorite to watch. She would often make up stories for certain ones, judging by what they looked like, their age and their mannerisms. After strolling around, she would head to the beach.

Abby would drag out the pliable beach chair from the trunk to the sand, with backpack in hand, squat down and watch the world as it was. She believed soul searching was one thing that every human ought to make time to do. The water with its smell, its thunder and its pure beauty- all were in Abby's dreams for years to come. Now that she was the mom, she wanted Lillie to have the advantage of living next to it, simple as that. In her mind, this was where they belonged and no one could tell her different.

The dawn arrived and Abby stretched in her bed, surprised not to see Lillie around yet. She walked down the narrow hallway and peeked inside. There was her little angel, curled up in a ball, barely visible with all the covers.

126

Abby went into her new kitchen and looked for coffee. There it was, freshly made in the new pot. She thanked the brilliant inventor for the coffee maker with a timer. She looked out the window above the sink and what a sight to see. She opened it and the breeze moved easily through her hair. This was certainly meant to be, she thought to herself. She looked over the kitchen table, making sure all the wine and glasses had been put away. She despised waking up to any trace of alcohol left behind, especially with Lillie here.

Abby went to open the front door to let some light in and leave the storm door closed. She turned the knob, an unusual feeling ran over her entire body. She immediately let go and casually walked to the window of the living room and saw nothing.

Her stomach began to turn inside out and she had a gut feeling that something was terribly wrong, something was out of place. She tiptoed into Lillie's room, trying not to wake her. She looked over on that side of the house and there it was, there was the trouble standing right outside.

"Here's yo'r housecoat, Misses Anna. It's hanging right 'der in da' baf'room, jus' like I told you. My goodness." Bessie hollered to Anna in the kitchen.

Anna walked to meet her.

"Sure enough. What would I ever do around this house without you? I'm loosing my head. Geez."

"I wonders if Miss Abby and little Lillie slept good through da' night. I'm sure dey' did jus' fine."

"I'm almost positive they slept the best they have in months since they are in an actual home and not some hotel room." Anna stated, pulling the sleeves of her housecoat.

"I bet she's havin' more dreams. You?"

"Lord, no. She's probably too tired to dream. All that hocus pocus just freaks me out now, you hear?"

"Yes'm. Won't says another word." Bessie threw her head up and to the side, knowing that she knew what she was talking about. Misses Anna just didn't want to hear it.

"Thank you. Now, are you ready to go on the porch?"

"Yes'm. I's ready. Let's fill our coffee up in here 'for we go." So they filled their mugs up and began their daily routine. Even though it was a Saturday, it didn't mean anything to these two, just another day, only more people out and about.

Misses Anna sat in her usual rocker on the left, Bessie sat her cup down and picked up the broom from the corner. The planks on the floor of the porch had to be cleaned before sitting down or the dust and sand would drive Bessie nuts. She swept up right quick and then took her seat in the rocker on the right. The white, wooden table sat between the two with an ashtray for company, mainly Batson. A handful of pulled out fresh flowers lay beside it, Lillie had brought them in from the yard the day before.

"I wonder what our Gracie is doing right at this moment?" Anna began the conversation.

"She's sleepin' in, I'm sure. I'm am tired mysef' dis' mornin'."

"Oh hush now, not our girl. I'm sure she's up typing, writing or something productive. She's always been an early riser. Don't you remember anything? Every morning that child would be the one waking us up and she was always ready to go to school. It was Batson we had to drag to the breakfast table."

"Uh-huh, dat's right."

"Don't you think she's going to love Abby and Lillie when she comes home?" Anna asked.

"Yes'm, very much so."

"Well, I think so too. I think they'll get along splendidly. Maybe being around Lillie will get those maternal instincts going," she paused. "It might do the same for Batson. You never know."

128

"Yes, Misses. I know. You betta' quit hasslin' now or you is gonna ruin it."

"Oh, whatever. What will be will be. I know that and you do too. Batson and Abby are going to be together, I just know it."

"Oh, you do, huh?"

"Yes, I do. Wanna bet on this one?"

"If you really wan'to."

"Of course I do. It'll be fun. How much?"

"No, not money. You don't pay me enough to waste that. Ha, ha, ha." Bessie sneered and Anna nudged her.

"Let's make it this way. If you win, then I'll clean house for a whole week and wait on you. If I win, you have to sell that house o'er there in mudtown and move in with me. Sound good?" Bessie eyed Anna; this was a stupid bet anyhow. Maybe Anna was frightened of being alone. Bessie didn't understand it, but she agreed.

"Move in here? Wif' you?"

"Sure, why not? Hell, you're already here all the damned time anyway... can't get rid of ya," she teased.

"All right, Misses Anna. You've got yo'self a deal!" Bessie reached out to grab Anna's hand and they both looked down, noticing how frail they felt when their hands met and clasp onto each other. They let go quickly and never mentioned it.

Just as Anna opened her mouth up to start a new topic, they heard a car door slam and then it started. Both of them ran as fast as they could to the windows on the side of the house to see what was going on.

There stood Abby in the front yard, her arms waving in the air with a terrified, angry look on her face. Who was that man?

"YOU are unbelievable! I cannot even begin to understand the reasoning behind this... this charade!" Abby told him, trying so hard not to yell and embarrassed that Anna and Bessie would hear from next door. "How am I supposed to explain

129

this to Lillie?"

He shrugged, not sure what to say anymore. He had expected this sort of reaction before he had even driven down here. Her face still gave the same disappointed expressions when she got upset and her eyes glistened with hostility. She always did something with those eyebrows of hers, made her look like such a smart-ass. That look used to drive him nuts and often, drive him right out the door. Same ole' Abby, same ole' Will.

Abby was raving still. "I mean, to come here and try to do... what? What exactly did you come here to do? Make everything yours again? Ha! I seriously hope you are not that damned stupid!" She caught her breath and brushed her hair back. She could not even look at him. He stood there, leaning against the post on the porch, looking everywhere else except at her. Her hands on her hips and sweating like a seething bull, he knew better than to push too hard.

"I am going inside to get a cup of coffee and smoke a cigarette. I want you to leave these premises immediately and I'm not joking Will! If completely necessary, you may come back when I've cooled off and we can talk so I can see what the hell you want with us. I mean it too. Geez, you sure do have some balls to show up on my doorstep and right out of the blue too! Goodbye Will." She walked inside, shut and locked the door tightly behind her.

Walking down the hall, she looked in on Lillie. Amazingly, she lay in bed still asleep. She quickly grabbed her cup of coffee, squeezed the cigarette pack left over from last night in her free hand and headed upstairs in the loft. She refused to let Anna and Bessie see her face right now. She knew they heard, they probably saw his van. Upstairs she used some old wooden crates that were there when they moved in to sit on.

Her hands trembled as she lit one cigarette after another, listening with the closest ear for Lillie's sweet voice. She probably wouldn't even recognize him. Damn him for disrupting everything that I've worked for, he waits until the perfect moment to come traipsing in our lives.

He had looked the same. His hair feathered back, never moving and his eyes, well, you could actually see the white in them this morning. Abby remembered looking into those eyes, long ago, seeing big dreams and wonderful ideas of how their lives would intertwine forever and ever. There were nights when she would find him slouched in the recliner, his eyes halfway open, passed out. She'd put her hand on his chest, just to make sure he was breathing, often secretly hoping he might not be. When she nudged, he would always cough, harsh like hell, throat veins bulging for air.

When they were first together, she did make an attempt to wake him, bring him to bed. But after a while, she refused to even try. She knew how the night would end the moment he walked through the door. Those eyes were a dead giveaway. The more tired Abby got over the situation, the happier she was when he passed out downstairs.

If he slept with her, she would toss and turn. Abby remembered it like it was yesterday. She'd grab her pillow, a couple of blankets out of the hall closet, and make a pallet on Lillie's floor. There beside her baby Lillie she would sleep, but never soundly. "We're gonna be alright, my sweet girl. I promise you that. I promise, baby," she would say to her.

He would wake up fine, as if nothing had happened. In his mind, there was no problem. "There's nothing wrong with drinking a beer after work, Abby. Don't you dare try and tell me how to live my life. Do you hear me?" The argument was always the same.

The nights and days rolled on and Abby began to realize that life with him was never going to change. She would counter, "Can't we live a normal life? Look at this... the keys were left in the door all night! Where were you? Don't you even care?

We are your family, dammit!" Nothing worked, never would.

There were too many bad times, horrible times. Looking back, it was hard to believe she once coexisted with this person. The ashtray would be emptied on the floor, where his feet had knocked it over as he slept on the couch. She would find empty beer cans under the recliner, behind the couch, in the bath trash, even tossed to the side of the house. The television was left on continuously and his clothes reeked of alcohol and smoke. His face would go unshaven for days at a time, some days he wouldn't even shower. It was too much.

Constantly, it was only Abby and Lillie at home together. They were the family. Will was never around to bathe her, to feed her, rock her or most importantly, kiss her goodnight. The bills stacked high, the phone got cut off and disconnection notices were always coming from the power company. It was pathetic, disappointing. The only thing that kept her going was time with Lillie; she brought joy to every single day. Then one day, Will went to the store and never came back. Finally, it was over.

"Mama? Maa-ma?" Lillie called out. Abby answered her quickly and bolted down the stairs.

"Here I am, sweetheart. Mommy's right here." She brushed her hair back, "I didn't mean to frighten you. I was just upstairs in the loft checking out some things."

Lillie didn't seem too interested.

"Well, did you sleep good?"

"I'm hungry."

"Alright, let's go on in the kitchen and find you something. How about some oatmeal? Toast, too?"

"Uh-huh."

Abby mulled over what a crazy morning it had been so far. How did he find them anyway? She didn't know how to explain all of this to Lillie, but maybe she wouldn't have to. If she had any luck at all, he wouldn't come back.

She boiled the water for the oatmeal, buttered the toast and sat down beside her. Her curls were tight this morning, sticking to her scalp in places.

"So, tell me. How's the bed? Sleeps good, huh?" She reached over and caressed her hair. Her sweet baby, clueless of what had started off the morning.

"It's soft." She grabbed a cereal box to see the maze on the box.

"What do you want to do today?" Lillie sat half awake and shrugged, too early to think about much.

Damn. She didn't want to tell her about her dad and what they might actually have to do today.

The phone rang. It was Batson.

His voice sounded so good in the morning and she wished he were there. She imagined waking up to hear that voice every morning, how nice that would be. She told him about Will's visit, had to be honest about it.

Batson chest ached, his heart felt threatened. Would his chance with Abby be tossed to the side? Surely she wouldn't fall for this idiot.

"Well, what does he want? I mean, does he have a legal right to spend time with Lillie? Was that ever an issue before?" The questions poured on thick. "I'm coming out there." Maybe it wasn't his place to go, to be there, but at that moment, he felt it was. Abby needed someone there.

"I don't know if that's such a good idea. He's not violent or anything like that, so trust me, we'll be fine." Lillie kept shoveling in spoonfuls of oatmeal, no interest whatsoever in the phone conversation above her.

"No, I think I should come out. It's wise for someone else to be there."

"Okay, whatever. I just don't want any trouble."

"Of course not. But, what exactly does he want? Did he

say?"

"I'm not sure. He wants to see Lillie, I know that, but there's got to be more behind it. I was so angry, I really didn't give him a chance to discuss anything with me. I told him to leave and come back later, when I cooled off."

"How did he even find you?"

"I don't have a fucking clue!" She pulled the phone cord around the corner. "I start to get my life back together and now I get tugged into this!"

"I'm on my way."

Abby decided not to tell Lillie, her hopes set high on the possibility that he might not return.

Five minutes later, the phone rang again. It was Anna.

"What's going on over there, honey? Are you and Lillie alright?"

"Yes, mam. It's over. Lillie's dad just decided to show up out of the blue. I'm hoping he doesn't come back."

That's all she had to say. Batson was coming over and Anna felt assured that they would be fine once he got there.

Liz sat at home at her kitchen table, putting the finishing touches on a welcome gift that she had made especially for Abby and her daughter. She didn't feel obligated; she just wanted to get to know Abby a little better. She needed to see why Batson was so intrigued by this young woman. The gift was a nice gesture and she knew she would enjoy one if she had moved to a new town.

Liz was working on the satin bow that curled over the rim of the hand-woven basket filled with all sorts of treats. There were Godiva chocolates, herbals teas, specialty coffees, a small baggie of pralines, two apples, a Camilla coffee mug and garnishes to accent the seasonal theme of the basket. She sincerely hoped Abby would like it; she wanted them to become friends. Liz had led such a sheltered life, never left Camilla except to take the kids to Brunson, north about forty miles, to visit her grandparents.

Sam walked in and bent over her back to kiss her on the forehead.

"Hey, babe. Where are the kids?"

"I took them to Mama's for a while. I've got some errands to run. Isn't this pretty? What do you think about the bow though?"

"Yeah, love it." He laughed, knowing damn well that he didn't care about stuff like that. "Who's it for?"

"Abby, you remember- Batson's new friend. She and her daughter are living out on the island next to Anna, so I thought I'd run it by. It's a welcome gift."

"My wife, anything to spend money."

"Hey. You watch it."

"So, can I take advantage of my wife since our moments alone are far and few?"

"Sounds good to me. What 'cha got in mind?"

"Oh let's see. Follow the leader." Sam grabbed her hand and led her to their room, the king bed still unmade and ready. It felt good to be wanted.

They flirted with one another like kids. Sam grabbed her hips, tossed her gently on the bed. He kissed her bare skin all over; she tingled and raised her arms above her head. God, she wanted him. Yes. Yes. Yes, she did.

Chapter Thirteen

Will Logan drove his van around town. So this is where she wanted to live? She's probably already found someone to mess around with, I'm sure of it, he thought. Going in circles downtown, he really wasn't sure what to do with his time.

"Isn't there a bar around here somewhere? I need a drink before I have to deal with her again. She's still beautiful, but man, what a bitch. Lillie's my daughter too," he said aloud to himself. He found Mary's on the river and convinced the morning bartender to go ahead and serve him. Sherry was working.

Batson pulled into the driveway, pleased to not see any unfamiliar vehicles around. He stretched, took a deep breath and walked to the door.

Abby welcomed him in.

"Morning." She kissed him on the cheek. "What's that television for?"

"It's for y'all. I knew you didn't have one yet and this one was an extra. Here, grab the rabbit ears." They were slipping off the top. Abby did as she was asked and Lillie ran to greet him, tugging on his legs beneath the bulk.

"No, Lillie. Honey! Batson brought a TV for you to watch and it's very heavy. Look out."

Lillie let go and proceeded to direct Batson on where to put it. "It can go in my room."

"No, mam. You'll watch it enough here in the living room." He hooked it up and placed a blanket on the hardwoods for Lillie to sit on. He flipped the channels around until he found a children's show. She seemed pleased.

Abby waited in the kitchen for him to join her. She poured him a cup of coffee and asked if he'd had breakfast yet.

"No, I usually don't eat breakfast, only on occasion. I'll have another kiss though." He whispered, "I think you need one."

"I think I agree" she answered. He held her in his arms tightly and filled with relief. Now she was more than glad that he had come over.

"This feels so normal, I mean, having you here. Is that a good thing?" she asked him.

"I think so. I feel the same way." They sat, drank coffee and waited, neither quite sure of what to expect.

The hands on the oven clock moved slowly. It was almost noon now and there had been no sign of Will. Lillie had gone next door to play with Gracie's dolls and Anna and Bessie enjoyed her presence. Abby and Batson sat on the back porch looking out over the water and watching the ships and fishing boats out for the day.

Abby sighed, "We are going to love it here. This is exactly what I wanted." She lavished in the moment.

"Of course you are. You and Lillie fit in perfectly, it was meant to be."

"I'm so nervous."

"About what? This whole thing with Will?"

"Can you blame me?" He shook his head. "Since so much time has gone by, I'm curious as to where he's gone. I never know with him, you know." No, Batson didn't know, he had only prepared for the worst.

"Don't you worry about all this. He probably just wants to see Lillie for a little while and then it will be all over." That's what he was hoping for anyway. He wanted her to feel safe, to know that she could count on him.

She reached for his hand and there was a knock at the front

door. Her heart plummeted, her palms went sweaty in seconds and she rushed toward the front of the house.

Nope, not Will. Thank God. It was Batson's friend, Liz. His eyes flew wide open at the sight of her, his fear was obvious to Liz and she moved in the doorway with a smile.

"Hi, y'all. I brought this for you and Lillie to enjoy. Just some small goodies I threw together to welcome you here."

"Thank you so much, Liz. How nice of you to think of us." She was grateful, a new friend. "Come in, come on in. Please excuse the house, I haven't gotten my furniture in yet." She led her into the kitchen and Batson found the strength to say hello. She had a lot of nerve. Man, what was going through that head of hers.

"I'm gonna walk next door, check on Lillie. I'll be back in a little while."

"Sure. Thanks." Abby appreciated his offer.

"Good to see you, Liz." He walked next door, thinking how stupid it was to leave the two of them alone. She wouldn't dare mention anything about them, would she? No, she'd better not.

Liz felt awkward sitting across the table from the woman Batson was probably already sleeping with. She wondered if he held her like he loved her. What did she ever mean to him? Was he falling in love like she had so many years ago with Sam?

Abby sat with her legs crossed, her free ankle rolling in midair. They talked about the kids, school and where to shop. She watched Liz talk about Sam and they sounded so happy. She wondered why her marriage couldn't have worked out like that.

"So, tell me now… you and Batson are an item, huh?" She couldn't help herself. Abby flushed, she wasn't expecting that one.

"Well, I don't know if you could call it that, but I suppose so. He's a great guy, although, I'm sure you know that." The comment caught Liz off guard. Of course she knew that, a lot better than she did.

"Yes, yes he is." She flashed to an image, she in his bed, cold, naked, wanting more. His lips discovering her body, just as Sam's had only hours before. "He's quite a catch, always has been. We all went to school together."

"Yes, I know. He's told me about it, especially some stories of he and Sam as kids." She continued, "I think it's great that you all are still so close." Close wasn't exactly the word for it. "All my high school friends have pretty much gone different ways. God, it's been so long ago." She got up to get Liz some more coffee.

"I actually have one good friend that I keep in touch with, but she's all the way out in Colorado. She's a wild one." Abby remembered, "Like we all used to probably be at one time or another."

"Yes, I remember those days. Can't believe I remember as much as I do sometimes?" They laughed. She liked Abby, absolutely nothing wrong with her.

"I'm so glad you came by. Batson will probably bring Lillie over here in a minute; you can meet her. You'll have to bring your crew by, Lillie would love that."

"Sounds great. Actually, I thought it'd be fun if you and I could go out, a girls' night out?" Liz hoped she wouldn't regret the invitation. After she asked, she thought about how much it might piss Batson off. Oh well, so what.

"How fun! Why don't we do something later tonight? I've had a really hectic morning and believe me, I need some fresh air." In short, she told Liz the situation with Will. She needed a break from Batson anyway, not in a bad way, just some space. "You think you could find a sitter on such short notice?"

"Well, I'll see." Liz was surprised at the reaction, she felt guilty. Maybe coming here had been an ugly thing to do. Batson was going to have a fit. "Sure though, I can work something out."

They exchanged phone numbers and it was a date, a girls night out. Batson walked in through the back door, Lillie in his arms. She tucked her head behind his neck when she saw Liz. Lillie wasn't too cooperative with the introductions; it was time for a nap.

"She's a doll. Well, I've gotta run. I'll call you later?" Liz wanted to hurry home; she hoped to have some more time alone with Sam. Her body ready to feel him again and again.

"Sounds good. Thanks again." Abby waved to her as she got in her car.

Will continued to pound down beer after beer. Sherry was becoming concerned and tried hard to make some conversation. It was now three o'clock in the afternoon and he was plastered.

"Can I call a cab for you?"

"A cab? Hell no, darlin'. I don't need no damned cab." His eyes red like blood, he knew better than to show up at Abby's like this. Hell, he couldn't even remember how to get there. He decided he'd be better off to get a room for now, he'd see Lillie tomorrow.

Sherry watched him walk out the door and signaled to the cop by the door to watch him.

"Don't kill anyone on your way to wherever you're headed, buddy." The cop said, putting forth a most minimal effort.

Sam was there when she walked through the doorway and the kids were still at Grandma's.

"Hey there. Get your errands out of the way?" She stood still, a sneaky smile on her face. "What is it?"

"I'm ready for a repeat of this morning, how about you?"

"Come here, girl. Now, I don't know about that, we'll have to see," he teased, he was always ready for her and she loved to be spontaneous. Her body moved above his right there on the

141

seat of the couch, she felt him push into her. She closed her eyes, Batson watching her move, taking it. She rubbed his chest, pulled his shoulders towards her breasts, and lay her cheek to his. He was making love to her, not Abby. God, he felt so good, so real.

"What! What did you just say?"

"I didn't say anything." She tried to think.

"Oh, alright. Nothing. I thought you said something." He pushed her harder and harder, the thought of Batson running through his head. The better it got, the further he forgot about the words she had whispered in his ears. God, no. It couldn't have been what she had said.

Abby told Batson about her plans and he about fell to the floor. He insisted Lillie stay with him at his house. If she wasn't at home and the car wasn't parked out front, maybe this Will character would leave them alone. He didn't think it was a good idea for Lillie to be right next door; it could lead to trouble. Abby agreed.

He couldn't believe Liz had suggested such a thing. Was she nuts or what? Just because he wasn't fucking around with her anymore, she had to go and stir up some trouble, make him a walking disaster. He never got around she and Sam like that, it was just too sticky of a situation.

Abby showered and got ready. Batson and Lillie were content in the living room on the floor, watching TV. She hollered his name.

"Yes?" He got up and peeked into the bath.

"Nothing, I got it. You could get me a glass of tea though." She stood there in the nude, her towel covering the most private of parts, asking for tea. "Like what you see?"

Batson did more than like it, he wanted it. He wanted to touch it, feel it next to him. "You call me in here for tea!" He walked away and she giggled. The sight of her in that towel and he nearly fell out. Unlike Liz remembering, fantasizing about him- she was nowhere near his mind, only Abby. Abby with her amazing body, beads of water trickled on her arms, her hair hanging down her back. He went to get her tea and saw Lillie still glued to the TV. Couldn't happen now, that was for sure.

Neither Abby nor Bats could believe that they hadn't heard from Will. How weird was that? He stopped in that morning, insistent on seeing Lillie and then not coming back. Strange, very strange.

Abby was relieved that Lillie would be at Batson's place. She and Lillie could sleep in the guest room for the night. They dropped by Anna's to tell her the plans for the evening. She looked surprised at the idea of Abby going out with Liz.

Yes, Anna was well aware of the situation with Bats and Liz. She wasn't born yesterday, always noticing the past tension when the three ran into in each other. Liz was taken though. She didn't know the details of their relationship, didn't care to, but she knew it wasn't love.

Chapter Fourteen

"Yeah, I know where he lives. Give me ten minutes." Of course, I know where he lives. I just got done fucking him last week! What does she know? I can't be like this... What's wrong with me? This whole thing is crazy. How could I say his name while I was making love to Sam?

She knocked at the door, the front one. She couldn't remember the last time she came in through the front. The few glasses of wine she'd had before arriving were helping the tension tremendously.

"Ready to go?" she asked.

"Yep." Abby kissed her baby goodbye and Batson reassured her for the fourth or fifth time that she would be fine. Lillie was working with the Play station hooked up to the TV. "I love you. You be good for Batson. Mommy won't be late. Are you sure you're going to be alright here?"

"She'll be fine." Batson saw her concern.

They walked to Liz's convertible parked out front and headed to grab a bite to eat before going anywhere else.

They got along fabulously. Liz recommended Captain Jack's for dinner and Abby agreed – she didn't want to seem picky. They sat in smoking and Abby's long ago habit was quickly coming back. The red wine gave them the giggles and it felt good to both of them to be out.

"I think I've needed this for a long time." Abby smiled.

"Me too. Even growing up right here, I never get with my old friends. It's quite a treat, isn't it?"

"What was it like growing up around here? I mean, around the ocean and all?" Abby wanted to know since Lillie would

145

be raised here, she'd never had the chance to.

"Who could complain... you're right near the water, so peaceful. Other than that, it's not much different than anywhere else. The tourists come from all over. I suppose we often take advantage of what all we have to offer here."

"Then you get outsiders, like me, moving in."

"You're not an outsider. You only came across the border; they have more beaches in South Carolina. You're a southerner, right? What made you decide to come here anyway?"

"Just loved it every time I visited. It was the closest beach from my hometown. So, after Will and I split, I saved and saved and well, here we are."

"Wow. I admire you. You must have a lot of guts to pack everything up and just leave everything you'd ever known behind." Liz envied her strength; the concept was farfetched and hard for her to understand. Liz always had someone looking over her; she never had the chance to be independent. First, she depended on her parents and then and now, Sam. Sam still took care of her.

"There wasn't much left for me back home. My mom and dad are there, but I had to make a move on my own. I was in a rut there, needed to sow some roots somewhere else, if that makes sense. I came to Camilla when I was younger to getaway, so I've returned for good this time."

"Good for you." She blew Liz away.

"I think so. I've worked hard to get here. I'm working downtown at a law firm now, called Wolfe and Richmond. Do you know of it?"

"Sure, I do. I've stayed at home with the kids mostly, not many career opportunities for me. Well, I work at this bakery once in a while, but that's about it." Liz was proud of the fact that she got to be a full-time mother – she loved it. The kids needed her, but mostly, she needed them.

146

"That's the hardest job of all. I kept Lillie until she was two."

"Really?"

"Uh-huh. It was the hardest job I'd ever had." She remembered those days like it were yesterday, the laundry, the cooking, cleaning, following Lillie's every step and picking up after her. It was exhausting.

"Enough about all that. Where should we go tonight?"

Where have you been so far?"

"Well, I went to Mary's, that's about it. She hadn't been out to bars in a long time, but it felt nice to have the chance to. Now that she had a new friend to go off with, it made her feel young again.

"Okay, since you've been to Mary's, let's go to Bernie's. It's a favorite of mine and it's down on the river too."

"Fine with me."

The moment they walked in, Abby felt like she'd stepped back in time. She had come to this bar many years before on one of her weekends in Camilla. She mentioned it to Liz and then went to check on the wall to see if her name was still there. In huge black marker with fat letters was her name, Abigail Mann, faded, but it was still there. Below it was the year, 1984.

The bar was crowded, the music blared loud and smoke filled the air. The conversation between them was beginning to thin out, so it was a relief to sit back, relax and listen to the music.

A female singer led the band with her deep, raspy voice. They sang old music, some tunes from Van Morrison, Fleetwood Mac, The Temptations, even one from Janis Joplin. This was a lot more exciting than Mary's had been.

"She's great." Abby complimented.

"Yeah, she's been working up here a long time. I love the live music. It's especially nice when you've been cooped up in the house all day." Her mind drifting somewhere else, the music stirring her memories like ice in a glass, crashing against each other, not enough room.

Abby watched as the singer tapped the beat on the microphone, moving her feet, swaying to the rhythm. Will had left her mind, but thoughts of Lillie erupted from down in her chest. Her heart ached and she wished she could be home with her; this going out was probably not the smartest thing to do. She went straight back to the pay phone to call. Batson said they were fine, she had fallen asleep on the sofa and he was going to carry her on into the guest room.

"Good, I'm just paranoid about all this. Something doesn't feel right. I mean, suppose he sees my car there. I don't know, I'm freaking out." Her stomach fluttered with nausea.

"So tell Liz to bring you on back." He was right, Abby was ready to go. Batson wanted to see her. She hadn't made love in over a year, but maybe tonight would be it. Tommy had been her last, right after she and Will split up. She needed it; her body ached in its absence.

By the time she returned to the bar where they had been sitting, Liz wasn't there. Where could she have gone? That was odd. Abby took a sit and waited, maybe she had to go to the car for something or the bathroom, that was probably where she was.

Impatiently, she waited, her head turning from side to side, anxious to get to Batson and Lillie. She asked the bartender. Did he know where she'd gone?

"No, sweetheart. I'm sorry, there's too many in here tonight and, of course, I can't keep track of who's coming and who's going." Smartass, it was just a question.

Abby walked around the bar looking for any sign of her but with no luck. This was really getting strange. She walked outside, and then decided to walk on back to the car. Maybe she was waiting for her there.

The sky was dark, the streets were empty and she was frightened. She passed a payphone but decided to wait. Liz was surely at the car.

She could see no sign of the car in the distant parking lot. The car was gone, no sign of Liz, no sign of anyone. Abby began to panic, she felt like someone was watching her. There was not a single soul anywhere around. She held onto her purse and ran towards the streetlights on Main, then rushed back to Bernie's.

The bartender looked overly pleased to see her return. Oh yeah, she was sure he was.

"Any sign of her?" she asked a second time.

"Nope. Sorry, lady. I told you before…" she walked off.

Damn. Where could she have gone? What if something had happened? It had been officially forty-five minutes now. She decided to phone Batson back and tell him the deal; she would have to get a cab.

"Hey, it's me." There was horror in her voice, like she'd witnessed a crime or was running from the criminal. "Liz is nowhere to be found. I got off the phone…"

"Abby, I know." His voice began to sound clearer as she listened more carefully. The truth would have to come out; she wouldn't believe anything other than the truth. Damn it. Damn Liz and damn himself for doing something like this! "She's here. Call a cab and I'll pay for it when you get here."

"What? What did you say?" She couldn't believe it, what was going on? "She's there? Is that what you just said?" Maybe they had simply gotten lost from one another, maybe she couldn't find Abby and decided to check there. No way, there was just no way!

"Yes, she's here. I'll explain when you get here." She threw the phone down, more concerned to get to Lillie and get the hell home than deal with anything else. What was going on?

She called the cab.

Minutes before Abby had called, Liz stood outside the back door, thinking to herself. What am I doing this for? Am I going crazy again… willing to throw it all away for Batson? Fuck, I can't help it. I didn't know these feelings would ever surface. I love him, now I have to tell him. She screamed aloud, "I love him!" It didn't matter who heard, she couldn't stand to hide it any longer. She knew it this morning and this afternoon when she made love with Sam so passionately. The magic between she and Sam was no longer; Batson was all she could think about.

She beat on the back door. It startled him, she could tell. She froze for a moment, her hair tousled and cheeks flushed with streaks in scarlet red.

"Liz? Liz, what are you doing here? Where's Abby?" His heart pumping ninety miles an hour.

"I can't do this anymore, Bats."

"Do what? You are hammered. Where is Abby?" He held his finger to his mouth to shush her. Lillie was fast asleep.

She wiped the black from her eyes, grabbed a beer from the fridge and Batson hassled her for an answer.

"She's still at Bernie's, I guess."

"You guess? You left her there?" His voice rose in anger, this was not some psychotic game here, some fatal attraction.

"Let me explain…"

"Explain what, Liz? What is there to explain? I just want to make sure Abby is all right."

"I want you, I want us. Don't you see? I've always wanted to be with you. Sam and I, we just don't work anymore. Seeing you with Abby, I realized that – it's driven me to this."

"What the hell. You're jealous. It's eating you up because

for once I have found someone that I care about and now you've gone and ditched her downtown, where she knows no one! My God, Liz, what the fuck are you thinking?" This was it, the big blast, the final straw. Abby would never respect him again. The truth was surfacing, rubbing right in his face. If he didn't explain this, he knew Liz sure as hell would!

Chapter Fifteen

She cried a river when Batson had told her the truth. The words hurt tremendously. She looked him dead in the eyes, "Don't you call me ever again! I don't even want to see your face. I have no respect for someone that screws around with their best friend's wife. You are both nuts! Where is my daughter?"

Neither Batson or Liz could stop her. She wiped the tears from her eyes, it wasn't even worth it. She gently picked up Lillie from the bed, furious with herself for falling into such a mess. Lillie stayed asleep in Abby's arms and Batson opened the door for her.

"Abby, please listen to me. Don't go."

"You blew it. I thought you were a good guy, someone I could trust." Her heart was throbbing, her life took another blow and she wasn't going to deal with another heartache. Maybe it was even a mistake to move here.

The ride home was a slow and painful drive. Lillie's head laid in her lap, while she whimpered. She would be better off alone.

She thought about Will and wondered if he was hiding somewhere, watching her. It didn't even matter now. She carried Lillie on her hip, unlocked the door and put her to bed. She double-checked all the windows and doors, all were locked tight. Home at last.

The bottle of wine was still half-full and Abby poured a huge glass to wallow in her disappointment. Fuck him. Fuck her. Fuck them both. She made an ashtray from an old ceramic bowl, sat on her bed and bawled.

Tommy would never have done something like that. Who was she kidding? Yes, he probably would have, but she could still love him afterwards. How much did she wish he were there, right then? She could almost see his head full of blonde hair lying on the pillow beside her. Even after the years that had gone by, she remembered every bit of him... his fingers, his hands, the way his body looked, sweaty and naked next to hers. She could almost hear his voice, his laughter and feel his warmth.

She looked at the clock on the nightstand, one o'clock. If she had his number she would call. No, she couldn't. Every time she was in a rut, she called.

Back at Batson's, Liz lay out on the couch. She had already undressed into nothing and lay still, waiting for him to hold her, tell her that he felt the same. She would be disappointed.

"I don't understand you, Liz. Where did all this come from? For Christsakes, what is Sam going to say?"

"I can't be with him, Batson. I don't love him like I used to. I don't care what he thinks right now, all I want is to be with you. Come here now..."

"Get away from me, dammit."

Abby awoke the next morning to a dream with Tommy in it. They were horseback riding, everyone was. His horse raced to get directly beside her. She turned her head towards the movement and for a moment, his lips brushed against the side of hers. Then, he was gone. She woke up to the reality of the situation from the night before.

She didn't even want to step outside her door. Anna and Bessie would be all over this one. It would come out sooner or later, just not today. She couldn't deal with it.

The coffee was made and she grabbed a cup to enjoy in bed, a novel beside her bed. Soon, Lillie joined her and they cuddled. Lillie was all she had. Life would go on without Batson Cannon, that was one thing she did know.

Chapter Sixteen

The days of fall were gone and past. It was early December and Christmas was quickly approaching. Abby had gotten all the Santa stuff for Lil and had it stored safely next door in Anna's storage building. The situation between she and Bats had dissolved quickly, but they would only speak on occasion. That dreadful night was pretty much forgotten. Abby had been humiliated beyond words and she believed it would never work out between she and Batson.

Will never showed his face again. After that morning, Abby told everyone that he'd probably just given up. It was still hard for her to accept sometimes, since she knew it would hurt Lillie in the long run.

Gracie was home for Thanksgiving two weeks ago and she and Abby got along fabulously. Anna couldn't have been more thrilled. Gracie was over every morning for coffee and Abby appreciated her company, as she needed a friend now most of all. They promised to write, but she would be back for Christmas.

Anna's hope of having Abby and Lillie as part of their family was coming true, and she couldn't imagine not having them around. They belonged to the Cannons now. This Christmas, Anna and Bessie had already spent an enormous amount of time and money on Abby and Lillie. She promised that their first Christmas in Camilla would be a special one.

Abby's parents had planned to visit for the holiday and she was ecstatic at having Christmas in her new house. Abby's dad wasn't in good health now and had to retire at the end of October. The stroke had done it. Abby's mom had plans to stay home and tend to him. Abby and Lillie had already been home twice to check in.

Sam and Liz had split up or, rather, he had left, devastated when Liz admitted her love for Batson. After the initial shock, he knew what she had done could never be forgotten. Sam said he'd seen it coming. He knew what she had said that day when they were making love. The last thing Abby heard was that Sam was living in a condo out here on the island, dating some bartender from a club on the south side. Liz let him have the kids whenever he wanted. She had a job at the hospital now, but Abby never spoke to or about Liz, only choked on the thought of her.

Today was a Wednesday. Abby already looked worn out from the holiday bliss and Patty had to comment on it.

"My goodness, you look exhausted. Is everything okay at home?"

Abby tilted her head up from the morning paper, "Sure, just fine. Why?" God, did she really have to hear this?

"Well, you just don't look like yourself."

"It's stress, got a lot going on right now. Especially with Christmas and all, my parents are coming..." Patty seemed satisfied as Abby walked on past, her head still buried between the two sheets of paper.

The desk had a stack of paperwork on it and the office supplies she had picked up from Office Depot yesterday, those would need to be put away. Her eyes drooped as she plopped in the comfy office chair. She looked up at the wall, staring into the white nothingness.

No sooner had she gotten settled with her coffee and about to begin her day when here came Patty. Geez, what now?

"Look, Abby! This came for you." She handed over a huge plastic pot with a fully bloomed Poinsettia in it.

"Oh, my, who's it from?"

"No idea. The florist just delivered it a second ago. Certainly is beautiful though." She left the plant on the desk

158

and walked out.

Abby searched for a card and finally found it buried down in the prickled green leaves. She pulled it out slowly, excited to see who thought this much of her to send it.

The card read,

> *"Dear Abby:*
> *Just something to brighten your holidays. From someone who loves you, Maizie."*

Abby was flabbergasted. Who the hell was Maizie? It had to be a mistake, a different Abby, the wrong address. She showed a small smile and put it on her bookshelf near the window.

Thom passed by her on the way to the kitchen.

"Good morning. Did you see the folders I put in your box?" He was such a gentleman, so courteous and a marvelous person to work for.

"Yes, I sure did. Did you see the surprise I got?"

"Yes, I saw Patty bringing it up. Who's it from?" Thom asked quickly. He had to get going or he'd be late for court this morning.

"I don't have a clue, no card," she lied.

"Well, have a good day. Sorry to be so short, court's at nine." He waved her goodbye. Well, someone was thinking of her or not. Either way, the delivery had made a difference.

The day was soon coming to an end, Abby and Lil sat at the kitchen table eating dinner, soup and sandwiches. Someone knocked at the door. It was Batson.

"Hi, stranger." Abby opened the door to let him in. "Is something wrong?"

"No, not really. I just wanted to see if I could spend some time with you this evening. Would that be okay?"

She was at a loss for words. They hadn't hung out together

since… well, it had been a long time. Sure. Christmas was close and besides, she was flattered to see him at her door.

"Have you eaten?"

"Yes, thank you.

"Hey, Lillie." He hugged her. "I ate over at Grandma's with her and Bessie. You guys go ahead, though." Lillie finished her plate and went upstairs to play in the loft, leaving the two of them behind.

"I brought you something. It's out in the car, let me go get it."

"What is it?" She followed him.

"A bottle of wine for us to share, for old times sake. Maybe we could make amends. You know, get past all that has happened." His voice slowed, "I want us to be close again, I have missed you."

"I've missed you too, our friendship that is." She held onto his words.

Later, they sat on the back porch like that night that seemed a million miles away.

"I think I really messed up, Abby."

"Let's don't go there, that night and all its fury, its memory."

"Well, that thing with Liz, it has destroyed my friendships with you and Sam. I told her weeks ago that it would never work. I'm sorry, I know you don't care to hear about it." She saw the hurt in his eyes, overwhelming regret and guilt. "I didn't know it would all happen like it did. I should have told you about my past with her sooner; I just didn't think…"

"We all make our own mistakes. God knows I've made my share."

"I know, I know." He put his arm around her shoulder.

Before she could even begin to know what was happening, he had his hands on the sides of her face and turned it toward his. He leaned into her and she relented, wanting to feel him next to her.

"God, I've missed you so." His voice soft and sensual, that was all it took. She led him inside.

Abby lay down gently on her bed and he lay beside her. Together they held each other, tied up with arms and legs, kissing one another like they had never been kissed. Abby kept reminding herself how she would probably regret this, but the passion was unbearable. She needed him and he had never wanted anything more.

The clock said it was three in the morning and tomorrow was another day at work. She wondered if anything would come out of this, then he touched her arm.

"Can I stay the night?"

"Stay? Bats, I don't know if that's such a good idea. What about Lillie? In the morning, I mean."

"Abby, I want to stay in this room more than anything. I want to wake up with you beside me, have breakfast with you, and be able to touch you all over again before you open your eyes in the morning." She looked deep in his eyes, waiting to hear more, clinging to everything he said. "Abby," he paused for a breath, to clear the air, for the moment to be right, "I love you."

The morning came far too quickly and Batson did as he said he would, he made love to her once again. Abby had nearly forgotten how good it felt to be so safe in the arms of a man. She no longer cared about what happened in the past or all the humiliation she had felt. His body mounted onto hers and she liked it, his body...so warm, his eyes... digging so deep into hers.

Thirty minutes later, it was time to get Lillie up and dressed for school. She walked barefoot into the kitchen and saw Batson sitting at their table drinking coffee.

161

"Batson!" She still had her gown on, arms latched around a doll of hers and ran to hug him.

"Good morning, my princess. Where's your mama?"

"She's picking out my clothes." She took a seat in front of the bowl of oatmeal and started to eat.

He meandered into Lillie's room and grabbed Abby from behind. While kissing her neck, he whispered into her ears, "Can't you be sick for the day? Come on, I don't want to leave you."

She pushed him away with a childish grin, but liked the idea. "Let's do it," she blurted out.

Batson kept Lillie busy in the kitchen, while Abby called in and left a message at the office. She felt spontaneous and tingled all over at the thought of it.

Abby took Lillie to school and rushed back home to enjoy her sick day. She wondered what Anna and Bessie were going to think of all this and then shrugged it off. She remembered the words Batson had said to her in the night, that he loved her. Did he really mean it? Did he love her? Did she love him? Oh God, she wanted him… couldn't wait to get back to him. She got heated thinking of it and pushed the gas pedal a bit harder.

Chapter Seventeen

In a hotel room in Baltimore sat a beautiful woman, Maizie Stockton. She was rummaging through paperwork strewn out on her bed and a laptop placed between her bare legs. The phone was ringing off the hook as she prepared for the ten o'clock conference call. Her golden short hair curled close to her ears, as her eyes stayed glued to the screen. The two long legs hung out to the sides of the double bed, and she bent down on her elbows on the bedspread looking forward.

"Ugh! Why can't anything go right for me this morning?" she hollered to herself.

Looking out the window, she saw the haziness of this city. Maizie was from Oklahoma and she couldn't get used to the dry salty air. She had been there for as long as she could remember, then finished graduate school in business and took a fabulous paying job with Aflick Corporation. Aflick dealt in international trade and affairs. They took Maizie in on account of her extraordinary referrals. She was brilliant with people, yet stern and determined at the same time. Maizie never put up with anyone's crap, she just never would.

She hopped off the bed and started to undress before her shower. She looked down at a brass frame that she had brought with her. Inside was a priceless photo, a photo that meant more to her then nearly anything else. The young girl in the frame was around five or six, an old newspaper clipping. Maizie had clung to it for many years now. The time had finally come. When was it ever going to be the right time? She wanted to meet this girl in the photo, wanted to know what she was like and who she was.

She fit the photo frame gently inside her briefcase to take it with her for the day. There would be a busy luncheon afterwards and she'd have time to grab a bite away from the crowd and think.

Chapter Eighteen

When Abby returned to her house, she noticed Batson's wagon still in the drive. He was still there. This was really happening. She felt guilty for a minute or two, knowing that she had just taken Lillie to school and here she was taking the day off to be with Batson. It seemed like she should have her there with her, maybe she would go get her after lunch.

Batson was open arms as she walked back inside. He had taken it upon himself to start breakfast with eggs, bacon and grits. The table was set and he had lit the candles and turned all the blinds.

"What is this?" Abby asked. "Our first intimate breakfast together, I presume."

"Yep. Like what I've done?"

Abby nodded.

"Well, you'd better get used to it because I'm staying around this time. There are not going to be any more problems for us... not any more."

She like the sound of that and had already decided to forget the whole situation with Liz on that horrible night. They ate quickly and then lay in bed, drinking coffee and smoking cigarettes. The television was still on in the living room from Lillie's early morning cartoons. It seemed like a normal day... in paradise.

Abby wondered if Anna and Bessie were curious as to where Bats was this morning. She assumed they would understand that he was at her place, but encouraged him to phone so they would not worry. Batson did as she asked and Abby listened to the uh-huhs and yes'ms.

Camilla cooled with Christmas rapidly approaching. Abby showed Batson all the presents she had picked out for Lillie so far and explained that it might be wise to spend part of her day off wrapping them. It would at least make her feel better about taking the day off. He agreed only after he had his way with her. She deserved some time to herself, time to spend frivolously.

Abby remembered the words he had said only hours earlier, the words that stuck inside her head. "Abby Logan, I love you." Could it be true? She pushed the thought out of her mind and told herself to delight in the fact that she had someone to spend time with like this. It felt incredible to relax and be open with someone again, someone that wasn't like Will had been. If anything, Batson was totally opposite from him.

He held her tightly in his arms under the covers and she fell back to sleep. The phone interrupted their late morning snooze, Abby reached over the man in her bed to catch it. Batson groaned.

"Hello. Hello?" Abby asked twice, regripping the phone.

"Hey, sweetheart. It's mom." Abby wasn't exactly in the mood to chat and assumed the obvious. "I called the office and they said you weren't feeling well. What's wrong?"

"I'm fine, Mom. It's a cold or something."

"Did you take Lillie on to school?"

"Uh-huh. She's fine."

"Well, good. Well, I was just worried and didn't mean to wake you. Your dad is... well..."

Beginning to get alarmed, Abby rushed her, "Dad is what? What's wrong with dad?"

"Well, he is back in the hospital again and its just... it doesn't look well. He had another stroke in the night and they came to get him about twelve."

"Oh God, no. Mom you should have called me last night. All right then, I'm making arrangements to come home. Let me call you back."

"No, now honey, there is absolutely nothing you can do back

here. You stay there and keep your own. Everything is going to be okay, I can feel it. We have all been saying our prayers and the church is doing so much to help me out with all of this."

"Mom, no. I'm coming back. I don't want to hear anything else about it. I'll call you back when I find out when we'll be leaving."

"Abigail, it's not necessary. Really."

"Yes, mom it is necessary. Tell dad we love him and we are on our way. I love you."

Batson leaned up and Abby began to cry.

"It's my dad. He's not doing well."

"I heard." He held onto her tightly and tried to comfort her but she pushed away, eager to get going.

She began pacing the floor, searching through clothes in the closet and some scattered on the floor, running in and out of the bedroom. She was a mess with panic.

"Abby, now calm down. You've got to sit down and think of what all needs to be done before you go. You're ranting and raving with panic. Slow down, let me help you."

"Ranting and raving?" She hollered, "My dad could be dying in the hospital right now and you are telling me to calm down! Stop ranting and raving?" She took a deep breath, "I'm trying not to." She looked pathetic, like a child, like the way she looked when he first saw her. Batson stood behind her and crossed his arms over her chest and squeezed.

"It's going to be all right, I promise. I am here for you. Just tell me what to do." She looked into his eyes and the tears seemed to fall even faster. He had hurt her before and now, suddenly, he was back in her life willing to help out again. She needed his support now more than ever.

"You can, um… go get Lillie at school. I'll call them."

Friday, December 18th, the paper printed out the obituary. Mr. Oscar Carlson Mann, Jr., passed away last evening, December 17th at St. Mary's Hospital. It read into a few details of his life, naming all living relatives and where to send all sympathy cards, flowers and any donations.

The house filled with a mess of people and Abby wasn't sure how much more she could handle. Poor Lillie didn't have a clue what was happening and Abby's mom was a basket case. The doctor had given her Valiums or something to calm her nerves, but they didn't seem to be helping much.

Abby dealt with death unbelievably well. Death was never frightening to her, even as a small child. She kept herself up with the faith that everything happened for a reason. Without her knowledge of it, she was a lot like Bessie, holding her faith close to heart.

Batson had stayed at home. Anna had sent a beautiful floral arrangement with a note card signed with all of their names, including Gracie's. Anna had called Gracie and told her the terrible news. All of the Cannons prayed for their dear Abby, hoping that she would cope with this sudden death of her father and soon return home, safe and sound.

The firm also sent flowers and Abby had assumed that they understood her delayed absence. She wanted to stay with her mom for a couple more days and possibly bring her back to the island. Christmas was under a week away and this was so exhausting and heartbreaking.

The beautiful plant was still sitting on Abby's shelf at work. Patty watered it while she was gone and wondered if Abby ever found out who had sent it.

Maizie was on a plane back home to Oklahoma. An enormous blizzard was falling directly over parts of Kansas and Missouri, she hoped the pilot wouldn't have any difficulty landing in Tulsa.

She pulled her briefcase out from between her feet, opened it to the photograph once more. She wondered if the girl in the picture had gotten the plant she had sent. It had been a spur-of-the-moment idea, but one that she wanted to do. Anyone else would have thought she was crazy to send something to this so-called sister that she had never met, even worse, one that probably didn't even know she existed. Would Abby accept her? Did she even know about Maizie? When would she get to see her? Ever?

The last time she had talked to Marie had been nearly five years ago. After much researching and an abundance of long distance calls here and there, she had finally tracked her down.

Thirty-three years ago, Marie Bloomfield had given birth to a healthy eight-pound baby girl. Maizie was her name. Her adoptive parents liked the name so much, they had decided to keep it.

Marie was only seventeen when she was born and her father would have had it no other way. This is what Marie told her when Maizie had called five years ago searching for answers. Marie never told Carl, she had met him a few years after Maizie had been born. No, it wouldn't be a good idea to visit now. Carl would not understand. Maizie asked her if she had any brothers or sisters and Marie finally let her guard down.

Maizie deserved to know about Abby and Abby about her, although Marie had never gotten around to it with Abby. It was just something that Marie liked to leave alone, in the past. Enough time had elapsed; it was now time for Maizie to meet her one and only sister, the girl in the picture.

Marie had always been curious about her first little girl, just unsure about their paths crossing. She cried in confusion after Maizie had phoned. She remembered that voice on the other end of the line, hard to believe it was the child that she had once given up, left behind. Maizie was something she could never let go of, not again.

169

"Hello." Abby answered the phone for what felt like the hundredth time of the day. People continued to come by, bringing food, flowers and offering their supposed words of comfort.

"Hey there, my sweet. How are you? Everything going okay?" It was Batson, sending his condolences.

She sighed in relief, a moment back into reality.

"Hi. Yeah, well, it's going as well as can be expected. Mom is taking this extremely hard. I mean, I try to talk to her but it's like she's hysterical or something. God. And Lillie is into everything, she doesn't understand. I don't think it's healthy for her to be here and in this situation much longer."

"I'm so sorry. You're sure you don't want me to come up?"

"Yes, I'm sure. Tomorrow will hopefully be easier. I just," she stopped, "I can't believe he's actually gone, you know? And it's so strange being in this house without passing him, sitting in his old recliner or messing with the junky tools in the garage." She tried to dry her tears and pull herself together. "And then there are all these people, in and out of the house. I know Mom is about to go nuts."

Batson tried his best to commiserate with her. He knew how hard all this must be. He thought it was probably more difficult for Abby because her father had been a part of her life, whereas, his parents had not been.

Abby told him they would be home soon enough, making him miss them even more.

Chapter Nineteen

Christmas Eve was painful for the whole family. Abby had persuaded her mom to come back to Camilla with her and Lillie. Marie had church friends back home that were going to clean up everything at the house, pick up the papers, and gather the mail. Abby had decided not to go back into work full time, but she'd stop by to check in. She didn't want to get behind on paperwork and Thom was thankful for her dedication.

Marie got along ideally with Anna and Bessie. Abby appreciated Anna's eagerness to spend time with her. It gave Abby time alone, some with Lillie and a little bit of adult time with Batson. Anna was regularly asking her over for coffee or to play cards, anything to help her deal with her sorrow. She could empathize with Marie and understand her pain.

That night Lillie went to bed early, excited that Santa Claus would be arriving in the night. The tree lights were glimmering through the front window and Abby and her mom sat on the couch side by side. A variety of candles glimmered scattered on the tables and the fresh smell of pine carried throughout the house.

Marie had been silent for most of the evening, but especially through dinner, taking breaks to go out back and wipe her tears. Abby was so grateful that she had agreed to come home with her. Being in their empty house back home would have been too much for anyone.

"Want to help me wrap a couple more things?" Abby asked, hoping to ease the wave of memories she knew was going through her head.

"Actually honey, I think I should turn in for the night. Tomorrow's a special day for Lillie and I want to feel up to it, alright?" she asked with weary eyes and a slight smile that took immense effort.

"Sure, I understand. There are extra blankets in the closet in my room if you get cold. Are you sleeping with Lillie again?"

"Yes. Good night." And just like that, she was gone.

The clock on the wall that Batson had given her was striking eleven and Abby began wrapping the smaller gifts and arranging them all in front of the tree. Stockings hung from the stairway leading up to the loft… all three of them. Abby had picked up one with "Nana" stitched on it for her mom, hoping the gesture would make her feel more at home.

Batson was right next-door at Anna's and Gracie was on a flight right home at the very moment. Abby was excited to see her again. She and Gracie had some good girl talks when she had been home for Thanksgiving. Of course she told Gracie about the episode with Liz and how she had come by to visit, making an attempt to be friends again. That didn't turn out well at all. Abby never thought about it anymore, it wasn't worth thinking about. She knew she had Batson in her corner now and Liz Borders was not part of the picture any longer. Sometimes Abby thought about Sam though, wondered how he was doing. She felt sorry for him. So she was glad to have Gracie coming home, at least for a little while.

"Mama! Mama! Santa came, come and see!" Lillie practically jumped on top of Abby, still in a deep sleep.

"Okay, okay Lil. Wait just a minute. Where's Nana?"

"In my bed. She told me to come and get you first."

"I have to get the camera." Abby rubbed her ringed eyes. It felt like only minutes had passed since she first lay down. Slowly she slipped on her bedroom shoes as Lillie tugged at her legs. It was five o'clock and still dark outside. Then looking into Lillie's bright eyes, filled with excitement, she woke up immediately with a rush of adrenaline.

172

"Happy Birthday, dear Jesus!" Lillie sang while she ran up and down the hall, knowing better than to go near the gifts until Mama was ready. "Happy Birthday to you!"

Abby met her mom halfway down the hall, Lillie jumping up and down while Abby got the camera ready.

"Oh, Lillie! You must have been awful good this year!" Marie commented on the living room.

"I have! I have!"

"Come on in and see." Abby signaled for her to come out.

Time with family was always a good time, even without her father there. Abby knew that he was in their hearts and looking down on them. Lillie was always Grandpa's girl. She asked where he was constantly. Marie had to walk out of the room every time when Abby tried explaining where her Papa was.

A couple hours later, all three of them walked over to Anna's for a Christmas brunch. Bessie had been up since daybreak stirring up all the mouth-watering casseroles, homemade biscuits with red-eye and a salty country ham. She had platefuls of sugar cookies that she and Lillie had baked together days before.

All the food was in the oven warming as Gracie kicked open the door with duffel bags thrown over each shoulder.

"Merry Christmas!" She dropped her luggage and everyone rushed in to get hugged. She was getting so thin and Anna complimented on her new short haircut. Gracie pushed her fashionable glasses up further on the bridge of her nose and Bessie kissed her on the cheek.

"Here's my new friend!" she announced. The two friends hugged. Abby helped her bring her bags into her room and Gracie lay out on her bed.

"Abby, I am so sorry to hear about your dad. I'm sorry I wasn't here." Her sincerity meant so much. Right now, all she needed was her friendship.

Christmas day snowballed into event after event. Abby,

Gracie and Lillie went next door to help Lillie put together some of her new toys scattered below the tree. They returned just in time for the phone call from Will, amazingly, calling to wish them a merry Christmas and to check on Lillie. Abby's heart throbbed with compassion for Lillie; it had to have confused her. She found herself remembering Christmas mornings years ago when Lillie was a babe. Will managed to be sober on Christmas and for that, she was always thankful. The Lord did work in mysterious ways. It was the one day when she knew she could count on him, the one day they could be a family.

Marie helped clean up the kitchen with Bessie and Anna went out to the beach with Batson for a cool, crisp walk. Even now, she needed to step out of the holiday bliss to take a breather. This was the hardest time of the year without Joe and Batson and Gracie's mom and dad. The hurt never went away, their absences could never go unnoticed. Memories trickled in Batson's head as well, but spending this time with Grandma Anna always made things feel better. The absence was something they could share.

The two walked to the end of the pier and noticed several fishermen doing their daily duty. Christmas had not seemed to disrupt their routines... nothing ever did. Most of them were wrinkled and old and with the fog so thick, they barely looked alive. Batson figured that most were widowed, no family to spend the day with, he felt sorry for them. He recognized the black man that he had seen on the riverbank during the summer months. Curiously he walked closer, leaving Anna holding onto the railing and looking out over the sea.

"Catch anything this morning?" Bats asked the man, being friendly. He didn't feel obligated to speak, just wanted to make an effort since today was Christmas.

The man looked up and then back down, pointing to his bucket of ruddy water- no fish.

"Oh. Well, have a good one and Merry Christmas." That was all Bats could think of to say.

Anna asked him about the gentleman alone on the dock. Batson explained to her that he didn't know him. Anna smiled. She knew him, an old friend of a friend.

Chapter Twenty

Only a week after Christmas and everyone was getting back to their routines. Marie had insisted on going home. She said she had to deal with things sooner than later. Abby finally agreed with her and when she left, it was heartwrenching.

Lillie was back in school, Gracie was flying back home to Chicago tomorrow and Batson was busy with his office work.

It was Monday afternoon at the office and everyone was glad to be back. The new year brought new expectations of what they could do to make their lives bigger and better. Resolutions were plentiful. Thom's goal was to cut back on the caffeine and Patty planned to start at the gym, but Abby kept her hopefuls to herself. She wanted to let go of the past, all her anger at Will, and at God for taking away her father.

That evening, Lillie was going to spend the night with Anna and Bessie so Bats, Abby and Gracie could spend time together. Gracie wanted to go out to eat somewhere first, have some cocktails and enjoy time with them before she had to go back.

The restaurant they went to was like a ghost town. Everyone had spent all their money over the holidays and retail would suffer for the first few months of the new year.

Gracie talked incessantly about her professional job as a journalist and it all sounded too busy to Abby. How she wished she had finished college and had a chance at a real career. Gracie got to travel, meet new people and do what she loved to do most, write for a living.

Batson sat beside Abby patiently waiting for their time alone. The last month of the year had been a dreadful experience for her and he wanted to make her feel a little normal again, get her back into the swing of things.

"So you guys will have to come and visit me sometime." Gracie finished her story with the invitation. "When I come back home, are y'all going to be making wedding plans or what? You seem pretty serious here."

Abby went beet red at the comment. That was the last thing on her mind and after her deranged relationship with Lillie's father, marriage didn't seem like an option.

"Possibly." Batson did not hesitate at all. "Abby, are you okay?"

"Um-hum."

"I didn't mean to embarrass you, we're just joking around here," he told her and she seemed to relax. The reality of a marriage to Batson sounded dreamy but still so far away.

"No, you didn't. My mind was just somewhere else, that's all." She smiled and Gracie smiled back.

Gracie broke into the silence, "Let's get a cooler full and go down to the pier, like old times Bats! Come on, it'll be fun."

"Gracie, it's freezing down there!"

"Hey, don't be a fruitcake! Besides this cold is nothing compared to Chicago. I think I can handle it if you guys can." She was determined. Once Gracie got something stuck in that head of hers it was a go. "Can you handle it, Abby?" As if she couldn't!

"Of course. I'm up for anything tonight. It's your last night here, so we might as well live it up!"

"I couldn't agree more!" Abby had not been out with her like this when she was home over Thanksgiving. To say Gracie was outgoing would be an understatement. She found herself almost jealous of Gracie's love of life, her spontaneity and zest... it was just as Abby had been before she had Lillie. She figured Gracie was probably a lot wilder than she'd ever been – getting high or puking your guts out from taking shooters was no doubt minimal to her. She could remember some of those wild days but obviously the party life that Abby once lived had been drowned with some of her memory of it as well. She laughed to herself and they headed out to the pier.

Batson drove and so the two girls wouldn't have to worry about limits. Batson watched as Abby kept up with Gracie and Gracie with Abby. The two were a sight to see.

Gracie ran as fast as she could down the pier with her arms wide in the air, V-shaped. She looked so free with herself. Abby laughed and giggled at the other end.

"Is she always like this?" Abby asked him.

"Always. She's a bordering alcoholic, I just keep hoping she'll wake up from it."

The look on Abby's face took a drastic turn. She was shocked at what Batson had said, not suspecting anything of the sort.

"Look at her, Abby." She was dancing in circles, laughing at the stars in the sky. "She's amazing! Grandma and Bessie don't know about it though. She gets away with murder, always has."

"I would never have thought... I mean, I just assumed we were celebrating her last night."

"You would have caught on sooner or later. She hides it well though at home and all. But don't hold it against her. You just have to take her as she is – love her that way."

Abby ran after Gracie, the two girls embraced and galloped in circles. Her dream of the sea goddess was becoming a reality, the alcohol surging through their blood like poisonous serpents. Batson smiled, he knew Gracie had found a friend.

Batson stayed at Abby's that night, they slept soundly in each other's arms while Gracie passed out hours before in Lillie's bed. The night ended around one o'clock and Batson insisted on staying, not that Abby didn't want him to. She was just waiting for him to ask.

Only hours earlier they had made love madly like they had

not been together for years. Abby grabbed hold and did not want to ever let go. She loved the way he wanted her so desperately. She could see his mouth when he whispered the words again and again, "I love you. I love you," until finally he took her head with both hands, looked into the deep brown of her eyes and said it once again. This time, she said it back. Abby did love him.

When she first came to Camilla, first laid eyes on him, she fought so hard not to get involved. It was crazy not to get involved with Bats... he was just what she needed. He was her security.

"Would you marry me if I did ask?" Batson taunted her.

Taken off guard and half drunk still, she answered, "Yes, yes. I believe I would." Batson shushed her with a finger to her lips.

He smiled, knowing she would say yes, or at least he hoped she would. This time it felt right, this one was meant to be. Liz had been lust, pure lust. Abby was the one for him, now all he needed was to give her time. Time to accept him and trust him before he would ask her to be with him for the rest of his life.

Maizie sat in her apartment situated on the fifth floor of the high-rise in Tulsa. The flight had been a smooth one coming back home. It was almost midnight and she sat up on her couch, sipping Merlot from a stemmed glass and asking herself how to go about contacting Abby.

She rose, poured the wine down the disposal and reached for a beer out of the fridge instead. A bottle of Smirnoff sat neatly above the sink in the cabinet and she brought it down to her level, filled a shot glass full and gulped it down. Maizie was not an avid drinker but tonight she had a lot on her mind. The image of Abby flustered her routine, but it felt like she was getting closer and closer. This was her sister for God's sake!

The vodka felt like fire in the back of her throat, she chased it down with a sip of beer and took her place back on the sofa.

Maizie's apartment was close to immaculate with furniture that she paid out the ass for, paintings that she had gotten at low cost from her brother's art institution and knick knacks made of crystal scattered here and there as if they were just something she had picked up at Kmart. Her bedroom was done in floral everything, from the monogrammed towels in the bath to the afghan laying nicely folded at the end of her canopied bed.

Tomorrow would be the day, she told herself. Or would it be? She had chickened out so many times before, afraid of rejection. Marie had rejected her, why wouldn't Abby?

She thought of this sister of hers, living on an island? How nice that must be! But she worked at a law firm doing secretary work… how could she possibly afford that? It had to be quite expensive living that close to the coast. The private investigator she hired down there had done a marvelous job of finding her. Maizie had told him that she didn't want any pictures of her; she wanted to wait and see her in person… see if she recognized her, like if she passed her on the street or something. Tonight she found herself wishing she had asked for pictures- too intrusive though, an invasion of her privacy.

The alcohol was doing its magic on her as she flipped the radio, jazz station. Maizie would end up staying up most of the night, worrying and pondering how to approach this situation.

Five o'clock a.m. There was a pounding on the front door. Who in the world… Abby looked out the pane on the side window. Oh no, this was going to be trouble. She went to wake up Bats.

"Bats, get up! Get up!" she hollered to him. "Get uppp!" Confused he rose to his feet and went to the door, while Abby, still in her gown, stood behind the kitchen walls peering out to see.

181

It was Sam! God, thank God Lillie wasn't here.

The moment Batson opened the door, Sam grabbed his arm and slung him in the yard. The moon was still shining and you could see the two figures dancing with one another in argument. Abby went to get Gracie and the two girls watched out the window.

"You bastard you! How could you do this? What... has this become a hobby of yours, fucking around with other men's women? Well, is it?"

Batson was at a loss for words... there was no explanation and no time for one either. Sam was enraged, orange fire in his eyes and the devil hard at work. Abby was frightened and neither she or Gracie knew quite what to do.

"Should we call the cops?" Abby whispered.

"Not yet, let's see how far they plan on taking this." Gracie knew Sam as their one childhood friend and hoped he wouldn't do anything stupid. "I'm hoping they will work this out. He's obviously drunk though and that scares me. Sam never gets this hammered. In fact, I've never seen him behave like this." That comment frightened Abby even more.

They watched Sam's mouth seemed to get wider and wider, louder and louder. He danced around Batson like a boxer, tapping his shoulders as he went around.

"Sam, I don't want any trouble from you now. It was all a mistake. This is not the right time to talk about this."

"Yeh, you've got that right... a big damned mistake. Do you have any idea what this mistake of yours had done to my life? My family? Huh? Do ya?" Bats shook his head, trying to go along with everything Sam said. He knew if his old friend was drunk enough to come over like this, he was drunk enough to pull anything. "For starters, I don't have my family anymore... they're gone. That perfect life that I worked so hard to build for me and my kids and Liz too – I don't even get to be a part of it anymore because of your fuckin' ass sleeping

182

around with my Liz! She's my fucking wife, Batson! Mine!"

For a moment, he seemed to stop and think. He walked over to his truck, reached in for a cigarette and leaned on the door. "Don't you move, Cannon. I'm not through with you." Batson saw the agony soaring over his face and he hated himself for what he had done. But what could he do about it now? Liz had a part in this too, what was he going to do... go harass her next? Batson could see the smallest of tears in the corners of his eyes. Sam looked crazed, brutally insane and a furious rage.

"Sam, I'm so sorry. Man, you've got to believe me. I mean, what am I supposed to do about all this now?" Batson tried to sound as compassionate as possible; he knew Sam was hurt and confused. Damn, why did I do this to him? How could I?

Batson turned his head towards the house for only a moment when the sound blasted through his chest. Not believing the jolt of it, Batson looked into Sam's eyes for explanation, all he could see was anger, no regrets. It all happened so quickly. He collapsed to the earth, still breathing, looked up at Sam, once his grade school friend, his pal, who, in a flash, vaulted in his truck and wheeled off. Not understanding fully what he left behind- Batson with a chest trickling with blood.

Minutes ticked by so fast and Gracie and Abby both flew outside. "Oh my God! Oh my God!" Gracie screamed. Anna swung open her front door, awakened from the thundering noise. "Call 911! Call it now! Hurry! It's Batson... we need an ambulance!" Gracie ran inside to get towels to stop the blood. Anna, in shock, dialed the number and Bessie went to help.

Bessie stood above Abby watching her boy slowly die. Abby held him tightly under his head, gazing into his still open eyes- it was like a nightmare. She looked up at Bessie for something- help, reassurance, then looked back down at the man that had told her he loved her only a few hours ago. "Oh God. Hold on, baby. Hold on. Everything is going to be all right. Oh God! Batson, look at me… just keep looking at me. Oh God, please!" She was crying as she pressed onto his chest, the wound felt high up and she knew. It was his heart. Seconds later, he was gone. "I'll love you forever," she whispered to him as she cried a sea full of tears.

Chapter Twenty-One

Only a week had passed since Batson had left them. The funeral was a short one with a crowd of people offering looks of sympathy. He was buried just a short distance from his Papa Joe. Anna looked like she had aged ten years sitting in front of the casket, head falling down almost between her knees, just as she had at all the funerals. Gracie and Bessie had their arms wrapped across her bent over back with Gracie looking down at her feet. The rain hammered on the coarse carpeting edge and on the well-kept grass beyond. The preacher finished his sermon and guests cramped together under the small space of the mortuary canopy to listen to the closing words.

Abby felt guilty afterwards because it seemed she had cried more for Batson in the past week, than she had when her father passed. Every minute, every moment, she thought of Batson. Their short-lived time together had been, for the most part, incredible. She was forever thankful for the final night they spent together. Whenever she shut her eyes, she could see his bewildered eyes, glued to hers, not knowing the eyes would soon close for good. Those were the last and final minutes of his life; the memory would stay with Abby for the rest of her life.

Anna was taking it extremely hard. She wondered if she would survive them all. She felt better knowing that her loved ones were in God's heaven, united again. What was wrong with this family anyway?

Gracie had expected Anna to beg her to stay, but it was just the opposite. She wanted Gracie to get back home, return to her normal routine. Bessie agreed. The longer she stayed in Camilla, the easier it would be for her to remember. Remember her brother's comical remarks, to remember his compassion, his support and protection over her, making sure he was there to pick her up. To see his face, his smile, his happiness... everywhere.

Lillie had gone to stay with her Nana for a few weeks, until the initial shock of Batson's death eased. Gracie had chosen to stay with Abby for a week or so, despite Anna's request. The two kept one another company, spending many days starting with a drink at noon and more throughout the day. The numbing aftermath helped both women cope with the loss of their one and only Batson.

Abby took extra time off from work. Thom was not exactly pulling in the number of clients that he had hoped at this time of the year. He, too, was coping with the loss of his old friend.

Sam Borders was taken into custody that next morning, while sitting in his condominium on the island. The police found him sitting Indian-style on his bed, his hands pressed on his forehead, leaning down, still holding the gun that earlier had killed Batson in his lap. The officers concluded that if they had arrived any later, he would have been found dead. Sam would get what was coming to him.

Abby was uncertain about where Liz was living, she assumed she and the kids were still at their old house. Abby felt sorry for the kids. They were continuously in her prayers. She was sympathetic towards Liz as well. Abby couldn't imagine being in her shoes. Liz did not come to the funeral, too sticky of a situation. Abby was sure she would have liked to, since her confession of love for Batson had fully unveiled. For Liz to show up would not have been appropriate under the circumstances.

The days streamed by without Batson in them. Keeping up with Gracie's habit was more than Abby had bargained for. The two rarely went out, instead stayed hidden behind the barriers of Abby's house. When they did venture out people would stare with faces of pity.

Two days before Gracie's scheduled flight back to Chicago, Abby woke her from sleep at the first break of light.

"Get up, Gracie. Come with me."

Disoriented, she rose up from Lillie's bed.

"What are you doing? Why are we getting up so damned early?" Grouchy and trying to focus her vision, Abby led her into the kitchen and pressed her rear end down in the chair.

"We are going out today." She accidentally slammed the coffee cup in front of Gracie's place at the table and filled in with the hot brew.

"Out?" She was still focusing. "Out where?"

"Fishing." Abby stated, plain as day. Gracie looked at her as if she had lost her mind.

"Fishing? You have lost it, haven't you?" Her head pounded from the mixed drinks they'd had the evening before. "Then if we're going fishing, I'd much rather prefer a Bloody Mary instead of Folgers. Is that possible?"

"Nope." Abby grinned, pleased with her self-discipline and dominating voice. "Now, finish that cup. I've got more in a Thermos waiting in the car."

Gracie rolled her eyes at her friend, hoping the Oyster Bar would open earlier than usual, she could get a real drink. What had Abby gotten into anyway?

The car was packed down with fishing poles from Anna's shed that were halfway outside the back seat window. The temperatures were in the low fifties and it felt much colder with the wind tied in.

They dropped by a gas station on the way and picked up the bait for the unusual excursion. Abby picked out Batson's old tackle box filled with a variety of gadgets, wire, hooks, rubber fish and sinkers. She parked the car and out they walked to the end of the pier at Hudson Pointe. The same pier they had danced on nine days ago.

Abby nodded at the skilled fisherman already set in their places, most sitting on warped oyster buckets. Gracie walked right beside her, dragging her feet and letting her head hang low. The perfect spot was in the corner at the ending point of the pier.

The day trip had officially begun.

"This one is for the love of my life!" Abby swung the line out as far as she could. She had not a single tear in her eyes when Gracie looked over at her.

Gracie followed with her line and admired her strength.

"Did you really love him, Abby?" Gracie was sober now.

"At first I didn't know if I did, but in the end, there was no question. I knew it."

"Knew what? That you loved him?"

"That he was the one for me," Abby stated clearly and with confidence. "He was."

Both concentrated on the water and their poles bobbing through, remaining calm and serene.

"He told me he loved me only days before he left." When she said it, she realized how it sounded. Like he left only briefly, as if he would be returning. That thought tore at her heart, Gracie could tell.

"Did you tell him you loved him?"

"I did. Only I didn't tell him until that night, when we were in bed together. He asked me if I would marry him if he ever asked and I told him I would." Abby remembered whispering, 'I love you', over and over when Batson was lying in her arms, slowly dying. Gracie didn't need to hear that.

Gracie teared up.

Abby looked over at her, noticing. "Now, don't do that. No more tears, all right? This day is for us, to remember the good, not the bad."

Gracie turned her head the other way and took a deep breath.

"You've got it," she paused, "Sister."

Abby giggled and wiped a sliding tear from the corner of her eye.

"Well, you would have been, you know? I mean, if you and Batson had ever gotten married, you would have been my sister."

Abby looked into Gracie's eyes, "I thought I already was." She meant it.

Maizie departed the plane and filled out paperwork for the rental car she had arranged for. She purchased a local map and made her way to the hotel where she was staying. Driving along she thought of Abby like she always did. Was this the right thing to do? Should she call Marie first? Maybe so.

"Misses Anna, where is you at?"

"Out here on the porch. Come join me?"

Bessie was shocked to see Anna out on the back porch, as it was nearly one o'clock. She hesitantly stepped on the first creaky board, careful not to step on any of the cracks.

"Well, dis' is a surprise! What on earf is you doin' out here at dis' time of de day, Misses?"

"Sit down and be quiet. I'm listening to the water."

Bessie did as she was told and readjusted the hankie atop her indigo head. She placed her hands in her lap, gently overlapping her fingers. She sighed.

Anna turned her head and looked at her.

"I know you're wondering what in heavens I'm doing out on the porch at this time of the day, aren't you?" Bessie looked forward. "Well, I'll tell you then if you really must know."

Bessie faced Anna with concern and curiosity.

"It's just that, well, this is my most beloved place- out here. You know that. It just seemed silly not to enjoy it more often."

Bessie was not sure whether to question her decision or just

189

nod. She nodded. She could ask her if it still reminded her of waiting for Joe, but she didn't feel it was her place to. Obviously, her old friend had come to terms with it all.

"Used to be I'd sit out here all day long, remember?" Bessie nodded.

"I would see my Joe pass on the fishing boat and watch him wave as they went by." She closed her eyes, picturing it momentarily. "Then he would pass by again on his way in, blowing that God awful horn, remember?" Bessie nodded a second time.

"So, now you've decided to deal wif' it?" It was a direct question and Bessie waited for her to answer it.

"Well, Bessie… you and I have been around a long time and for years and years after Joseph died I couldn't bring myself to come out here. Like I was waiting for him to come home again, you know?" She nodded. "Now that Bats is gone," she stopped to catch her breath and her lips quivered, "well, all I have are my girls… Gracie, of course, and now, Abby and little Lillie. I have to live for them. Sitting in that old house ain't living, ain't living at all. I need to get out and relish in it, remember all the things that I used to love about life."

"Yes, you does Misses. I is so glad to see you so sc'rong." Bessie could not begin to express her admiration of Anna, her life long friend.

Gracie and Abby returned with their fishing gear, both smiling from ear to ear. The screened door slammed behind them as they walked in. Abby was proudly wearing her newly bought straw hat that curved above her ears.

"Grannie? Hello?" She peered back at Abby as they searched the house.

Finding the two women on the porch, they joined them by sitting down on the old floorboards, obviously exhausted.

"Well, hello girls. Catch anything?" Anna asked.

"No. A couple bites maybe, but that's it." Abby answered.

The air was silent, except for the hoarse, wailing cries of the birds flying overhead. All of them looking out to the edge of the sea, no one speaking, just watching. Something was missing, the man of the family. They would all make it through though, that was life, right?

"Guess I'm headed home tomorrow." Gracie broke the stillness.

Anna and Bessie nodded, while Abby was still searching for something out over the water. She wished only to see him one more time, just a moment. She closed her eyes and saw his face, his lips saying those three words. Tilting her head back to wash the sadness back inside, she then turned to enter the conversation.

"I hate that you have to go. We need you here, Gracie." She said it with a serious expression.

"No, Abby, dear. It's best for her to go back, get her life back on track." Anna replied. Little did she know how off track Gracie's life was, if anything, she needed her family.

"Yeah, I need to get my things together." She stood up, almost weary on her feet and walked off the porch over to Abby's.

Bessie remained in her chair, laying back into it with her eyes closed. Abby looked at both of them and noticed how old they looked. It was a horrible thought, but a truthful one.

"Are you doing okay, dear?" Anna asked her.

"Yes. I'm just ready for Lillie to come home. She'll be here tomorrow." She stopped momentarily, looked out at the incoming tide. "I'm going to help Gracie with her stuff."

"You do that."

Marie Mann was in her kitchen taking a string mop to the tile floor. Lillie had a mess of puzzle pieces strewn out on the carpet in the next room. Marie looked in to check on her, seeing the recliner that not long ago had Carl relaxing back in it, half asleep.

Everywhere she turned, she felt him beside her. The ladies from the church had cleaned up most of the house and were gracious enough to help her with his clothes. That had been difficult, the smell still covering each sleeve, each collar, cologne in place on his ties. She was thankful she had Lillie to keep her mind on other things. For the most part though, she had gotten her house put together since his death. Now, she had her daughter to worry about. Losing Batson and her dad simultaneously was an immense tragedy. Abby hadn't told her much about she and Batson's relationship, but from what she could tell, Abby would be lost without him.

The phone rang three times before Marie answered.

"Hello."

"Hey mom, it's me."

The conversation continued. "Lillie is fine, playing with puzzle pieces here on the floor. What do you need?"

"I need a favor. When are you planning on leaving?"

"I had planned on coming on in the morning, is that alright?"

"Well, actually, I need to come up there. Need to get some things."

"Alright honey. That's fine. What is it you need to get?"

"You'll see when I get there. I'm leaving tonight. Gracie is leaving early in the morning and so she's going to stay with Anna tonight. I thought I'd give them some time alone before she went back home."

"Okay. What do you want to do about dinner? Do you want me to cook?"

"No, we can go grab a bite when I get there, my treat."

She argued on that one, of course. Marie always insisted on paying for dinner. Abby was soon on her way.

192

Gracie said her good-bye to Abby and they hugged tightly.

"You call if you need me. I'm always here for you, remember that," Abby said, her hands clasped on her shoulders.

"And me for you. I'll be back soon." Gracie smiled at her, "Remember, our plan!"

"Our plan!" Thumbs up in the air, they squeezed each other again and Gracie walked next door to Anna's. She turned around to wave but Abby was already inside.

Their plan! A brilliant idea was brewing and no one knew about it except Abby and Gracie. Abby couldn't wait to start on it, but it would take time. There were many things that needed to be done before this idea would ever actually show itself.

Maizie had the house address and decided to take a ride. Abby wouldn't recognize her anyway... or would she? No, absolutely not. Abby didn't even know she existed.

She followed her map, the radio blaring instrumental high notes as she lit a cigarette. She crossed a rustic bridge, made of iron, linking the inland to the islands. The seascape view was illuminating and the whole atmosphere moved Maizie. The mystical space surrounding her was like taking a breath from heaven. For a brief moment, Maizie envisioned Abby's profile in the clouds surging across the sky above. The smell of soggy sand and salty ocean water was staggering the further she drove. She was drawn into the lush landscape on all sides. With the windows down, she heard the roar of the waves crashing down upon one another and imagined the brisk brush of sand tingling her skin.

This drive into her sister's part of the world was exhilarating. Maizie drove further into the small island where Abby lived and down the street marked with the matching name, Barefoot Trail.

Thoughts filled her head... what if she were home? What

if she was standing outside? Was she driving to slow? Maizie suddenly felt intrusive. There it was. She slowed. This was it, it had to be.

Maizie stopped the car incidentally to have a glimpse. Enough time to see the window boxes, unoccupied at this time of the year and the screened, front door opened to the side. Maizie's emerald green eyes shifted to the rundown car parked in the gravel. The driver door was open and she assumed Abby was either leaving or had just returned from somewhere.

A figure passed the open door of the house and it was too far to see. Maizie watched curiously as her chest rose with air. She couldn't bear to drive forward, not yet. One quick look is all she wanted, no more than that. One look would have to do for now.

There she came in denim jeans strolling down the steps and into the yard, having not a care in the world. Abby looked young and bright. Her hair was long and dark as the wind blew through it. Abby glanced at the car and waved friendly, as if she knew the woman. Maizie slowly drove off, too frightened to stop. Now wasn't the right time. She could feel it. Maizie needed courage to confront Abby. She finally decided to contact Marie first.

Abby finished throwing her things into the back seat and honked the horn as she drove out of the driveway. She wasn't sure when Gracie would be home again. It would be soon enough, as they had big plans.

Inside Anna's house, Bessie was busy with laundry and Anna lay in her bed with one of her library books. Things seemed to be getting back to normal. Abby had volunteered to go through Batson's apartment when she returned and would arrange to auction all his furniture and other non-personal belongings off. The money would be donated to various charities in the area that they had all chosen.

Gracie had packed up all her things tidily, ready for the morning to come. The three ladies stayed up late playing poker, partnered it with a few too many Bloody Marys, and were in bed by twelve.

Chapter Twenty-Two

The weeks lingered and Abby often couldn't find the strength to get out of bed on weekends. With Bats gone, everything had changed. He had been her hope and now he was gone, now hope seemed too hard to reach for. Tossing and turning in the cotton sheets, Batson flew through her dreams like an angel. She was positive he was there with her, his spirit folding around her like a field of wild energy.

Some mornings, Abby would make her coffee, sit at that old breakfast table, and just talk to him, as if he were right there reading the paper. She wasn't sure why his absence was hitting her so hard. Later she figured it out. He had been the man that she had once dreamed of marrying as a girl. She regretted not having the chance to have met him sooner.

Lillie went about her business. Her life was the same as it had always been. Abby took her to school every morning and returned to pick her up in the afternoons. Only on occasion did she ask Abby was she was crying, after too many times asking… she stopped.

The law firm was filled with distraught clients coming in and out for appointments, probably costing them out the ass just for an hour or two. Abby admired Thom for his compassion towards the majority of them. He was straightforward and aware when financial difficulties were an issue for his clients. Thom set all of his own fees, so Abby really wasn't sure what the normal fees were.

Patty was her usual self. She and Abby had recently started going to lunch together quite frequently. Patty remembered Abby and Batson's outstanding lunch date, rain or shine. She invited Abby to join her the day she returned to work. She would go on about the Sunday school groups at her church and even a singles night that met on Mondays that she thought Abby might like.

"No, that's not for me, Patricia. I don't think I'm up to anything right now." Patty understood.

When Gracie first left she was in relatively good spirits, at least she did not have a drink before leaving the airport. Unfortunately, the reality of his absence was sinking in, depression followed soon after. Time would have to do the healing.

Anna and Bessie struggled on with life just as it had always been. Only now, Anna stayed locked up in her bedroom more often. She had gotten into this pattern of closing her door, not letting anyone in except Bessie. Her behavior drove Abby up the wall, like she was hiding something from her. Anna acted like she did not even care, oblivious to the outside world.

Abby thought about Anna quite a bit. She could imagine how overwhelming all of this was to her. But why had she shut off the rest of the world into a dark, barely living, drowning state of mind? Doesn't she know that life does goes on? Can't she see that there are still people here who love her? People who are living for God's sake- not dead! She sighed.

She grabbed her journal out to clear her head, realizing that months had passed since she had written. When was the last time?

> *Dear Diary,*
> *Has my world caved in completely? I don't feel like writing down all the troubles that have passed, I'm only using you for my outlet. I pray to God for strength but sometimes I don't think he hears me. I need that strength!*
> *Being, it's a sudden feeling of being lost again. Like where do I go from here? God, I miss my dad. I miss*

Batson. And right now, I miss me. Where did I go?

Gracie has her outlet and now that she is home, I'm sure she'll use it. I can't allow myself to drink like that any more. It doesn't solve anything, right?

Nope. I know myself all too well. I'm a mom and I can't lose sight of that. Some things in life are more important... things are going to change around here, they have to.

She tossed the handwritten book under the mattress where it belonged. Lillie was snuggled tight in her bed and Abby decided to put on a pot of coffee. Was she crazy? It was ten o'clock at night, but who cared?

She leaned against the counter watching the streams fall into the pot from the filter. The smell was heavenly and fresh. She grabbed the pack of cigs on top of the refrigerator, deciding since she can't have a drink... she would smoke instead. They would compliment the coffee.

The kitchen table had Lillie's used lunchbox, pieces of discarded junk mail, not important enough to open yet, and the four frilled placemats beneath it all. Abby cleared it all off. She remembered purchasing a huge pad of art paper for Lillie to color on; it was in the top drawer of the hall desk. She spread a huge sheet covering the entire table.

The bell on the coffee maker beeped, the pot was full and ready. Abby spent the next four hours hovered over that table. She was building the dream that she and Gracie had pondered over.

The sheet had doodles and scribbles all over it. In the middle were shapes and designs filled with creative lettering, to the side was a list of Abby's productive brainstorm. She was a firm believer in brainstorming for ideas, like a flashback from her school days.

Chapter Twenty-Three

It had been three weeks since Maizie's impulsive trip to Camilla. She had not called Marie yet. There was a panic button still pushed inside of her and she would not let go.

The workload was heavier than usual and she was now visiting Houston for back-to-back business meetings with a set of new clients for the company. Even sitting around the conference table with ten to twelve people could not keep her mind off her faraway sister.

Lunch soon arrived and Maizie took a cab back to the hotel. She dialed Marie's home and luckily she was there to answer.

"Marie?"

"Yes, this is she," she answered, recognizing the voice as soon as she heard it.

"This is Maizie."

"Yes, I know. How are you, Maizie?"

"Good. You?"

"I've seen better days. It's been a long time since I've heard from you." Marie was curious still. Where was this other daughter of hers and why was she calling once again? Had she heard about his death? Was she in trouble? She listened carefully as Maizie spoke.

"Yes, I know. I... I'm calling about Abby." The words lingered on her lips after they left her mouth. Maybe this wasn't such a good idea after all.

"Abby?"

"Uh-huh. Does she know about me?"

Marie almost dropped the phone. So much had happened lately and now, now she was going to want to contact Abby. Marie felt lightning strip through her entire body.

"No." Marie stopped, not wanting to have this conversation.

201

"No, Maizie, she doesn't. Before you say a word, I know. I know it's my fault. Are you wanting to call her or something?"

"No, I don't want to call her. I want to see her, to know her – to be a sister to her." Maizie fought the tears from the corners of her eyes, pushing them back in.

Marie knew this day would one day come. Maizie agreed to give Marie time to explain the situation to Abby. Marie told Maizie about the family's recent hardships and that it was going to take some time to let this sink in.

"I don't know how she will take it, you know. I mean, Abby is a very stubborn person. She takes after her dad." Marie swallowed on her last words.

"Just try. Please Marie, I've never asked for anything from you. This is my sister for God's sake… I want to know her. That's not too much."

"Yes, yes, of course not," she sighed out loud.

"What? What is it then?"

She went dead silent.

"Marie? Are you still here?"

"Um-hum."

Her desperation was overloading, "Well, um… can I see you too?" There. She got it out. It was out in the open and for Maizie to decide.

Maizie held the phone down to her lap, overjoyed and still unsure what this might bring. Her adoptive parents were elderly now, a full-time nurse assisting both of them at home. She never wanted to hurt them. That had always been a huge concern before, but now, it seemed the timing couldn't be any better.

Marie told Maizie she would call when it was time. Maizie was ecstatic. This was going to be hard to wait for, but well worth the wait.

Chapter Twenty-Four

"I'll have it in by nine-thirty tomorrow morning, I swear it."

"You'd better, Gracie. This is an important piece, girl... don't you let me down."

She walked down the hall, briefcase in hand with a newly purchased suit, looking far from the island girl she once was.

People passing by waved to her and she hooked up with the happy hour crowd waiting outside for a cab together.

"What's the plan?" Asked a young reporter, blonde hair, a fake tan and accent that made you want to put a piece of tape over her mouth.

"Don't care. Whatever y'all are in the mood for." Gracie hooked up the backpack mechanism on her briefcase. It was nothing fancy. She bought it for herself when she first moved up here, backpacks were the easiest to tote.

The crew headed to a small pub on the other side of town and before Gracie knew it, time had slipped by. That damned piece! God, she had forgotten. "I gotta run guys. That piece is due in the morning for Wilder or he will have me canned."

"Hey, Gracie. I got a fresh bit on that one." A nice-looking co-worker spoke too soon. Any favor to help her through, just let her stay for another hour.

"Really? Can I use it?"

"Of course. Got it from a friend of mine," he said quietly in her ears. "Sit down, relax. Hey! Waiter. Bring her another, put it on my tab."

"Thanks." Her tension eased quickly, her body loose again and ready for another round.

Patty rang Abby's desk upstairs.

"You have a phone call."

"Who is it?"

"Not sure. They wouldn't say, but it's a woman."

Abby immediately assumed it was about Lillie. She had probably gotten a sore throat or something.

She answered the call, "Abby Logan."

"Ab, it's me." It was Gracie.

"Hey honey. What's wrong?" She could hear the huskiness through the line.

"Everything is wrong. Being up here is wrong."

"What do you mean? Are you at work?"

"Nope. It's all over for me. I'll have to tell you about it later. Can you come up?"

Silly question. There was no way she could come up. She had Lillie in school and work had let her off so much already.

"Gracie, you know I can't. Can't you come home? Why aren't you at work?"

"I suppose I'll have to. I just didn't want to disappoint Grandma."

"You won't. Whatever is going on, she will understand. She needs you too, you know."

"Yes."

"Pack up your things and head on home. Call me when you get to the airport and I'll come pick you up."

The day finished itself out slowly. It was now spring and things were starting to bloom. The cool fresh air put everyone in a better state of mind and brought in happiness.

Abby picked up Lillie at school and went on to the grocery store for their weekly trip. Lillie had recently made a habit of tossing random boxes of cereal, snacks and candy into the buggy. The cashier loathed at the amount of things she would no doubt have to replace on the shelves.

"No mam. We don't need that. You already have a box still unopened at home." It was the grocery store routine, every mom probably goes through it, she thought.

The bag boy was in the process of overfilling the plastic bags, while the young girl finished scanning the remainder of items on the belt. Lillie stood right beneath Abby, clinging to her legs as usual.

"Abby?" She heard the voice but was almost afraid to turn around. It was a familiar voice but one from long ago, years it seemed.

"Liz. Well, hello." Abby felt her throat bubble up and then swallowed hard.

Liz stood behind her cart with all three children huddled around her. Both women were at a loss for the right thing to say.

"How have you been? It's been a while, hasn't it?"

"Um-hum."

"These are my kids." She pointed to them as she said their names, "This is Billy, the youngest, then this is Brandy and my oldest back here is Jonathan."

"Well, this is my Lillie."

"Yes, hi Lillie. I believe I saw you once before."

"$122.34, mam," interrupted the cashier, not wanting to back up her line.

Abby wrote the check and pushed the cart full of bags out of the way. For some reason, she waited. Did she want to talk to Liz? It would be a friendly thing to do.

She had thought about the whole situation with Batson many times before in her head. The incident with Sammy was not Liz's fault, all she had done was fall in love with another man. Abby had fallen in love with that same man.

Liz joined her and they walked out into the parking lot, side by side and with the kids dragging along.

"I know this is very awkward for us both."

Abby nodded in agreement.

"But do you think, we could somehow start over... like on

a new foot?" Liz looked different, more sensitive in a way or maybe more humble. "We have both been hurt in this Abby. It might help if we could somehow be friends."

Abby fought the tears building in her head. There was still so much pain and resentment. She remembered how excited she was when they had first met... a girls' night out. Along with that memory, she recalled being left and hurt immensely in the same night.

"Friends? I don't know, Liz. So much has happened."

"Just think about it, okay? Here, let me write down my number in case you ever want to talk." She began scribbling it down, "I don't go out anymore, but I would really like for us to get a cup of coffee or something. My counselor said it might help if we can come to some sort of reconciliation." Counselor? Reconciliation?

Abby put the number in her purse and went her own way to their car to unload.

"Who was that?"

"Just someone I knew before..." she stopped and began crying.

"What's wrong, Mommy?"

"Nothing, sweetheart. Mommy's just having a hard day. Get in your seat, please." Lillie obeyed and they headed home.

She hated to get upset in front of Lillie. It did nothing but confuse her.

She glanced over to Anna's as they pulled in the drive. The house looked desolate, dead. No one outside and no lights on.

"Huh- that's weird. No messages." Abby said aloud.

"Who's supposed to call? Nana?"

"No, baby. Aunt Gracie."

Abby called Gracie's apartment but got no answer. She assumed she had already left and was on her way. Gracie would call her as soon as she arrived in Camilla, she promised.

Marie phoned Abby requesting to visit for the upcoming weekend. She needed to get away for a while and wanted to take Lillie shopping for new summer clothes. Abby didn't argue. Money was tight right now and she couldn't afford many new things for Lillie, let alone herself.

"Sure, Mom. That would be great."

"Good, I'll be up there Friday around noon. Can you leave the key under the mat?"

"Yep. Drive careful." That was that.

Lillie was thrilled to be going shopping. She was much more feminine than Abby had ever been as a child.

Abby started a bath for Lillie, threw on her housecoat and slippers and put on the teakettle for hot tea.

Minutes later, Lillie was playing in the tub while Abby tried to soap her down. She must have gotten to play on the playground at school. Her shoes had clumps of dirt inside; even her hair had pieces of sand stuck to her head.

Gracie never called and Abby began to worry. She pondered over the idea of telling Anna about their phone conversation earlier that day, but decided not. What good would that do now? Make her worry too.

Bessie pulled the sides out from the game table in the living room and got everything ready.

"You ready yet?" she hollered into Anna. She snapped the TV knob to off and walked in to the room.

"Course I'm ready." Bessie placed a bowl of popcorn to the side and both took their seats. Gin rummy was about to begin.

The interstate leading south towards Camilla looked the same as it had two years ago. Even in the moonlight, you could easily notice billboards plastered on the sides that blocked the view for miles. The south had some of the most ridiculous ones… most promoting different beaches and islands, others promising fantasy clubs for adult men, food places, antique shops, oceanfront beach properties, etc. They could not leave well enough alone.

Gracie's eyes itched with weariness and fatigue. The U-Haul dragging behind her swayed sporadically, causing her to tense up, frightened it might come loose. The enormous weight of it should hold it down, she told herself.

Batson was with her, she could feel his company. He was glad she was coming home; it's where she should be. Grandma Anna needed her there and right now, she needed to be there too.

Gracie was confident this was the right move. No more cold, snowy struggles to get to work and no more deadlines. This would not be her final move. She eventually wanted to write again with a paper or magazine.

Being home would mean a new lifestyle and hopefully some stability to help her get better. She wasn't happy anymore, only depressed. Just as Anna, it felt like life as she knew it had disappeared.

Driving along, she saw a pit stop. Gracie meandered over into the right exit lane and took a parking spot right up front. She needed to make some calls. The first was to Abby, she would be sick with worry.

At nearly four in the morning, the phone rang numerous times before she finally said hello. Gracie told her she was coming in; she should be there by six. Abby was relieved. Was Gracie coming home for good?

The thought was overwhelming but Abby was elated about her being here. She couldn't go back to sleep now.

"The coffee will be on. I'll be waiting up for you. I'm so excited that you're coming home, Gracie."

"Me too." Gracie hung up. One down, one to go.

Gracie reached into her side pockets for a number written on a red card, a sponsor card. The number belonged to a Brenda Morrison.

She looked around her to see some scary surroundings. There was a lineup of trucks parked on the side, with little lights lit up like nightlights and the coffee bar to the right was no doubt open 24 hours. Inside she saw a rough-looking girl ringing up a few tickets, showing her stained teeth when she smiled and pouring refills for the customers.

Gracie looked back on the card. Just go ahead and call the woman, she is there to help me.

"Hello."

"Hello, hello Brenda. It's Gracie."

"Yes, Gracie. Did you make it yet?"

"Not yet, about two more hours. I just stopped to call and grab a quick cup of coffee."

"Alright. Get your coffee and get going, girl. Call me when you get there. I've got a lady's name for you. She's a sponsor in Camilla to help you out. Hang in there."

"Okay. Will do." Had it come to this? Did she need a sponsor? Yes, she did. Don't be a fool, Grace. Whatever it took, she was going to do it and no, there was no looking back.

Gracie walked in to get her coffee and felt like an exhibit with eyes on every inch of her. Some of the men had long hair, some old enough to be grandfathers.

"Man, that pisses me off," she mumbled, sickened by her surroundings. She fumbled in her wallet to get some change.

"What is it, honey?" the young waitress asked her. "Here's your coffee."

"Does everyone have to stare? Is that like a requirement to be a truck driver or something?" Gracie asks sarcastically, not too loud, but loud enough for the few people sitting at the counter to hear. No one spoke a word, not even the girl.

Gracie grabbed her coffee cup, stared right back and walked out the door checking behind her. She rolled her eyes to herself, still pissed off at the behavior of some people, started up the van and took off towards the interstate.

Abby had been up and made coffee. She was baffled at the idea that Gracie had loaded up her stuff and was moving back here. What brought this on? And what about her job in Chicago? Did she leave all of that just to come home? She flipped on the TV to watch the morning news. Katie Couric was always a favorite of hers and the Today show was just about to start.

Abby had never been to New York. She often thought about one day taking a trip there, just to say she had been. She decided long ago to wait until Lillie was old enough to enjoy it, then they could go.

She remembered when she was pregnant with Lillie, all her expectations, and aspirations. She wanted Lillie to be cultured, to travel and see new things, like to read and see plays at the theater… the whole nine yards. Abby still believed they would get to do those things, all it took was time, money and planning. Of course, the job at the law firm wouldn't be able to support these dreams, but something would. Abby could feel it; good things were about to happen.

She walked out the front door to smoke; it had become a habit again. The hands on her watch were at six and ten; Gracie should be coming in soon.

As soon as that thought went through her head and by the time she lit her cig, Gracie pulled up.

The U-Haul was dragging behind her and wiggled through the gravel and stone. Gracie was waving through the front windshield and Abby sighed with relief, thrilled that she had made it safely.

The two ran to each other and embraced.

"I'm so glad you're here."

"I'm glad to be here. Damn, that's a long haul. I had forgotten."

"Well, come in and get some coffee. We'll unload all your stuff tonight when I get off work."

Gracie ran back to the car to get her duffle bag and purse, and then joined Abby inside.

Through the kitchen window you could see the fog hovering over the still waters. Gracie stood looking out while Abby took a seat at the table.

"You know, it's weird what you can remember. As a child, the mornings are something I can remember distinctly, almost like just yesterday." Gracie told her. "Like even in the morning fog, you know that water is there even though you can barely see it. That fog is a like a blanket over it, ever think of it as that?"

"No, not really. But I see what you mean."

Gracie turned, showing her face.

"I fucked up Abby."

"What? What do you mean? You didn't fuck up."

"Yes, I did." Gracie looked at Abby directly in her eyes. "I lost my job. I, um… I got fired."

"Fired! For what?"

"I copied someone else's work. I mean, not exactly word for word, but it was obvious what I wrote came from this other piece. My boss had seen it before and that was it… I was out of there." She sat down and placed her head inside her hands, leaning on the table. "Everything I had worked for- gone. I went and humiliated myself in front of everyone. Everyone knew."

Abby was at a loss for words. "I am sure they all didn't know, Gracie."

"Yes, Abby! Yes, they did." Abby rubbed her back to comfort. "But you know what? It all happened for a reason, like a sign to get my shit back together." Abby listened to every word. "I used to be so quiet, well-mannered and disciplined. Somewhere along the line, I've lost myself. Do you ever get like that?"

"Of course, Gracie. Everyone does at some point in their life, that's just part of it."

"Well, do they drink it away? That is what came along with mine, kind of like buy this item, get this one for free. A deal that I could not refuse! I'm serious, Abby. Get it!" She sat up straight, and then with seriousness in her eyes, "I am serious, Abby. I'm an alcoholic but I'm fighting to get better. I have to make a call."

With that last statement, she got up and called. Abby was astonished at her confession. She went in to check on Lillie and to give Gracie some privacy.

Abby dressed in a new suit she had found at the second hand store, real professional-looking. Lillie got her things together for school. Aunt Gracie fixed her breakfast for her and then put pink barrettes in her hair to match her outfit.

"Aunt Gracie, will you be here when I come home?" Lillie asks with hopeful eyes.

"I sure will."

"Good, we can play!" Lillie skirted around in her seat at the table.

"Slow down, honey. Are you ready now? We've got to get going or Mommy's going to be late." Abby interrupted.

"Yes, mam."

"Good girl. Let's go." She paused and looked at Gracie, "If you need anything, just call the office. You can put your things in the loft upstairs. It's quite cozy up there, believe it or not."

"Thanks. First off, I think I need to go over and talk to Grandma. I'm sure they will be up by now."

Abby smiled at her and walked out the front door. Gracie went in to freshen up before confronting Anna next door. She knew Anna would be thrilled to know she was home for good, but concerned about the reasoning behind it.

"Misses Anna, you needs to git up and out of 'dat bed now. I'm telling you, if you don't git up, you is gonna sink right in it."

"Bessie, I don't need to hear your lectures. Don't you think I know that?" Anna said, obviously frustrated. "You got the coffee on?"

"Yep, you just gotta come and git it."

"Yes, yes, alright. I'm coming."

Neither had looked out front or they would have seen Gracie's load parked in front of Abby's. Instead, the two sat routinely at the table and sipped on their coffee before going out on the porch.

Chapter Twenty-Five

"Did you talk to her yet?"

"No, not yet. I'm going there this weekend to stay and thought it'd be better to do this in person."

"Yes, I suppose so. Well, take this number down and call collect if you need to." Maizie gave her the number in Denver. "Please call me as soon as you can, I'm on pins and needles here."

"Of course, I will."

"When should you arrive?"

"I'm leaving here in about an hour or so. I should be there around lunchtime."

"God, I'm so nervous."

"Maizie, for whatever it's worth... I'm sorry about everything. There is just so much that I want to say to you, not so much an excuse, but just..." she hesitated, "I just want to see you, that's all."

"No need for explanation. I'm sure you did what you thought was best. I'm over blaming you. Just give me the chance to meet you and my sister, it's very important to me. You could never understand."

But she could understand. The child that she had carried with her as a young girl was at the other end of the line, begging for a chance. Marie cried uncontrollably after she hung up the phone.

How was she going to tell Abby? Would Abby hate her for telling her so late? She looked up to the sky for strength and then bowed her head. She was overwhelmed with joy; her two daughters were coming together. Marie Logan never thought she would see the day.

Abby sat daydreaming at her desk. The room was a blur and the visions in her mind were clear as water. Batson laughing with her, loving her, and then brushing her hair out of her face. She glanced out the window to see people strolling by on the sidewalk and then one couple holding hands on the bus bench. Batson, why did you ever have to leave me? Will I ever find love like ours again?

She opened the top drawer of her desk, rummaging through sticky pads and pencils until her hands found the photo. She held it up to see it fully, she and Batson at Christmas time standing in front of the tree at Anna's. Batson had his arm placed around her, keeping her from harm and both smiling happily like a fairy tale about to happen. Damn, that dream flew right out the window.

Abby closed her eyes to hold the tears in. Then her mind wandered to Will… where was he now? He hadn't called since Christmas. She shivered with the memory coming into view, and then forced it out of the way.

Concentrating on the paperwork on her desk, she went back to work, attempting to finish several folders before lunch. There was a devastating divorce case that Thom was presently working on with details that made Abby cringe. A family from the suburbs was calling it quits. Thom was representing the wife who was filing adultery. They had three children, all under the age of ten.

The wife, Delores Grainger, had only been a housewife. She had no professional skills and if Abby remembered right, she could not even type. Where did this leave her? Sure, she could go back to school, try to make a living doing something, but with three kids? Abby felt so bad for her.

After all, she had first hand experience of what it was like to be a single mom. How would she make it? Was it even worth it to leave?

Her thoughts went adrift again, only this time she pictured

Tommy. Ah, the one love of her life. Every time she thought of him it always made her homesick, homesick for youth, innocence. Briefly, she thought about calling him or actually calling his parents to see where he was and what he was doing. They had always adored Abby. Then again, she would be running back to the comfort of that old fling… it would never work.

"Abby, call on line two," Patty beeped in.

"Abby Logan."

"Hey sweetheart. It's mom. I'm here."

Abby had forgotten about her plan to visit.

"Hey. Sorry, Mom. It's been a long night. Is Gracie there?"

"No, she's not. The back door was left unlocked and so I just came on in that way. You forgot to leave a key for me." Not just the key, forgot period!

"Yeah, well, she's staying with us too. It's a long story, tell you about it later. Why don't you go on and pick up Lillie at school and then come and get me for lunch? Sound good?"

"Sure. Whatever you want to do. What's the name of that street again? Where Lillie's school is?"

"It's off Tupelo, right off the highway."

"Oh, that's right. What time?"

"I leave for lunch around one usually, but whatever time you get here is fine."

"So you're going to be staying with Abby?"

"Yes, mam. Just until I can find a place of my own and get back on my feet."

"Gracie, what happened up there? You can tell me."

"Grandma, nothing happened! I just wasn't happy, that's all, okay?"

"Well, alright then. I see you can't talk to me anymore. I'm just glad you're home, baby." Gracie rolled her eyes at the comment and hugged her.

"Don't you worry so much, all right? Everything is going to be just fine. Just us girls, right?" She smiled. Anna nodded and Bessie sat beside her holding her hand.

"Hello." Gracie picked up the call.

"Hey, it's me. Forgot to mention, my mom is in town to visit for the weekend, so she's next door. I just didn't want her to startle you when you went back over."

"Oh, alright. Abby, am I imposing?"

"No, of course not. We can all fit. She's picking up Lillie and we are going to eat somewhere for lunch, so she'll be leaving there around twelve or so."

"Okay."

"How'd Anna take the news?"

"Oh, she's glad I'm home you know." Then she whispered, "I didn't tell her everything, didn't see the need to."

Abby understood. "Oh, alright. Whatever. I'll see you when I get home tonight."

Liz walked in the park with Billy, the others were in school and she had the day off from the hospital. The day was perfect, a cool breeze coming through and daffodil blossoms gathered underneath the tall oaks. Mothers were out everywhere strolling newborn babies or meeting their husbands for lunch.

She had to go see Sam in a little while. A family visitation is what they called it, although she had not taken the kids yet and wasn't sure if she ever would. The prison was a terrifying place, even for her. The visits were something she always dreaded. They were nothing but painful, reminders of the evil that once evaded him. First she would take Billy to her mother's and then pick up a little package to take him, full of cookies, magazines or books.

The sight of Sam in such a miserable place nearly killed her the first time she had gone. He was good-hearted and the guilt that she caused him to get to that uncontrollable point was devastating. It seemed like it was all they talked about in the beginning and now it hardly even existed.

Sam was no longer angry with her; she couldn't have stopped those feelings for Batson. Love is the one feeling we have no control over.

Often it was like watching him die a slow death inside those dismal walls. Sam was cursed with hate for himself and almost ached for God to take him, forgive him, and have mercy on him. It was a horrifying sight, this man that she loved, now suffering like this. But then she thought of Batson, loosing his life because of the anger and jealousy of this love she had for him.

Liz kept going around and around the park sidewalk, no one daring to speak to her. Everyone that noticed her stared, whispering comments to themselves or to the ones with them. Liz held her head up high though, she had to stand her ground, be strong.

The kids had already fallen victims to rejection and cruel jokes at school. This had altered all of their lives, Liz dealing with it all in stride. She was the mom, the leader, and the one in control now... someday she hoped they could all have normal lives again. She remembered cookouts and birthday parties, block and Tupperware parties, storybook time at the library with other stay-at-home moms, afternoon movies and soccer games... all to be enjoyed with friends from Camilla. Not anymore, that was all a thing of the past since the incident.

Time would heal the open wounds, she told herself over and over. Liz and the kids were at church every Sunday, rain or shine. God was their only savior from the ridicule and viciousness surrounding them. One day their sun would shine... it would have to.

Marie walked up the stairs to the schoolhouse. The paint on the stairs was cracked and without question, could use a fresh coat. The door was appropriately decorated with Easter eggs and Marie found it hard to believe that it was already April. Lillie's birthday would be here on June 10th, five years old already! Goodness, where had the time gone?

As the door flew open with ease, she could hear the voices of the children inside, music notes flying high through the halls. The walls were hidden with bulletin boards decorated with colored paperwork, pictures of classmates and painted fictional characters. Teachers had hung polka dotted and striped borders along the edges to make it look even more festive.

Marie was pleased to run into someone finally, a young girl from the back hall.

"Can I help you?" the girl asked her in a pleasant voice.

"I'm here to pick up my granddaughter, Lillie Logan. Do you know where she is?"

"Yes, mam. Follow me. They just got up from their nap." So Marie followed her through a maze of more bulletin boards and the painted tiles below her feet. Seconds later they arrived at the door of the classroom.

"You can go on in." The girl said, waving simultaneously to the teacher waving back through the glass pane in the door.

Miss Brenda came to greet her. Abby had called a few hours back to let them know that she would be coming.

"Hi there. You must be Lillie's Nana, right?" Marie answered her by nodding. "She has had a nap already, just let me get her things together and she'll be ready to go."

All the trimmings on more walls inside the classroom amazed Marie. To one side were two lines of cubbyholes, each with a name written in marker. She searched for Lillie's name and finally found it between Ethan and Ashley.

"Nana!" Lillie came dashing towards her with arms wide open and Marie indulged her with a bear hug.

"Lillie, help me get your things together now. You won't be back until Monday, so let's get what you need to take home," Miss Brenda was prompt and attentive.

"Yes, mam." Lillie answered her.

Marie waited patiently and soon she was ready. Miss Brenda commented on the pleasure of meeting her and Marie was satisfied that Lillie was in such a good school.

Abby stood outside the office pacing back and forth on the sidewalk and then looking up and down the street for Marie's car. The temperature was already rising; she could feel the sweat building on her body. Turning her head back, she glanced at the realty company there on the corner. Anna had elected one of the longtime agents to takeover until she made a final decision of who would run the agency. Abby wondered if they had emptied out Batson's office upstairs, where the window faced east and you could see directly down here on the sidewalk.

While she stayed lost in thoughts, she hardly noticed when her mom's car pulled in between the two parked cars on the curb. She smiled at both of them and hopped in the front seat.

Marie reached over to hug her daughter and brushed a quick kiss on her rosy cheek.

"What do you feel like? To eat I mean." Abby was starved and ready for a good lunch. She looked in the back, "Hey, baby. How was school?"

"Good. We got to paint with the big kids." Abby laughed and switched her eyes over to Marie.

"What did you think about it? Nice school, huh?"

"Very nice. I was very impressed." Marie complimented.

"Alright, what shall we eat?" Abby thought for a minute, then suggested the pancake house down the road. "Breakfast food sound good?"

221

"Yummy!" Lillie hollered from the back.

"Mommy thinks it sounds yummy too. Breakfast for lunch. Yes, let's do that." Marie simply nodded and followed Abby's directions on how to get there.

Lunch was enjoyable and Marie had asked Abby about taking Lillie out shopping while she finished up at work. Abby agreed, giving her a list of things to look for, for herself.

"Abby," the words were slow coming out, "I need to talk to you about something later tonight. Nothing bad, I don't want to frighten you, but rather something good. Or at least I think so." Marie had to say something now or else she might be hesitant on telling her at all.

"Okay. What is this all about though? Something about daddy or the house?" Abby rummaged through her mind, trying hard to imagine what it could be.

"No, no. Nothing like that. Just trust me. It's nothing bad okay. Just surprising, that's all." At least Marie didn't think of it as bad. The news would certainly come as a shock, but she knew it would pass and Abby might even be anxious to meet Maizie.

Abby's eyes squinted and then relaxed and Marie could tell it would weigh on her mind for the rest of the afternoon.

"Okay, then. We'll talk later about it though, right?" Abby wanted a definite yes.

"Yes, yes, of course. Don't let this bother you now, that's not what I had intended. Just be patient and you will find out tonight."

Abby went back to work, finding it hard to think about anything else. What could it be?

Gracie sorted through the trailer filled with assorted pieces of furniture, the two stained glass lamps that she adored, artwork galore, boxes of clothes neatly marked as summer or winter and some accessories that had once looked so nice in her town apartment there in Chicago. She carried in what she would need while staying with Abby and left the rest in the trailer.

Taking a break with a glass of iced tea, she thumbed through the Rolodex in her mind for a guy friend that could help her unload the rest at the storage unit. Gracie picked up the phone to call Jordan, a close friend who was probably working and of course, after reaching his machine, he was. He owned and managed a local plant nursery, so she tried there.

The time was set and he would meet her at the storage unit. She was thankful for old friends. Batson would have done it if he were here, she thought to herself. He would have dreaded it, but he would've done it. Brothers were always good things to have around.

She became silent just thinking of him. His memory would be with her always, there was no stopping it.

"Alrighty. Time to get a move on." Gracie said aloud, although no one was home but her. She looked down at the dirt and dust that had accumulated on her white t-shirt. "Oh well, I'm bound to be nasty… I am moving." She laughed.

Gracie took her tea glass in hand and tromped up the wooden stairs reaching the loft. She began organizing what she could, putting clean sheets on the mattress and box springs that had to be dragged up. Keeping a few art pieces, she leaned them against the wall.

One of them was undoubtedly her favorite, a picture of a pier with a lowly fisherman leaning on it. His skin dark from the sun and worn from age. She had bought it at an antique store on Levell Street for twenty-five dollars, if she remembered right. Not an expensive one by any means, but to her it was worth a lot more. It reminded her of Papa Joe and she placed it where she could see it.

A three shelved bookcase sat beside the bed, Gracie dusted it off and put some frames with old photos on them. The one of her mom and dad on top, a small one of just her mom beside it, a snapshot of she and Batson as kids on the middle shelf and then some books on the bottom. It was already beginning to feel like home.

Over in the corner were books and a folded white sheet of paper. Gracie would never pry, but this was her room now, right? She quietly unfolded the paperwork on her bed, looking over her shoulder to make sure no one was behind her.

"Oh my God! I can't believe she did this!" She smiled, elated that Abby had taken their idea to heart.

There were several sheets that had been neatly put together. Abby had drawn floor plans. How she knew how, Gracie did not know. It was amazing. The top sheet had scribbles of names that Abby had come up with, "Dawson Bridge, C & L Fishcamp, Cannon's Java Joe's," even "Lillie's Lookout." Gracie liked the last one the best so far. Then she saw different styles of writing, like calligraphy, letters at random she had tried out with different colored pens and magic markers.

The second sheet must have been her practice sheet. She screwed around with the ruler and pencil in all sorts of directions, measuring out different rooms, rest rooms and the kitchen. Abby made sure to include the most important thing of all, porches. Porches on every side of the structure and windows everywhere from what Gracie could tell.

The final sheet was immaculate. Gracie was in shock! Abby was really into this, this dream that after many drinks they had conjured up while in the moment.

Gracie put all three pages back together just as she had found them and decided to wait and talk to Abby when she got home. How exciting it was all going to be… it would one day become a reality, she could feel it in her gut.

"Bess, can you come out here?"

"I'm a'coming," she spit while walking towards the porch

door. "Yes'm?"

"Come on out here n' sit with me."

"There are things to be done in here, Misses Anna."

"Don't care. Sit with me."

Bessie gave in and took a seat in the chair beside her. Her eyes red and sunken, her skin wrinkled like a prune.

"What is it?" she finally asked after several minutes of silence.

Anna looked over to her, "I need your help."

Bessie listened whole-heartedly.

"We need to clean out my closet in my bedroom. I've been putting it off for far too long and now, I want to do it today. I can't fit anything else in there."

Bessie held her mouth closed, trying not to let it fall open. What was going through that stubborn head of hers? Why did she want to do this all today? She nodded.

"Did you make iced tea?"

"Yes'm."

"Alright, good then. Go fetch us a couple glasses and I'll meet you in the bedroom."

"You got it."

Bessie did as she was asked and fixed two glasses of tea, adding a touch of lemon juice and a mint leaf in each.

She had always served tea that way, made it more of a treat.

Chapter Twenty-Six

Maizie stewed in her room. She called down to order some food from room service for lunch, as it was a couple of hours behind their time in Camilla. Maizie could not leave the room, scared they might call while she was gone.

This is crazy. They might not even call until tomorrow and I'm pacing around like a hen waiting to lay eggs, she told herself. But she remained, who cared. She did not have another meeting scheduled until next week and that was in Tulsa again.

She ran a tub while waiting for her food, took advantage of the complimentary bubble bath and slipped in.

Finding it hard to keep her mind of things, Maizie snatched her book off the back of the pot and read line after line.

She dozed off with her head tilted over the side of the tub and woke to the knock at the door.

"Oh shit!" She draped the oversized towel around her as she hurried out, yelling, "Hold on. I'm coming! I'm coming." Her voice faded the closer she got to the door.

There in the doorway stood a younger guy, probably in college, with a cart adorned with linen and covered with dinner and drinks on top.

"Room service?" he asked out of courtesy, knowing this was the right room. She held her towel up, looking up as he towered over her. Oh, sometimes she wished she were young again. Many months had passed since she had been in the company of a man.

"Yes, hi. I ordered all that. I'm starving you know. I'm Maizie." What the hell, give it a try.

The guy, obviously uncomfortable at first, took a second and then introduced himself.

"Busy tonight? I mean in the kitchen, of course."

"Yes, Mam. We've got a tour group staying on the second floor."

"Well, come on in. Let me get you a tip here." She took her time looking for her purse, which sat in plain view on the nightstand.

He waited patiently and actually enjoying the view of this older woman roaming around in her bath wear. Her skin looked smooth and silky, her hair curled up at the nape of her neck… yeh, he could handle that.

"So, how old are you again?"

"Uh, I didn't say. I'm 22. I go to school here."

"From this area?"

"Yes… grew up here." He watched her move and nervously caught contact with her eyes… they were all over him. He noticed how she took her time. "What about you? Where are you from?"

"Now, that's not important is it? Tulsa, I'm from Tulsa. I'm a sales rep for a company out there."

"Wow, big stuff huh?"

"I guess you could say so. Here." She handed over a five, holding the towel up with the other hand. He eyeballed her every move.

"I like your name, Maizie. If you need someone to show you around Denver, just call me." Damn, he was cute.

"Well now, I'd need your number to do that, wouldn't I?" she teased him and could not actually believe she was contemplating sleeping with this younger man. What the hell, you only live once.

"I get off at eleven, want a visit? I mean, we could go out or something," he asked her without a twitch anywhere on his body, calm and collected. She looked older, but not that much older. He guessed her to be in her late twenties or so.

"Sure, sounds good. But I am waiting on a call, so we might

have to stay in. It's a Friday night you know, don't you have friends or someone to go out with." The conversation lingered and she knew after the words had escaped her mouth that she hoped he would come back to her.

"Yes, of course. But that's what I do every weekend." He had the grin of a fox and she quivered at his ego. "Enjoy your dinner, Miss Maizie. I'll see you later."

Later would be good, if he actually followed through with it. True, he was young but she was only 33 and looked a lot younger. How easy was that anyway. She took off her towel, laid it out in a perfect square on the bed, pulled up the cart and sat there naked eating her Cordon Bleu with a side of pear salad. What pleasures. At least he would take her mind off of things for a while.

Abby drove on home in the five o'clock traffic. She never had to really sit in it because under normal circumstances, she always had to pick up Lillie first. Since she was going straight home she had to go over the bridge and hit the traffic right on target. Cars were backed up for what seemed like miles and she was so anxious to get home.

When she finally got there, Gracie's car was gone but Marie and Lillie were there. At first, she felt an urge of worry, wondering where Gracie might be. Abby was not so confident that she would pull out of the alcohol so easy. It was most definitely going to be a struggle for her as it would anyone that had a problem with it.

"I'm home," she announced walking through the doorway with her briefcase on one shoulder and purse on the other.

"We're in here." Her mom's voice hollered from the kitchen. Abby joined them and smelled the baked cookies while walking through the living room.

"Hey girls." Lillie jumped up to hug her. "What have we got here? Chocolate chip, huh?" Lillie shook her head in agreement. "Good, my favorite!" Abby grabbed a warm cookie off the cooling rack and helped herself to a glass of milk. "Can't beat that."

"Want to see what all we picked up today?" Marie knew Abby would be thrilled with what she had picked out for her.

"Um-hum," she mumbled, the chocolate melting in her mouth.

"Go get Mommy's bag, Lillie. It's lying there on the sofa."

Lillie did as she was asked and returned with the paper bag from Penney's.

"Did you pick out something for Mommy?" she asked Lillie. "Yes!"

Abby pulled one article out at a time. Two colored sweatshirts, a pair of black sweatpants, and three pairs of thick socks- all on sale and for next winter. Abby kept digging… a shirt embroidered with, "World's Best Mom," Lillie had picked out especially for her. "Oh, honey. I love it. Thank you so much." Lillie hugged her again, proud that she had gotten something for her mom.

"And she paid for it all by herself too!" Marie acknowledged, sure that Lillie would like the compliment. "There should be one more thing in the bottom." Marie waited to see her reaction.

Abby reached and felt the small trinket box in the bottom of the bag. "What is this mom?"

"You'll see. Lillie, why don't we see what's on TV, okay?" She walked Lillie in the living room and turned on the Disney channel, surely there would be something on there she would like. Then Marie looked in the kitchen to see if Abby had gotten it out yet.

Abby sat there looking at the inside of the small box, not understanding what it meant.

"Hold on, Abby. I'm coming." Marie joined her daughter at the table and Abby held the charm in the palm of her hand.

The silver charm shined and glistened, with the word engraved on it that made no sense to her.

"It's for your charm bracelet."

"I got that part, Mom, but what... what does it mean?"

Marie took the box and charm from Abby's hands and held her hands close to hers.

"There's a story behind that charm and I'm not sure how you are going to see it, but here it goes." Abby could feel her body tense up, afraid of the unknown.

Marie proceeded with her story, "A long time ago, before I even met your father... well, I got into some trouble and..."

Abby interrupted, "What? What are you telling me? Just say it, blurt it out! I don't need the whole story- tell me!"

"I'm trying, Abby. Please hear me out, be patient."

"I'm confused. Oh my God... this is very important, isn't it?"

"Very." She paused for only a moment, now ready to release what she had held in for so long. "Abby." Abby looked up into her eyes like a child about to hear some horrifying truth. "Abby, you have a sister." There she said it, it was out. Now she could see where this would go.

Abby sat there for a moment, frozen, not taking her eyes away from her mother's for a single second. The words had not yet sunk in and she waited until finally they were there to stay.

"A sister? A sis... sister?" She questioned the word, the title, the relation.

Marie nodded and began sobbing. "I tried to tell you the story behind it all first. She was mine. I had her two years before I even met your father. My dad forced me to let her go. I had no other options, Abby." Abby sat there, now concentrating on the lines in the kitchen floor, listening.

"I was so young, so ashamed and so terrified. Abby? Abby, please look at me."

Abby glanced up, looking for some reasoning behind it all.

231

Why hadn't she told her sooner? Why now?

"Abby, your father never even knew. I could never find a reason to tell him." At that, Abby grew angry. How could she have not told him? "I know you don't understand all of this, somehow I tried to pack it all away, never think of it."

"How could you give her up, Mom?" Those were words that pierced. Marie had no explanation, not then and not now. Abby looked in at Lillie, reminding herself of how precious she was as a baby. Give her up? Never.

Silence filled the room and they sat there, still and apart. The storm was coming, the walls closing in, and the news more real as the minutes passed one by one.

Abby gathered her strength and spoke again, Marie wiping the tears still falling. "What brought all this on? Why did you decide to tell me now, after all this time?" She took in a deep breath and almost whispered, "How come you never told me before? Jesus."

The last question was too difficult. There was no good explanation that would excuse her from not telling Abby or her father. "She's, um… she's been looking for you." That did it. The look on Abby's face was irreplaceable; Marie saw the desperation in her eyes. They widened almost with excitement, but truth was, the shock was sinking in.

Abby stared at her hard and tears built up in the corners of her brown eyes. "She's… she is looking for me?"

Marie nodded. "What? Where? Where is she?"

"She was raised in Oklahoma and she contacted me about five or six years ago. Recently, she called again and this time… the timing was right."

"Oh my God. Dear God." Abby took another minute of silence. "Well, what is her name?"

"She still has the name I gave her when she was born. They kept it." Marie paused; this was a moment for sure. "Her name is Maizie, Maizie Stockton."

232

"Maizie, M-A-I-Z-I-E?" Marie nodded.

"Mom, I think I need some time."

"Sure, I understand."

"Will you watch after Lillie? I think I need to go lay down."

Marie signaled for her to go ahead. First, Abby stood up, reached on top of the fridge and grabbed her cigarettes. The ashtray was right beneath them, so she took it too and headed towards the back of the house to her room.

Gracie rushed in as Abby slowly closed the bedroom door behind her. "I'm here... finally!" She caught a glimpse of Abby's shadow. "What's wrong? What has happened?"

Marie called her into the kitchen and told her to let Abby be for a minute. "What's wrong, Mrs. Logan?"

"It's a long story, I'll let Abby tell you about it when she gets up. Come on, we need to put something on for dinner." She stood up from the chair, telling herself to be strong. "Lillie, honey? What sounds good for dinner?"

"Pizza!"

Gracie giggled at her and Marie rolled her eyes with humor. "Hey, sounds good to me. Want me to call it in?"

"Sure, why not." Marie left to pick up some Cokes and Gracie called in the pizza.

Abby stayed in her room for the remainder of the evening, answering to the knocks on the door only a few times. Once for a glass of water, the second time to tell Lillie goodnight.

"Wait a minute. Lillie, come back in here." She motioned for her to join her on the bed, "Will you sleep with Mommy tonight?" Lillie said yes, without much hesitation and Abby whispered to her, "Good, I need you to cuddle." And so, both were tucked in under the covers and Abby held her baby just like she used to when she was small. "I love you so much! Do you know that?"

"I love you too, Mama."

Gracie looked at the travel clock that she had brought with her, 2:16 a.m. She had tossed and turned ever since she had laid down. The blanket was thick laying over her; she tossed it to the side and went to get the paperwork that Abby had worked hours on. She had never told her that she had found it.

Spreading it out on the floor, she took a pencil and went to work, making circles and designs on the blank sheet behind the three before it. The images were fresh in her head and she had trouble making it to the paper before they vanished.

The building would sit beside the ocean, with fish of all sorts swimming in the shallow waters around it. Gracie penciled fins and shells, sandpipers and sand dollars, waves, sails and sandcastles. The artwork turned out better than she had imagined. She set it to the side and fell asleep with the lamp still on and pencil on the nightstand.

Abby slept like a rock. Lillie's head tucked between her arms, breathing softly as the ocean air washed against their faces.

The water pounded on the damp sand, Abby dancing once again. No one was with her this time. Only her alone. Above her, closer to the dunes, sat Lillie in a hole of sand with her hands digging into the dust. The wind caught her curls and tossed them to and fro, she waved to her mama. Both happy and free. The perfume from the water drenched them with faraway aromas.

Abby's head turned around looking for the man that had been watching her before. She quickly forgot about him, carelessly bouncing her feet through the sand and wading in the cool waters. Then walking slowly from the end of the beach, he came towards her. She instinctively put her hand to her hairline to shade her eyes from the sun and focus in on the figure.

He was a stone's throw away; still she could not see his face, only his shadow. The glare was too strong. Who was this stranger? Was he an outsider or did she know him?

Confusion partnered with frustration and Abby rolled into her pillow, holding on tightly. Her eyelids fluttered, recognizing the outlines of her furniture in the dark. The sheer veil flapped as the wind blew in the tight crack at the base of the window. Abby was rescued with a breath of reality... aggravated with herself for not finishing the dream. That always happens, she thought.

Remembering the earlier conversation with her mom, she wiped her face and got up for a drink of water, taking the cigarettes with her. The sun would be rising soon, so she chose to stay awake.

The air was cool outside as she stepped on the back stairs of the porch. The light rays from the moon still descending down onto the still water. She meandered out on Anna's dock and sat down weakly on the edge at the end. Her legs dangled over the water as it brushed in.

There Abby remained quietly, not to bother anyone, staring out to sea. Maizie roamed in her thoughts. The whole idea of her was so overwhelming and the shock would take some time to wear off.

She lay back on the wooden dock, closed her eyes and felt her body flow back and forth in rhythm with the sway of the dock. She could see Batson with her eyes shut, not in his final moments, but rather their meetings with one another. She imagined hearing symphony music as she looked into his eyes, prancing on her toes in the sand. And those bold eyes of his, the ones that captured her heart many months ago, over a year now, glaring into hers. God, how she longed for him, to feel his strength beside her and being able to love him.

Abby dozed off and woke to the warmness of the sun shining on her exposed skin. A new day had begun. Tomorrow would come soon enough, but today was here already... make the best of it.

Maizie looked over at him, lying there in her bed. It had been fun but now it was time to start worrying again. He had a bird chest; the kind that stood out from the rest of his body but his face was soft as baby's skin. Cute, but oh, so young.

She tried to be quiet as she got up to order breakfast and coffee, laughing to herself at the thought of what the next room service guy might look like. She told herself that normally these situations never happened, but honestly, sometimes they did. One-night stands were best suited for someone like Maizie. Not to say she slept around, it was just easier this way… no attachments, no strings, that sort of thing.

Maizie had had a couple serious relationships in the past, but her work was the top priority. Love never seemed to stand in her way. Sometimes it bothered her, she would miss having that stability of someone being there and then the feeling would pass.

She called in a couple orders of pancakes, a side of scrambled eggs, two orders of bacon and a carafe of coffee with cream and sugar, two cups. Little did those kitchen guys know one of their co-workers was in her bed asleep and about to have a breakfast date with one of their customers. She giggled at the thought.

The sex had been unbelievably exhilarating, younger man with all his stamina probably could have gone all night long. The wine had taken a burden on both of them and he held her closely in his robust arms.

He stirred as she hung up the phone. His weary eyes looked into hers and she joined him under the covers. Another roll in the hay would be nice before breakfast and anyway, he offered.

Maizie was quiet as a mouse as he pulled her closer and closer. The phone rang and it was Marie. Maizie pushed him away and concentrated to the voice on the phone.

"I told her." Marie whispered into the phone, peering out the kitchen window to make certain Abby had not moved from

236

her spot on the pier.

"She knows?" Maizie needed to hear the words once more to make sure.

"Yes, she knows."

"How'd she react?" Maizie's hands tensed, as everything around her seemed to disappear.

"She's still in shock. It was hard on her but I think she'll come around. I need to go. I'll call you later, okay."

"Yes, alright. Keep my number handy. I'll be here for another couple of days." She hung up and laid down flat on the bed, the young hands wandering over her body wanting more. She stared at the ceiling, tingling from his package making it's way inside of her again, reaching further and further.

Chapter Twenty-Seven

"I'm exhausted." Anna sat on her double bed sorting piles of pictures and boxing some of the debris that made its way out of the closet.

She and Bessie had stayed up until wee hours going through the majority of it, shedding a few tears and sharing the stories of days gone and past. Bessie had slept on the couch and Anna in Gracie's room. Now the two were back at it again.

"Look at dis'." Bessie tossed a picture of Anna in her housecoat posing at the front door. On the back was written, "Our first house."

"Yes, I thought this would be just our first house. Turned out to be our only house." Maybe so, but Anna couldn't picture herself anywhere else but here. Sorting through all this had revived her exhausted heart. She found it gratifying to see the faces of her loved ones in such blissful, memorable times.

There were hundreds of pictures taken of Gracie and Batson growing up, playing on the beach, Christmas mornings, Easter egg hunts, costume photos from trick-or-treating, Prom dates, dances, every occasion you could conceive of. The baby books were priceless; reading through the notes that their mom had written in the given spaces brought back good memories. Gracie's graduation with her distressing haircut, Batson's first Trout catch with Papa Joe, Gracie digging to the bottom of her stocking Christmas morning, snapshots of the two with Santa, at swimming lessons, Batson at his first job at the Burger Palace, Gracie's piano recital, Batson with his softball team, birthday parties with elementary schoolmates... all were priceless.

To see her Batson was difficult, Bessie stood behind her as they passed through the photos together. Her hands held

Anna's shoulders when she broke down and then wrapped her arms around her when she cried uncontrollably. The memories were missed and Anna remembered some as if they were yesterday. She could see the fear in Gracie's eyes when she had trouble with a bully girl at school, Batson's when he was going in to have his tonsils out, the stitches, the principal's office, the days at the doctor's office for regular checkup shots, the braces, the skinned knees… all the times, good and bad. But all had been good to Anna; she was the privileged one who got to participate in those special moments, the one survivor.

In one large box put to the side were memories of the late Mr. and Mrs. Cannon, in marriage, as children and then with Batson and Gracie. Their marriage certificate and death certificates, cutouts from the local paper of that horrifying crash and several family photographs, always taken by a professional. One clipping had a picture of them standing in front of the aircraft, the one that eventually carried them both to their deaths. Anna thanked God everyday that the kids had not been with them on that doomed voyage.

Her only son lost control of the plane late that afternoon and the water called out to them as the plane dove, unstoppable into the deep waters. The Coast Guard took days and nights searching for the remains, unable to come up with anything. The ordeal had been devastating for the whole town and something no one would ever forget. The ocean would hold them forever, hand in hand, at its desolate bottom. Anna gingerly added a few pieces to their pile atop the box and moved on to something else.

"Good morning girls." Gracie said as she walked in and helped herself to a cup of coffee. "What in the world is all this stuff?" She also helped herself to a handful of photos from one of the piles. "Look at this! You can see where I cut out a big chunk in the front of Batson's bangs! He almost killed me for that, so did you!" She pointed the finger at Anna.

"I had forgotten about that. And remember, we had pictures the very next day!" Anna filled in her side of the story.

"So, what possessed you to go through that rummage of a closet?"

"Just needed to be done, that's all." Bessie looked over to see her nonchalant expression. "What are your plans for the day?"

Gracie sipped her coffee and made a face because of the hot coffee dribbling down her chin. "Damn," she mumbled. "Sorry, it's hot! Um, well, I told Jordan I would come down to the nursery and help out for a little extra cash to help get me going. Abby's mom is visiting you know and I think there's something going on. Abby was upset last night but I didn't have a chance to talk to her."

"Hum. Wonder what it is?" Bessie asked. She worried about everyone but herself.

"Don't know. She seemed better this morning, but very quiet, keeping to herself. I figured it would all come out in the wash today." Gracie hoped it would.

She took a deep breath and decided to go ahead and ask Anna about the money. The project would take quite a bit to be built and all. She would ask for a loan, but she knew she'd never have to pay it back. Family business was family business.

"Grandma, I've been thinking about something. Well, Abby and I have thought of a good idea... a new business." She slowed down, not sure how to ask properly. Was there a proper way to ask for money? Probably not. "We want to open up a small restaurant with a fish store inside, kind of like that place we visited in Savannah that one year."

Anna listened closely, insisting on making Gracie suffer just a bit.

"It would be built out here on the island to bring in more tourists, but could also become a favorite for locals." She shrugged her shoulders as if she wasn't sure where to go from there, "Um, we still need to see a builder or contractor about costs, an attorney to lead us in the right direction and um…" Her voice trailed off, her head hung low, and then she raised it ever so slightly, enough to swing her eyes up to look at Anna. Anna's eyes were attentive and she acted as if she hadn't caught on to the main point of her story.

"Yes dear? Keep going, we're listening." Anna pressured her.

"Alright, you know darn well what I'm getting at now… it's going to take money, money that we don't have. We need a loan."

"A loan? Bessie, have I not always loaned out my money to the kids?" Bessie nodded. "Do I ever get repayment?" She teased on until Gracie began to get aggravated.

"Grandma! Stop it now. Can you help us out or not? We are very serious about this. Abby doesn't want to be at that law firm forever and having our own business would give me the chance to freelance a little or write a best-seller. Now, will you help us?"

Misses Anna remained silent, focusing on a photo from the largest stack. Bessie went about her work inside the closet.

"Of course I can, sweetheart. Find out how much you need to start with and then let me know. Starting a business is a lot harder than either of you might think. We will need to sit down and discuss your plans. And don't take me so serious, I thought you were over all that."

"This is serious. It's going to be fabulous." She hugged Anna and kissed her on the cheek, whispering in her ear, "I love you so much."

"I love you too, dear. You know I'm always here when I can help and I understand things sometimes that you don't think I will. I'm old, but I'm a wise one. You remember that, you hear?" Anna smiled at her.

"Yes, mam. I know you are." She tied one of her shoelaces that had broken loose. "I'm off to the nursery. Need anything?"

"Look n' see if dey' got some petunias for the boxes out back… or jus' anything purdy," Bessie requested from the walls of the closet. "Surprise us!"

"Yes, mam." And she was off to work for the day. Anything to keep off the bottle that haunted her every hour, every day, and from now on. Gracie wished and prayed those demons would bury themselves and be dead.

The weekend days passed by slowly. Abby kept to herself and Marie chose not to push it. Finally, Sunday night, Marie sensed Abby might want to try talking about Maizie again. The initial shock had worn off and Abby was rather interested in this so-called sister of hers. Abby did not blame Maizie in any way, shape or form… the idea of it all was quite moving for her though, propelling emotions she didn't believe existed.

"Do you remember her, Mom?" She stopped and dried off a dinner plate, "Maizie?"

"Abby, this is hard for me too. I just wanted you to know that, but yes, I remember her." She walked over to the sink and joined her daughter. "Look at me Abby. I want you to look at my eyes."

Abby did as she was asked and reached over for her mother's hand.

"She was my daughter. I was able to be with her for two days after she was born. I breastfed her, changed her diapers, held her close, but most important of all… I loved her, Abby. That feeling never goes away."

Abby listened, her skin tightening on her face and a yearning inside her. She still didn't understand. Why?

"It's just hard…" she rubbed her nose on the sleeve of her top, "it's just hard to believe, that um, that you could give her up, you know? I think that's the hardest part for me. Not that she exists or that you got pregnant before you met Daddy... just that you had the strength to give her away."

Marie wondered about that one herself but tried to explain it delicately.

Abby's ears were burning when she heard the rest of the story and in the end, agreed that her mom had done the best thing for baby Maizie. The teardrops were wiped clean and they leaned against the counter hand in hand.

"Now, I'm leaving in the morning for home. Another new week for the two of you and I just get in the way around here." Same ole' song and dance.

"Oh, Mom, you do not. Really, this has been one of the best weekends I think we've ever spent... and one of the hardest."

"I could not agree more."

"So, what about Maizie?" Abby inquired.

"Yes, well. I am going to leave all the planning to the two of you. In the morning, I'll leave the number where you can reach her. You can call if you want or you don't have to, it's totally up to you."

"What if I decide not to right now?" Abby was too nervous to think about it.

"It's totally up to you, honey." Marie repeated. "Really."

"What are you going to do? I mean, are you going to see her?"

"Might. Don't know." Marie saw the concern in Abby's eyes. It was like 'if you call, then I'm going to' kind of thing. "We'll see, alright. I'm going to bed now, you need to get some zzz's, too."

"I know, Mama. Good night."

"I love you." Marie said under her breath, while her slippers led her down the dark hall.

"Love you too." Abby whispered, but she wasn't sure she heard her. She knew she did anyway.

Chapter Twenty-Eight

Two months passed with a snap of the fingers. The air was humid and dry, typical for the middle of July. The heat irritated people and often sparked arguments over nothing meaningful. One man blessed out another man for getting to the pay phone before him, insisting he was first. A neighbor filed a complaint on his neighbor of fifteen years because his dog peed on a tree in his yard. Heat brought out the crazy in people down south. It was contagious, like a virus.

Life for Liz Borders carried on in the same fashion. The people of Camilla had softened their hearts slightly, not so many stared anymore. The kids were out of school for the summer and stuck together like glue. They kept the close friends they always had that lived nearby. Liz would take them to the pool on her days off or to the zoo. Liz was thankful they had each other and prayed for the next school year to be easier.

Several months since she'd seen Abby at the grocery store but she had not heard from her yet, not that she honestly expected to. Liz was eager to earn her trust back, even more, her forgiveness.

She had seen the new restaurant going up quickly on the south point of the island, but never would have guessed whom it belonged to. The kids were at a weeklong summer camp, so she walked all alone through the blistering sand and debris scattered on the shore.

The sign merely said "New Addition: Restaurant/Fish Camp... OPENING SOON! Her curiosity got the best of her and she crept up the wooden slats laid at an angle unto the foundation. Carpenters of all sorts were putting up baseboards and frames, it reminded her of Sam.

"Excuse me, Miss. Don't mean to be rude, but you can't be

up here." One of the gentlemen looked over at her as she heard the voice behind her. "You could get hurt and we'd be responsible."

"I'm sorry. Just seeing what it's going to be like in here." Embarrassed, she began going back down the slats.

"Hey! Aren't you Sammy's wife? Sammy Borders?" he called out.

Liz didn't know how to react to that. Technically, she still was, but nowadays, she was unwilling to be referred to as that.

"I'm sorry. I need to go." She hurried off without answering.

The dunes were beautiful at this time of the day, so natural looking with puddles of salt water scattered among them. Sand crabs roamed sideways and it took seaside talent to avoid stepping on one or two because they were so plentiful.

Abby and Lillie took their place in the sand. Two chairs, two towels, sand pail and shovel, tanning lotion and sunscreen, the whole bit. Today would reach above 100 degrees and it was almost too hot to even be outside in it. "A scorcher," the DJ on the radio repeated after every song. "Now here's another tune from those magical wonders we call, 'The Temptations'." Ah, beach music.

"Mama, when is Nana coming back?" Lillie asked. She had already been to the water and back approximately three or four times to fill her pail and had returned to her seat.

"I'm not sure, baby. Soon I'm sure." Truth was, she wasn't sure her mom would be coming soon. Marie had called her when Maizie had come to meet her. Abby wasn't ready to see her yet and she declined the invitation.

Even after the news had sunken in and Abby realized it was not going to change, she still needed extra time. Time to see that she was no longer an only child, to face up to the fact that she had a sister out there. A sister that desperately wanted to meet and see her. She would climb over that wall when she was ready to come to it.

"I want her to come." Lillie pouted.

"Let's see, when was the last time she came down?"

She thought about it for a minute, and then Lillie quickly spoke up, "For my birthday!"

"You know what... you're right! That was it, almost a month ago." Abby dabbed sunscreen on Lillie's rosy cheeks, "We'll see her soon, I promise."

Lillie returned to building her castles, talking to herself, pretending to be a princess or something. Abby relaxed in her lounge chair, taking in as much sun as possible. If she burned, which she rarely did, she'd lotion it up. This was only the second time she and Lillie had been out to the beach since the first of June.

She was in a stage between sleeping and daydreaming, though she saw the clouds passing by at a snail's speed. Abby couldn't fall asleep, for fear Lillie might wander off. As long as she kept talking to herself, she was fine, because Abby could listen out for her.

Willingly or unwillingly, she eventually napped a short while. When she opened her eyes, Lillie was still right there. She was such a good girl.

She tried hard to remember what thoughts ran through her head... it had been Tommy. Another dream about Tommy. Not surprised in the least, she dreamed about him on occasion. Strange to be dreaming of him when she had lost Batson, the one grown-up love she'd ever had. Always go back to the old ones and God knows that's no solution. But once upon a time... he was my one true love.

Abby tried to picture his face and was curious if he looked the same. I could give him a call. Nah, what would I say to him... 'Hello, I'm still alone. Things are pretty shitty. Want to come down for a visit?'

Not quite. The idea of having him there with her was a wonderful dream, but that was all it was. She couldn't imagine loving someone again, not like Batson. She wished for a long kiss to share or arms that wrapped around her, making everything else disappear, even if only for a minute or two. The simplicity of rolling over in bed, reaching to finger the back of someone else, things like that were what she missed… it was having someone here to love. That someone had been Batson. Even if only briefly, it had been him, only him.

Abby and Lillie soon headed for home to await Gracie's return. Exactly one month earlier, she admitted to Grandma Anna that she was dependent on the booze.

The day after working in the nursery, she had relapsed hard while frolicking with so-called friends of hers from the olden days. She phoned Abby every couple of days to let her know she merely existed. After about a week had gone by without seeing her face, she showed up to pick up a suitcase of clothes. Gracie had made plans to housesit for someone. Abby, not impressed by Gracie's actions, was quite worried about investing her time and effort into a business for the two to share. She decided to let Gracie learn for herself that this was not the way to live, and sure enough, she eventually broke down.

A week and a half later, she found herself cashed out, worn down and knocking on Anna's door for help. Jordan, from the nursery, came to pick her up two hours later and carried her to an alcohol and drug center near the County hospital. She was admitted to detox and would need to stay for thirty-two days. Tough break, but one break that might sober her up.

Anna was heartbroken after the news and without willingly admitting it, devastated that she had not caught on to the problem sooner.

On the third Sunday, Gracie was finally allowed a visitor's

day. The whole family, which included Anna, Bessie, Abby and Lillie, went to see her. The day passed by fast, full of outdoor activities, a picnic and lots of coffee. To see Gracie in a hospital for her drinking was tough on the heart, but the necessary support and love was clearly present.

"Soon it will all be over," Abby told her, rubbing the upper part of Gracie's shoulders. "You'll come out feeling so much better, I promise. Like a whole new Gracie." The words came out effortlessly, and once she had said it, realized how much easier it was said than done.

"I hope so, but the battle will never be won." Her eyes did not fall as deeply into her face as before and her skin tone had brightened since the last time Abby had seen her.

Now the day had arrived when she would finally get to come home. Bessie had washed all her clothes, put clean sheets on her bed in the loft and filled the fridge with Cokes galore, the caffeine had been absent at the hospital. Gracie would still get to stay at Abby's for extra privacy, since Abby worked all day and Lillie went to school, but Anna and Bessie would have their eyes on her for sure.

Lillie had worked on a huge sign the day before for her homecoming, carefully coloring in the lines of every letter, written out as, "WELCOME HOME GRACIE!" She and Anna sat on the sofa now, playing war with a deck of cards.

"Alright you guys, I'm going to get her." Abby looked at them. Anna and Lillie into their game and Bessie waved to her from the kitchen. This was her family. Not to push her mom away, but here and now in Camilla… these people belonged to her.

"Go get dat' girl and bring her home!" Bessie winked at Anna, making her lips rub together with tenseness.

"Drive careful, Abby." Anna smiled tenderly, looking like she had that day when she had fallen. Helpless, looking for someone. "I want all my babies home."

Abby waved to her and closed the door.

The dependency ward was set off from the actual hospital buildings. The road wound up around a mountainous hill, which led to what looked to be an ordinary house. From the front you could see the additions on either side and since she had been inside before, knew the hall in the middle traveled a long way back. Trees grew tall and shaded the majority of the property. Abby pulled into a guest spot in the parking area, strapped her purse on her shoulder and walked up the front steps. She stopped to take a deep breath before going inside, and then rang the button for service.

A black nurse with a nametag, Shanna, greeted her.

"Yes?" she asked through the intercom.

"I'm here to pick up Gracie Cannon."

"Oh yes. We have her packed and ready to go." The nurse seemed happy about Gracie's discharge. Abby was sure they were glad to see patients succeed and go on with their lives... hopefully for most, sober lives. Then, on the other hand, she was sure they were glad to just get rid of some as well.

She opened the door, which stayed locked electronically and showed Abby to the waiting room.

"I'll tell her you're here and she'll come out when she's ready." The nurse then kneeled down to Abby's level in the chair, "Sometimes it takes them a while."

"A while?" Abby asked.

"Yes. Staying in a place like this makes them feel very secure and safe from all the evils of the outside world. Believe it or not, leaving is just as hard as coming in." She said it with confidence. She had seen hundreds come and go, some two or three times.

"Okay. I'm a patient person." Abby started to look up at her as she said it, but the nurse was already walking down the hall.

Abby occupied her time flipping through magazines and glancing at her watch. Not much time had passed really but it seemed like an eternity. She thought about Gracie and then what the nurse had said, finding it hard to believe that it would actually be hard to leave this place.

She heard footsteps and immediately looked up. There she was. Denim jeans cut off at the bottoms, black top fitted loosely on her upper half and her hair hanging down on the sides of her face. Gracie held the brown leather bag that had accompanied her when she had first set foot in this place.

Abby stood up at the sight of her, not sure whether to hug her or not. Was this a sad moment or a happy one? Then looking at Gracie's expression… it was a happy one.

Gracie's arms reached out to her and Abby clung on tightly. Neither one saying a word yet, only holding onto the moment.

"Ready to go home?" Abby asked.

"I think so." She was surprisingly quiet, calm, almost humble.

"You gonna be okay?" Abby's tone went down a notch, unsure still about how to approach anything with her.

"Yep. It's just hard, but I'm gonna be fine." She turned around to the nurse that had shown Abby in. "Love you."

"We love you too, baby. Day by day- remember, day by day." The nurse said and when she did, Gracie cried tears of joy. She had made it a whole month here, now back into the real world, she would take it day by day.

One Year Later…

"Gracie, here. Take this to twenty-two for Becky." Abby signaled her through the kitchen window.

The restaurant was packing people in like flies. A year of being sober for Gracie and eight months for the newest addition to Camilla, The Lillie Pad. Life was good for all the girls now.

Lillie would be starting kindergarten in the fall with Mrs. Owens for her teacher. She was excited about meeting new friends, but for the summer, she played with ones in the neighborhood. Anna kept her under her wings while Abby and Gracie spent most of their time at the restaurant.

"Order up!" Yelled a fry cook in the back.

"I'm coming." Gracie called out. She was a food runner for this shift. "I said, 'I'm coming'." Running around frantically, she scuffled from table to table balancing plates up her arms.

The lunch hour dwindled down to only a small number of customers. Some sitting on the barstools lined along the wooden counter, sipping on the last swig of coffee, while others chatted over tables.

The small establishment was screened in for the most part, including part of the kitchen area. Ceiling fans kept the guests cool, along with ocean breezes that passed from time to time. It had been built like a beach shack, to accentuate the surroundings of the island and give off an airy sensation. The tourists would get their island experience that they came for and locals had a new spot to round up for coffee and good food.

Since only breakfast and lunch were served, the sunsets were private. Abby and Gracie frequently stayed late, after the staff went home, to decide on the specials for the next day and enjoy a cup of coffee without the hustle and bustle of people in and out.

After today's chaotic lunch, staying late was out of the question. It was time to head home.

Abby rarely drove her piece-of-shit car to the restaurant. She began her walk down the main road towards the house, when a car pulled alongside. Startled, she hopped to the side to see who it was... probably Gracie; she forgot to tell her something.

The glare from the sun blinded Abby momentarily and when she saw the driver, she stopped. Other cars passed and went about their business while Abby froze in her tracks.

"Abby?" She knew the voice before the body stepped out of the car. Abby did not reply.

"Abby, please... hear me out. I need to do this, to talk to you." She was alone; the kids must be staying with her mom or something.

"Yes, Liz?" She was tired and not exactly in the mood for some heart-wrenching discussion about Batson or Sam or anyone else. "What is it that you want from me?"

"I've tried to call you several times. Have you not gotten my messages?"

"Yes." For some reason, she felt ashamed and embarrassed. "I've just been so busy with the store and all."

"I can imagine." Her voice was sincere. "Abby, I just want us to talk, as friends."

"Liz, it's just too much to handle. I've got a lot..."

Liz interrupted her, "I know. I know. Can't we at least grab a cup of coffee or something?"

Abby took several minutes, thinking of excuses in the back of her head but none that seemed believable. She had forgiven Liz for everything that had happened and for some reason, Liz was reaching out for her.

"Um, sure. I've got to swing by the house first though to check in." Liz's smile broadened.

"Great. I can take you if you want. Hop in."

Anna lay on her bed reading her newest borrowed book, while Bessie sat on the couch playing solitaire on the coffee table. Lillie's feet dangled from a kitchen chair, with crayons scattered across the table.

Abby walked inside and took her apron off.

"Hey." Bessie acknowledged her presence without looking up from the deck of cards. "How'd it go today? Busy?"

"Uh-hum." No time for small talk, she had someone else to deal with. "Where's Anna?"

Bessie pointed her long finger towards the bedroom and Abby kissed Lillie on the head on her way back. Anna sat leaned on two large pillows propped against the headboard.

"Hey there." Anna looked up to her. "What's wrong?" She could tell just by looking into Abby's eyes.

"It's Liz. She's waiting outside. Wants to go get a cup of coffee or something."

"Well, go on. You know we'll watch Lillie."

"That's not it. I'm not sure I want to." She glanced down at her feet, noticing the pieces of food stuck on the tops of her shoes. "I'm having a hard time understanding what it is she wants from me. Says she wants us to be friends again." Advice, she needed some advice.

"Sit down right quick." Abby did as she was told and Anna took her left hand and squeezed it tightly. "Now, you listen to what I say and you can either take my advice or push it to the side, but what I say is true." Abby's eyes focused on Anna's. "God put us here on this earth to love, not hate. We are to forgive and not dwell. When someone comes knocking on your door for help… you answer it. If you shut them out, you're shutting God out. Do you understand?" Abby nodded.

Anna continued, "Abby, Batson is gone. The past is the past and if Liz didn't need you, she wouldn't be trying so hard to get to you. To live is to love. Without love, we wouldn't have life… do you see what I'm getting at?"

"So I should hear her out?"

"Listen to her, Abby. Listen closely to what she's saying to you. Not only will you probably ease her mind, but you might surprise yourself and ease yours as well. Don't you think I've had a hard time forgiving? God has taught me how. Every time I've lost someone I love, I've been mad... mad as hell. And it's been a hard time to understand why God makes some of the decisions he does, but that's not anyone's fault, Abby. It's his choice and his alone. So don't close that door. Leave room for an explanation and find the strength to forgive someone that you don't necessarily want to. Now go." With that speech, it was hard not to. After all, she was probably right anyway.

Abby kissed Lillie one more time and met Liz in the car. "Where are we going?"

On the way back to the restaurant, Abby thought long and hard about what wise Anna had said to her. The words rang powerfully inside... "Listen to her... to live is to love... don't shut her out!"

And that is what she did... she listened to every word, every syllable and every sound that came out of Liz's mouth.

Liz told her this was a healing process, to get everything out in the open, no repulsive feelings left to float. She wept timidly as she talked about Sammy, Batson and the cherished, past times they shared.

Abby watched, knocked down by her sudden honesty and humbleness. Her eyes loosened as the tales continued, word upon word, Liz exposed her tender heart. Abby felt the warmness of her hands, fingers rubbing over fingers, the touch of someone in need.

"So you see, Abby... I had to get this out, these haunting feelings. I couldn't spend the rest of my life, knowing how you hated me and couldn't forgive me."

Abby was overwhelmed. Part of her wanted to hold on to the anger, but the good part bled into the bad part... the part that wanted to overlook the past and move on. Then trying to put herself in Liz's shoes, she melted.

"Liz, life is about loving other people and I uh... want to get over this as much as you do. It's been over a year now and believe me, it's still a struggle. Maybe it always will be, but I'm willing to try, if you are?"

"That's all I want, Abby. I just want you to smile or say hello when you see me instead of turn your head. I would like you to answer the phone when I call. Maybe have a cup of coffee every once in a while, that's all." Liz looked at Abby with a truthful innocence, "Most of all, I would really like it if we could share this together, the memories."

Life was about love, right? At least that's what Anna had said. Whether we like it or not, it going to continue on with a variety of ups and downs, trials and tribulations. Abby took a vow that she was going on with it. Life was too damn short to dwell on in anger, too short to be resentful and too long to live with wretchedness built up inside.

Abby picked up Lillie, walked to their front door and tucked her tightly under the covers with her.

"Cuddle with mama?" Lillie's eyes were too tired to answer. Abby held on to her baby, just as if she were three months old again. "Lay like spoons."

Gracie's apartment was fresh with herbs and plants galore. The balcony overlooked the river, with two small wooden rockers for a wonderful view. She had ferns draping down on either side of the porch on white iron hangers and three window boxes attached to one another containing all sorts of flowering plants. On the right side of the balcony and directly inside the sliding glass door were shelves of herbs growing wildly. Gardening had become her passion outside the restaurant and her good friend Jordan led her in the green thumb direction.

It was a Sunday morning and Gracie had been awake since about six. The paper had not even arrived and she already had her coffee on. She filled a cup and took a seat in one of the rockers outside. Springtime was her favorite of all the seasons. The moist air roaming briskly through the screens on the windows.

Looking down on River Street, she could see no one out yet this morning. There was only a casino boat that had pulled in to dock for the night. Other balconies flourished with greens such as Gracie's, but she rated hers high above the rest, giving it top priority in the apartment.

What a day this would be! The high was to get into the 70s with a low humidity at this time of the year. What good would come out of today? she wondered.

Ten o'clock, Lillie was dressing for church. Abby had been dressed for a while now and was expecting a call from her mom at any minute. She always called on Sunday mornings right before they left for church.

Lillie came out of her room with a raveled pink ribbon dangling down on one side of her face.

"Look mom... did it myself," she stated proudly.

"Um-hum," Abby mumbled staring down at the classifieds, looking through the antiques section. She rearranged the ribbon to fall evenly.

"There now. Go look in the mirror and see if you like it better. When is mom going to call? It's almost ten after!"

Lillie returned and Abby then noticed she had attempted to fool with it again. "Oh well," she whispered to herself, not moving her mouth at all.

Minutes ticked by and Abby finished her coffee, began folding the paper up for a later reading time.

The phone rang. It was Gracie.

THE LILLIE PAD

Their conversation was about pretty much nothing, except she wanted Abby and Lillie to come over for lunch.

"Homemade burritos!" Abby motioned her finger sticking down her throat. "Sound good?"

"Sounds great!" Ugh. Burritos weren't exactly appealing this early in the morning. "Hold on, I think someone is at the door. Probably Bessie, wondering if we are actually going to church or not!"

The doorbell rang again. It was so quiet you could hardly make out the sound, one of those things that needed to be fixed.

Abby was taken off guard when she opened the door.

"Mom? Mom, what on earth?"

"Hey, sweetheart. Where's my Lillie?" She walked on in, closing the door behind her. Abby opened it back up, not recognizing the car or the person sitting in it.

"Who's that?" She was lost. "What's going on? Is something wrong?"

"Nope." Marie leaned over and kissed Abby quickly on the cheek. "You both look so pretty. But I don't think you'll be going to church today."

"What? What do you mean? Mom, what is going on? Tell me... tell me right now!" Abby felt invaded.

"Calm down now. Calm down. Flatten out your ruffles." She paused slightly, then smiling, "I brought someone to visit. Only for a couple hours if you allow it."

As soon as the words tumbled out of her mouth, Abby knew. Maizie. It had to be Maizie. Unable to say anything, she looked into her mom's eyes.

"Abby, hold my hand." Abby stood, frozen, not wanting to move. "Abby! Abby, take my hand, don't be afraid. If you don't want to see who it is, I'll turn around and we'll go."

"Quit it, mom! I know who it is... it's Maizie." Marie nodded, patiently waiting to see her reaction.

"Are you serious? You brought her here?" She began

259

panicking, "Look at me though! Look at this house, it's a mess! How could you do this without consulting me first? Oh, shit. Oh my God!"

"Calm down right now, Abigail." The tone in her mother's voice was stern and she obeyed. "I did it this way because I have wanted the two of you to meet for a long time now. Every time I've asked you about it, you put it off. You make excuses! Well, not today. Either you want to see her or you don't." The ultimatum. "What's it gonna be?"

Abby searched the room to see Lillie's reaction. She had never told Lillie about Maizie but now she would have no choice. She took a deep breath, her legs buckled and she landed on the sofa in a slump. This was so unbelievable, so surreal... she shook her head back and forth, and then covered her eyes with the insides of her hands.

"God, Mom. Can't you give me a minute?" The room was silent, almost hearing the vibrations bouncing off the walls when she spoke. "Please, I need a minute with Lillie."

"Of course, honey. I'll stand on the porch and you just open the door when you're ready for us to come in." Marie stepped outside. At this minute, she almost hated her decision for coming down, but it was the only way that Abby would ever accept it. She forgave herself immediately and joined Maizie in the car.

"What is it Marie? Is she upset?"

"Well... I didn't exactly tell her we were coming."

"You did what?"

"Yep, I knew this was the only way." Maizie looked at her like she was crazy. "Trust me, I know my daughter."

Inside Abby was running around like a looney.

"Mama? Mama?" Lillie had no idea what was going on.

"Sit down here, baby. Sit down beside mama." Abby pulled her on her lap. "Nana has someone very special with her."

"What's their name?" Lillie interrupted.

"Her name is Maizie. She's um... she's my sister." No other way to get it out, except to just say it. Lillie kept staring at her eyes; she needed to explain. "See, well... Nana had her before me and she grew up somewhere else. But she's here now and she wants to meet you and me. Is that alright with you?"

"Yes, Mama! Tell em' to come in, Mama. Go tell them!" She was glad someone was excited. Then and only then, realizing that she too, was excited.

She had not forgotten about Maizie, just put her on a back burner until she was ready to accept her. Well, today was the day.

Her heart raced, pumping blood fast to her head, making it flush. She licked her lips and quickly decided to change into something more comfortable before opening the door.

"Hold on Lillie! Don't open the door, I'm gonna throw some jeans on." No need to be all dressed up, right? Just be myself. The first pair came up with holes in the knees; she dug in the closet for a second. Abby sat on the bed, pulling the jeans to ride up her long legs. On her dresser, she saw herself in the mirror. Looking closer, she saw the face of Anna reflecting back at her. "Life is love, being able to love someone else is the most rewarding thing. You must never close the door on someone who needs you... if you do, you're closing that door on God." All the advice, all the arrows pointing in the same direction.

Around the room, on shelves, she carefully stared into the photographs filling her bedroom. All the ones of Lillie, several of she and Gracie, that one special snapshot of she and Batson, the wallet of her as a child, family photos of her mom and dad and then a black and white that she had recently taken of Anna and Bessie on the porch. She was living her dream and looked at all the people that had supported her along the way. Each person in all the photographs had showed her how to reach out, be brave, grasp onto what life has to offer and hold on. All of them were her family.

Only now, she realized one to be missing. That one was standing outside her front door, waiting for the opportunity to show her new things. Waiting for that moment to share as sisters.

Abby's heart was pumping heavily again, only this time, fueled with passion. A passion to reach out and grab this person, give her what she had to offer and love her as a sister. After all, life is all about love… or so that's what Anna says. And she's always right anyway.

* * *